**Praise for the novels of *New York Times*
and *USA TODAY* bestselling author
Diana Palmer**

"Diana Palmer is an amazing storyteller, and her
long-time fans will enjoy *Wyoming Winter* with
satisfaction!"
—*RT Book Reviews*

"The popular Palmer has penned another winning
novel, a perfect blend of romance and suspense."
—*Booklist* on *Lawman*

"Palmer knows how to make the sparks fly....
Heartwarming."
—*Publishers Weekly* on *Renegade*

"Sensual and suspenseful."
—*Booklist* on *Lawless*

"Diana Palmer is a mesmerizing storyteller
who captures the essence of what a romance
should be."
—*Affaire de Coeur*

"This is a fascinating story.... It's nice to have
a hero wise enough to know when he can't do
things alone and willing to accept help when he
needs it. There is pleasure to be found in the nice
sense of family this tale imparts."
—*RT Book Reviews* on *Wyoming Bold*

"Readers will be moved by this tale of revenge
and justice, grief and healing."
—*Booklist* on *Dangerous*

"Lots of passion, thrills, and plenty of suspense...
Protector is a top-notch read!"
—*Romance Reviews Today*

P9-DJL-205

Also available
from Diana Palmer
and HQN

Long, Tall Texans

Fearless
Heartless
Dangerous
Merciless
Courageous
Protector
Invincible
Untamed
Defender
Undaunted
Unbridled
Unleashed

Wyoming Men

Wyoming Tough
Wyoming Fierce
Wyoming Bold
Wyoming Strong
Wyoming Rugged
Wyoming Brave
Wyoming Winter
Wyoming Legend
Wyoming Heart

For a complete list of titles available by Diana Palmer,
please visit www.dianapalmer.com.

If you purchased this book without a cover you should be aware that this book is stolen property. It was reported as "unsold and destroyed" to the publisher, and neither the author nor the publisher has received any payment for this "stripped book."

ISBN-13: 978-1-335-04535-5

Recycling programs for this product may not exist in your area.

Unleashed

Copyright © 2019 by Diana Palmer

All rights reserved. No part of this book may be used or reproduced in any manner whatsoever without written permission except in the case of brief quotations embodied in critical articles and reviews.

This is a work of fiction. Names, characters, places and incidents are either the product of the author's imagination or are used fictitiously. Any resemblance to actual persons, living or dead, businesses, companies, events or locales is entirely coincidental.

This edition published by arrangement with Harlequin Books S.A.

For questions and comments about the quality of this book, please contact us at CustomerService@Harlequin.com.

HQN
22 Adelaide St. West, 40th Floor
Toronto, Ontario M5H 4E3, Canada
www.Harlequin.com

Printed in U.S.A.

DIANA PALMER

UNLEASHED

HQN

To the brave men and women in all branches of law enforcement, who serve throughout our country as peace officers, and who risk their lives daily to protect us from harm. And to our people in all branches of the military, who serve around the world with honor and dedication. With love and thanks.

Dear Reader,

You can probably tell that I have tremendous respect and admiration for the Texas Ranger Division of the Texas Department of Public Safety. I've written many books that feature them. *Unleashed* is the newest of my novels to feature a Texas Ranger as a hero—Colter Banks, who has had cameos in many of my stories over the years. Clancey, Colter's assistant in the cold-case office, is eccentric and sweet. I hope you'll like her. (He doesn't. LOL.)

I have dedicated this book to the brave men and women of law enforcement and to our military. My great-great-grandfather was a deputy US marshal back in the early part of the twentieth century. My husband's best friend is a former sheriff's department homicide detective and still serves as a volunteer sheriff's deputy. When I was a teenager, we played penny ante poker with my best friend's father's best friend, who was a lieutenant of detectives with the Atlanta Police Department. When I was a newspaper reporter, sixteen years' worth, I spent a lot of time around people in law enforcement. I gained great respect for them as I covered news stories in my county and surrounding counties.

I'm especially fond of the Cornelia Police Department, the Clarkesville Police Department and the Habersham County Sheriff's Office, all in northeast Georgia. I have friends in all three places. Brave men and women, past as well as present.

I've also known a lot of people in the military, including members of my own family and group of friends. That's a job that comes with hardship and grief, but we have some gutsy people, men and women, who bear it for all of us, all over the world. Big hugs, guys and gals!

I hope you enjoy the book. I like the way it turned out. I hope you do, as well. Love and hugs. And, as always, I'm still your biggest fan!

Diana Palmer

ONE

"Even a doctor couldn't read this handwriting," Clancey muttered to herself as she tried to decrypt a note jotted in the margin of a photocopied arrest record.

"What are you muttering about now?" Colter Banks asked from the doorway.

Colter was her boss, a Texas Ranger who worked cold cases for the San Antonio office of the Department of Public Safety. He was gorgeous: tall, narrow hipped, with powerful long legs and broad shoulders. He had dark brown hair and liquid black eyes. Those eyes were glaring at her.

She looked up with a disgusted expression on her oval face. She brushed away a strand of dark wavy hair from her forehead. Pale gray eyes glared at him. "I can't read this." She waved the sheet at him.

"If you'd like to resign…?" he offered, and looked hopeful.

"I can't resign. This was the only job available and I have to eat," she grumbled.

He took the sheet from her and frowned as he studied the note he'd placed next to a certain charge on the rap sheet.

"Ha!" she exclaimed.

He glanced at her. "What do you mean, *ha*?"

"You can't read it, either, can you?" she accused.

He lifted his chin. "Of course I can read it," he scoffed. "I wrote it."

"So, what does it say?"

He stared at it again. He had to puzzle it out or she was never going to let him forget this. While he stared at the scribble and tried to make sense of it, the phone rang.

He tossed the sheet back on her desk. "Phone."

"Excuse," she said under her breath.

He glared at her as he pulled his cell phone out of its holder. "Banks," he said.

He listened. His face grew harder. He glanced at Clancey, who was still waving the sheet at him, and turned his back. "Yes, I can do that," he replied. "Sure. I'll stop by on my way home. No problem. See you."

He put his phone back and looked pointedly at his watch. "I've got to see the assistant DA on a case I'm working, that Reed case from five years ago. We hear that Morris Duffy, who was suspected in his disappearance, may be getting out of prison a year early for good behavior, and soon," he remarked, missing the sudden worried expression on his assistant's face. "We could sure use a break in the case." He glanced again at his watch. "I'd better go on. Almost quitting time."

Clancey got her composure back before his eyes fell on her face. "You still haven't translated this for me," she said pointedly, indicating the sheet.

He glared at her.

"Well, it's not my fault you can't write," she said belligerently. "I'll bet the teacher who tried to teach you cursive threw confetti on the last day of school and walked you all the way to the school bus."

He glared harder. "I can write cursive just fine, thank you."

"Then what does it say?" she persisted.

"I'll take it under advisement and get back to you," he said nonchalantly.

"You can't read it," she said, and grinned.

"I could read it if I wanted to," he retorted.

"How am I supposed to type up this report if I don't know what you've written?" she asked reasonably.

"If they question me about it, I'll tell them you had a senior moment," he said with a deadpan expression.

"I'm twenty-three, not eighty!" she huffed.

"I thought you were twenty-two."

"I was, until last November, just after I came to work for you," she said. "Birthdays come once a year. You don't stay the same age forever."

He didn't react to the snarky comment. He slid his white Stetson over one eye. "If anyone calls, I'll be out until tomorrow."

"If they call, they'll call you, not me," she pointed out.

"You have the fixed phone, that antique thing that's attached to the wall," he pointed out.

"I have a cell phone," she said defensively.

"Does it have anything except numbers on it?" he asked with a sarcastic smile.

She glared at him. "I'm going to get a really fancy

smart phone as soon as I pay off my new yacht," she said belligerently.

He turned away before she saw the smile. "Okay, nasturtium. Have a good night."

"I am not a nasturtium!"

"A likely story," he muttered on his way out. "I'll bet my badge you don't even know what a nasturtium is."

"I do so!" she called after him.

When he was out of sight, she pulled the pocket dictionary out of her drawer and looked it up.

It was a flower. Well! Maybe he didn't dislike her as much as he seemed to. She wondered at the irony, because the meaning of her real name was the same as that of the nickname he'd stuck her with. She doubted if he'd paid any attention to her name on the job application. It had been, after all, the department's interviewer who'd hired her for this job.

She glanced at the sheet she still couldn't read and put it in her desk drawer. Tomorrow, she promised herself, she'd pin him down and make him take a crack at it.

Meantime, she typed up the reports she could read.

SHE WORRIED ABOUT the cold case Banks was working on. He didn't know, and she wouldn't tell him, but the victim had been her grandfather, Dalton Reed. She didn't want to share any of her private life with her bulldozer of a boss. Even in prison, her stepbrother, Morris Duffy, could have things done to her, or worse, to her little brother, Tad. He'd even threatened that when he went away. Keep your mouth shut, he'd said. Things could happen to the boy, even if he was in prison. He had friends. The threat was still enough to keep her silent.

She'd always suspected her stepbrother, Morris, of killing her grandfather, but the body had never been found. If there was a body. She grimaced. Her grandfather had always been punctual. If he said he'd be there at six, he'd be there at five forty-five. He would never have just gone away from his job and his family without telling anyone. Unless he was dead.

Dalton Reed was a former sheriff's deputy. Even after retirement, he'd been a volunteer deputy. He could make a guitar sing. Clancey still had his precious guitar. She'd hidden it while Morris lived at home, for fear that he'd sell it. After all, he'd made frequent allusions to its value. He'd also been covetous of her grandfather's antique Colt .45 in its equally antique hand-tooled holster. Odd thing, the gun and gun belt had vanished along with her grandfather. She'd thought at first that Morris might have sold them. But they were collectibles, and a lot of people in San Antonio—including many policemen and sheriff's deputies—knew about them. Perhaps Morris had been too cautious to put them on the market.

Clancey had loved her grandfather. He was the only good in her miserable home life. Her stepfather, Ben, had coddled Morris, his son from a previous marriage, as if he'd invented bread. He protected the boy, got him out of trouble all the time, refused to believe his own son had ever done anything bad. Tad had never gotten the attention from Ben that Morris had. The child got his affection from his half sister, Clancey, who'd loved him from the day he was born. After the death of her mother, Diane, not long after Tad's birth, Clancey and her grandfather had been Tad's protectors, until her grandfather's disappearance.

Tad had only been three at the time when her grandfather didn't come home. But a few days before that, Morris had viciously attacked Tad for crying during his video game. The little boy was screaming as Morris slapped him around. When Clancey had come running at the sound of the child's screams, she saw Morris, cursing, grab up a metal scoop that was used in the open fireplace. As she yelled, horrified, he swung it at the child and knocked him off the couch. Clancey ran to defend the little boy, and Morris swung the heavy scoop at her, breaking two ribs and bruising her as he swung it over and over again.

It had been a brutal act that still kindled nightmares. She'd had bruises and cuts on her face and arms, in addition to the broken ribs, and her back had suffered a torn muscle. There was a worse complication that sent her to the emergency room. Ben had come home from work just after the incident. He grimaced at Clancey's condition and reluctantly called an ambulance, recognizing that her injuries might be life-threatening. She begged Ben to let Tad go, too, but Ben refused. The kid would be all right, he said sarcastically. He was just bruised. Morris had told him, drugged up and wild-eyed, that the child and Clancey had been tussling and both fell off the sofa. Ben believed him.

Clancey was horrified at what had happened and sick with fear for little Tad. One of those vicious blows had caught the little boy in the head and he was bawling. She didn't want to tell the truth, out of fear of what her stepbrother might do, but the doctor on call at the emergency room quickly realized that she was a victim of a brutal assault. He dragged the truth out of her. She told him she was afraid for her baby brother, who'd also been a victim of the attack. The doctor had called the police.

Clancey hadn't wanted to cause trouble. The policeman, a veteran, did. He drove Clancey to her home after she was treated, questioning her about the incident. He insisted on seeing Tad, who was obviously injured. He said the child would need medical attention and called for an ambulance. Then he promptly arrested Morris, who was staggering and screaming curses at everyone, even a shaken Ben. Half the neighborhood came outdoors when they heard him yelling. Ben had pleaded with Clancey to tell the police Morris didn't do it, but to no avail. She explained to him that Morris had attacked Tad for interrupting his video game, then he'd beaten her up when she tried to save her little brother.

Ben said Morris would never hurt a child—those bruises were from falling when he'd been playing with Clancey. The policeman said that it was odd that the bruises on the child were shaped like the metal shovel from a fireplace set, wasn't it? He added that Clancey's broken ribs were hardly from a fall while playing. He sent Morris off in another squad car and went into the house to question everybody who lived there. Clancey was intimidated by Ben and said as little as possible, but her grandfather was a gold mine of information on Morris's recent behavior. He added that he thought the boy was on drugs and that he was selling them as well, to afford his expensive video console and the games to go with it. That provoked a violent reply from Ben. The policeman had calmed them both down and continued taking notes. The ambulance arrived then, and Ben climbed in with Tad, already complaining about the expense of it.

The kind policeman had told Clancey it would be all

right. They'd lock up Morris and he wouldn't be a threat to her or Tad again.

She wrote out her version of what had happened and signed it. So did her grandfather. Ben would be required to do the same, later. Her grandfather took her prescriptions to the pharmacy and paid for them out of his own pocket. They both knew that Ben wouldn't spend a penny on her. She'd turned on Morris.

But Morris was permitted bail while he awaited his trial, which they said could take months. Ben tried to mortgage the house to afford a fancy lawyer for his son, only to be reminded that Dalton Reed was co-owner of the property and until he could be found or declared dead, Ben had no right to sell it. He blamed Clancey for that as well, and he paid no more attention to Tad than was necessary. They'd kept the little boy overnight, to observe him after the mild concussion. Clancey had stayed with him. Her boss, who was then the detective lieutenant at a precinct close to Clancey's home, Cal Hollister, had gone to the hospital to sit with her. He was one of the kindest men she'd ever known, although she had no romantic feelings for him. A widower, he kept to himself and had nothing to do with women. But he liked Clancey. He was furious about what Morris had done and promised that he was going to speak to Darrell Tarley, the assistant district attorney on the case, and make sure Morris didn't weasel out of the very serious charges. The fact that Morris had used a weapon in the assaults made it a second-class felony, which carried a penalty, if convicted, that would put Morris away for several years. Clancey felt guilty for hoping the justice system would remove the frightening man from her life, and Tad's.

For Clancey, it was agony to live in the house, which her late mother had left jointly to Ben and her grandfather. The pressure of her unsettled home life affected her job performance, but Hollister, aware of her problems, protected her. She also had a growing health issue that Ben and Morris ignored. They barely spoke to her.

From high school graduation, she'd worked as a clerk for the San Antonio Police Department. The precinct where Hollister presided over the violent crimes unit was close enough to home that she could walk to work and back. At least Ben did finally understand that Tad was in danger every time Morris was interrupted at his eternal video games. He yelled furiously at the child, who cried even louder. It frightened Clancey that Morris threatened Tad. He wasn't tolerant of any noise when he was playing. If he lost his progress in the first-person shooting games he favored, he shouted curses at his little half brother. Ben, trying to ward off more trouble for his oldest son, had found a nice elderly lady who worked cheap to take care of Tad in the daytime and keep him quiet.

Morris didn't have a job, a fact that annoyed Clancey to no end. She worked a six-day week for a paycheck that was not as much as Ben made on his job. But she didn't dare say anything to either her stepfather or stepbrother. She was gun-shy after the beating Morris had given her. He seemed to like the fact that she was afraid of him. He told her once, when the others weren't listening, that she'd better hope he got off when the trial came up, or she was going to have some major problems.

It was only a few days after Morris got out on bond that her grandfather didn't come home from work.

Ben and Morris hadn't said much about that. They

talked to the detective who worked the case, denying that they'd seen the old man after breakfast the day he disappeared. Morris had been tight-lipped about the whole thing. He didn't even look familiar sometimes. He was jittery and had bloodshot eyes, and he talked nonstop. She wondered if there were mental problems that Morris and her father were keeping from her. Not for the first time, she was sorry that her mother had married Ben. On the other hand, if she hadn't, there would be no Tad. And Clancey loved Tad, more than anyone on earth except her grandfather. That they couldn't find the old man tormented her. She was certain that it had been something drastic, because you could set a watch by her grandfather's actions. He was never late coming home or going to work. It broke her heart when weeks passed and detectives moved the file aside because they couldn't find the old gentleman. They told Ben they suspected foul play, but they had no viable suspects. Odd, she thought, how Morris had looked when they said that. Very odd.

Ben had taken Morris's side over the assault on Clancey. He said Morris had been having a hard time with one of his friends, and he was sure Morris hadn't meant to do anything to his siblings. She knew better, but Ben never saw any problem with his son from a previous marriage. He loved Morris and defended him constantly.

Morris had things to say to Clancey afterward. He told her that she'd better never interfere again when he was playing video games, and that went double for Tad. Next time, he said ominously, he'd do a lot more to her. And he gave her a look that still made her uneasy years later. It was an adult look, as if he knew what was under her clothing. She'd folded her arms over her chest and left without another word. But after that, she caught Morris watching her sometimes.

Her grandfather had told her, before his disappearance, that Morris was running with a very tough crowd and he thought the boy was using drugs. He didn't want Clancey and Tad exposed to his friends, who sometimes showed up at the house when Clancey was at work. He'd been going out in the afternoons, after work, to talk to people about the gang Morris was getting mixed up with. He found a man who said he knew that Morris was using, and he also knew who was supplying the drugs. Her grandfather said that he was going to meet the man the next day after work and get the names from him.

Her grandfather didn't come home from work the next day. They searched, but they didn't find him. Clancey had bawled when they finally realized he was never coming back. So had Tad. Morris had been stiff lipped and silent, like his father. Clancey was suspicious of both of them. Neither had liked her grandfather. She was certain that Morris, at least, had some idea what had happened to the old man.

The charges against Morris were serious, because, in addition to beating up Clancey and Tad with a weapon, Morris had attacked the police officer who tried to handcuff him, yelling that it wasn't his fault, that they were framing him. Assault on a police officer was another felony, added to the two he was already being indicted for. Morris only had a public defender who, though eager, had little experience of trying cases. Ben was anguished that he couldn't afford a classy lawyer to help his son beat the rap.

A year after his arrest, because the court system moved

slowly, Morris was found guilty of second-degree assault and battery, and assault on Clancey and Tad, and assault on a police officer, and resisting arrest. He was sentenced to six years in prison after Clancey reluctantly took the witness stand and told the jury what Morris had done to her little brother and herself. There were photos of both of them, taken after the incident, which helped prove the case.

The trial had almost killed Ben, who was a maintenance man for a local corporation and didn't make much money. He couldn't afford to even go and see his son, sent to a penal facility hundreds of miles away. It made him even more bitter.

Ben had died soon after Morris went to prison, when Clancey was nineteen, in a freak accident, after he'd gone to some apartments nearby to talk to a man who had some information about the thugs that Morris had been running with. He told Clancey that Morris had been on drugs when he hit her, and that he was going to find out who had been supplying him. If he couldn't get his son out of prison, he was going to make the people who gave Morris the drugs pay for it.

Ben had been hit by a speeding car when he started back toward the lot where his car had been parked. The driver was never found, despite vague descriptions of the car by a bystander. It went down on the record as a hit-and-run. Ben was buried, with only Clancey and Tad to mourn him. Morris was refused permission to make the long trip to the funeral. Clancey had written to him, explaining what had happened and how sorry she was. Morris wrote back, a terse little note thanking her for her kindness. She wondered if being off drugs had improved him, just a little.

His attitude had been a surprise. Perhaps he'd gotten off drugs and was facing his past. Her boss, Cal Hollister, scoffed at her when she said that. Leopards, he told her, didn't change their spots.

Although Morris was out of the house and Clancey was in possession of it until Morris got out of prison—having more or less taken possession of her grandfather's half of the estate when he went missing—it didn't make her any less afraid of him. The incident had been traumatic for her. The doctor who treated her said that she needed therapy. She told him that she'd go to a therapist as soon as she paid off her new stretch limo. He'd laughed, but his eyes were sad.

BEN'S DEATH AND Morris's incarceration had put Clancey in the position of head of the family.

It was Ben's house that she and Tad lived in, which now belonged, on paper at least, to Morris. Half of it was still her grandfather's, because he'd never been declared legally dead. If Morris got out, Clancey worried about having to live under the same roof with him. Morris had always run with people on the wrong side of the law. Any money he got, he hadn't worked for, because he didn't hold down a job. No doubt he'd still be hanging around with the people who got their money in illegal ways. They were dangerous. Clancey didn't want them around Tad.

She was concerned about herself, as well. Morris had been attracted to her, and she was uneasy about living under the same roof with him. If he was using drugs, as she suspected he was when he'd beaten her, he was capable of even worse violence. She'd always wondered if he had something to do with her grandfather's death, because his attitude afterward, when the old man disappeared, was odd. He didn't talk about it and he avoided meeting Clancey's eyes when she wondered what had happened to him.

The thought of Morris getting out of prison and coming home frightened her. Prison changed men. No doubt he'd learned a lot about getting around outside the law. He'd probably made friends there, who would be even worse than the crowd he'd run with when he lived at home. Despite the nice letter he'd sent her after Ben's death, she was dubious about any real changes in his attitude. Men could pretend, to get parole. Hollister had told her that, sensing her concern about the future. He'd do what he could for her and Tad when Morris got out. He promised. Hollister could be scary. He had a mysterious past and he was friends with some equally scary people, despite his position with the police. But he was the best friend she had. He helped her get custody of Tad, so that social services wouldn't take him away, and he got her a small raise, which helped with expenses. It had devastated her last year when he was promoted to captain and moved downtown to a new office. She was happy for him, of course. But Clancey couldn't afford a car and she couldn't walk to work—it was much too far for her lungs. Hollister offered to drive her back and forth, but she felt she'd imposed on him enough. She heard about the opening in the Texas Ranger cold case office and applied for the job. Amazingly, she was hired as soon as the lieutenant interviewed her. That had been almost a year ago.

This job paid well, and she had benefits, as she'd had working for Hollister. They helped pay for insurance, and that was a blessing. She could still walk to work. But time hadn't eased her fear of her stepbrother. Banks had said he was supposed to get out soon. When was soon? And where would she and Tad go when he got out? Would he come after her? Her testimony had put him in prison. Her life could be in danger.

But when Morris got out, she comforted herself, she'd be advised by the victim advocates so she'd know about it. And he'd have a parole officer who would check on him frequently, and at unexpected times, to make sure he was keeping his nose clean. That sounded fine, but Morris could do a lot of damage if he was alone in the house with his stepsister and half brother. Although Tad was nine now, and she was twenty-three, Morris posed a threat to both of them, especially if he wasn't truly rehabilitated and started running with his old crowd of lawbreakers again.

She shivered, remembering. Morris knew how much she loved Tad, and she knew that if he planned to get even with her, Tad would be his means to do it.

So she worried incessantly about Morris getting out. The sentence had been for six years, but an attorney who knew his public defender told her one day in the office weeks ago that Morris had apparently been a model prisoner and there was talk that he might get out sooner. Banks had just confirmed that rumor.

One of her ideas about finding a home for her and Tad was to apply to the military. She would get a signing bonus that would provide a lot of new clothes and comforts for her and Tad. In addition, she'd get a place for her and Tad to live, where they wouldn't have to cope with Morris. There would be free medical care and dental, and insurance. The only downside was whether they'd take her. She had a health issue that she never discussed. But a doctor would spot it right away. Maybe she could find some way to deal with it beforehand.

Sure, she thought miserably, just like I've dealt with a better place to live and good clothes for Tad that didn't come out of thrift shops. Utilities and house payments and medicine and groceries took almost all her salary. Almost everything they wore had belonged to somebody else first. She didn't mind. She was grateful to have clothes at all. But it sometimes meant squeezing her feet into shoes that were a size too small or too large and jeans that she had to roll up because they were too long. She was luckier fitting Tad.

But he grew like a weed. He was tall now and getting taller by the day. Clothes didn't last him as long as they lasted her. And he'd been having issues at school that she didn't know how to deal with.

As a substitute mother, she was pretty much a dead bust, she sometimes thought. She loved Tad and she did everything she could to make him happy. But he got in fights and she didn't know why. He wouldn't talk to her about things that bothered him. He put on that sunny smile that she loved and said that she didn't lay her problems on him, so he wasn't laying his on her. Once, concerned, she had Cal Hollister come over and talk to him. She never knew what was said, but soon afterward, Tad stopped getting in fights and maintained a good average in his grades. Hollister, she thought, could work magic in one small boy.

Tad knew about Morris, of course. He'd only been three at the time, but he remembered Morris hurting him and knocking Clancey around when she tried to defend her little brother. He was afraid of Morris. So was Clancey.

He worried, as she did, what they'd do when their step-brother got out of prison.

Well, they wouldn't have to face it today, Clancey thought. And if she could ever work up enough nerve to talk to Banks about it, there might be a solution of some kind. It was just that Banks intimidated her. He was pleasant enough, from time to time, but she knew that he resented her. She didn't know why. He'd been antagonistic since her first day on the job and he'd tried infrequently to get her moved to another office. That would have been awkward, because she was the only person who applied for this job and he couldn't find anybody else—mainly, another man—who'd take it on. So he was stuck with her.

It worked both ways. Certainly, she was stuck with him, too! Big, arrogant, irritating Texas Ranger. He was so self-contained that he didn't even date anybody.

She knew why, of course. There was a lot of gossip about Colter Banks. He'd been in love with his best friend's fiancée. His best friend, Mike Johns, had been a police officer over in Houston. He was shot to death in an attempted bank robbery, along with his mother. He wasn't even on duty at the time. He'd just driven his mother to the bank.

Grace Charles, Mike's fiancée, had mourned him long and hard. Banks had comforted her and would have loved to take Mike's place, except that Grace suddenly enrolled with a missionary society and went to South America. She was deeply religious, something Banks wasn't. So he lost his best friend and his love interest. His sister, Brenda, had told one of her girlfriends about it when they came to take Banks for lunch, and Clancey had overheard them talking while Banks had gone to bring the car around.

Banks had asked for reassignment to San Antonio to get away from the bad memories. He seemed to have recovered. On the surface, at least.

But it wasn't Clancey's business. She put up with Banks because she had to, but he was too abrasively masculine to appeal to her. She'd had more than enough of belligerent men with attitudes.

SHE LOCKED UP the office and went to pick up Tad at the school he attended. They had an after-school class for students whose parents couldn't afford day care. Not that Clancey was a parent, but she sure couldn't afford day care!

"Hi, kid," she teased, ruffling his blond hair. "Did you miss me?"

"Not since breakfast," he teased, laughing. He was a tall boy. He came up to her shoulder now. He was beanpole thin and had blue eyes, like hers. He was always smiling. It made her feel good, just to be around him.

"How'd school go?" she asked when they were walking down the sidewalk.

"Better than usual," he replied. "I made an eighty on my math test."

"Very good!"

"And a fifty in history," he added with a sigh.

"We can't all be great scholars like me," she said with a haughty smile.

"Ha!"

She laughed and pulled him close to her side. "You'll do, kid," she said. "You'll do just fine. Mama would be proud of you."

They stopped in at the dollar store on the corner to get

Tad another notebook. Across the street, a tall man in a white Stetson was frowning as he watched them. Surely the boy wasn't Clancey's son. He scoffed at that idea. A little brother, probably. He'd never asked if her parents were still alive. He knew next to nothing about her, except that she was a pain in the neck at work.

Well, her private life had nothing to do with him, he thought as he continued on his way.

CLANCEY AND TAD walked the three blocks to the little house that they shared. It wasn't much, just a one-story shotgun house with three bedrooms and a walled-in porch. When Morris and Ben had lived with them, the men shared the master bedroom. Clancey and Tad had the smaller bedroom. Each had twin beds of an antique sort with metal headboards. The furnishings were bare. Faded curtains, faded sofa and easy chair, and an old rocking chair where her grandfather sat in the evenings while he watched TV with Ben and Morris. There was a fireplace with gas logs, and beside it, the implements that had been used years ago when there was an open fire there. She shivered as she looked at the empty wrought iron holder where a fire poker and a metal shovel had once stood. She remembered the shovel most. The police still had it, somewhere. It had been evidence in Morris's trial.

She averted her gaze to the rocking chair and the acoustic guitar on a stand in the corner. She smiled at the guitar, remembering evenings when her grandfather played for them. His rocking chair was just as he'd left it. She touched the worn piece of furniture with a loving hand and vowed that one day she'd find out what had happened to the old man. If Morris had anything to do with his disappearance, she'd find a way to make him pay for it. She blinked away the tears and went to the kitchen.

"What's for supper?" Tad asked, returning after he'd placed his backpack on his bed.

"Whatever we can find that won't put up much of a fight," she teased.

"I saw a chicken in a yard down the street," he said, his gray eyes twinkling.

"We are not chicken nappers," she said haughtily. Her own eyes began to sparkle. "However, if you can spot a beef steer, I'll go looking for a big bag!"

He grinned. Beef was rarely on the menu. It was mostly chicken, in a dish to go over rice, or canned salmon made into croquettes. Mashed potatoes and biscuits went with most evening meals. In the morning they ate cereal, because cornflakes lasted for several days. On the weekends, she made bacon and eggs and biscuits for breakfast. It was a frugal lifestyle.

"Oh, I wish we had a cake," she sighed, picking at her mashed potatoes.

"You could make us one."

"Dream on," she said sadly, thinking of the expense that even a pound cake added to the budget.

"Maybe we could get just a slice each at the grocery store," he suggested. "That's not as expensive as a whole cake."

She smiled at him warmly. "We can get two slices of cake when they send the Batmobile home and it's safely stored in our Batcave."

He made a face.

"It's ours," she emphasized. "I'm sure of it. Any day

now, some smarmy lawyer's going to come to the door and say they're bringing it right over."

"When dogs fly," he agreed.

"I'm sorry we're poor," she said gently. "I wish I had more education, so I could get a better job."

He went around the table and hugged her tight. "I'd rather have my sister than a Batmobile," he said huskily. "You're so good to me, sis. I don't care if we're poor. We got each other."

She bit her lip and hugged him back, tears threatening. "Yes, Tad. We've got each other."

He went back to his place and finished his supper. "Sis, what are we going to do when Morris gets out?" he wondered aloud.

Her heart jumped. The thought terrified her and she didn't dare show it. "We'll cross that flaming lava bed when we have to."

"It's his house, isn't it?"

"Yes," she said. "Well, until they either find Grand-daddy or prove that he's…dead. In which case, I'd inherit his half of the house. But that would take a lot of time." Her eyes saddened. "Tad, I've been thinking about the military. It's a good job, with great benefits. We'd get to travel…"

"No!"

He looked horrified. She stared at him blankly.

"All my buddies live here," he said, his face tragic. "We have this house, where we both grew up. Cal Hollister is close by if we get in trouble and need help." He sighed. "Our family settled here before the fight at the Alamo. You told me that. We can't give that up to go away to some foreign place. Please, Clancey," he added, his eyes huge in his face.

Her eyes narrowed. "That isn't why you don't want to go," she said suspiciously.

His thin chest rose and fell. His eyes lowered. "Mostly, the Army goes into bad places overseas. Lots of people in the military get killed."

"Oh. I see."

He didn't quite look at her. "You're all I've got, sis," he said softly. "I don't want to be put in a foster home. My friend Gary lives in one. He says it's awful…"

"I'd make sure there was no combat involved before I signed up," she began.

"What if they lie to you, just to get you to join?"

"You have a suspicious mind," she accused.

He grinned. "My sister works for the Texas Rangers," he teased. "Of course I have a suspicious mind. One day, I'm going to be a Texas Ranger and chase crooks."

"Really?"

He nodded. "Your boss looks real mean," he added.

Her heart jumped unaccountably. "When did you see him?" she asked.

"Last week. He was on television. They interviewed him about a robbery. He caught one of the bad guys. They said the case had been sitting for several years, but Mr. Banks worked it out from a slip of paper that had been found in a trash can after the robbery. He tracked down the thief."

"I remember," she said. She shook her head. "He's very good at puzzles. I think you have to be, if you want to work in law enforcement."

"I'm good at puzzles, too."

"In fact, yes, you are."

"Do you think your boss would ever talk to me, about being a Ranger?" he asked.

She felt uneasy. She didn't want Tad around Banks. She didn't know why. It was just that she hesitated to let him into her private life. She guarded it from everybody. She had, for years.

"Do you have homework?" she asked, trying to sound natural when her head was buzzing.

"I do," he replied. He grimaced. "A lot."

"You should get to it. Afterward, you can play video games until bedtime," she added.

"Okay!" He finished his milk and went tearing off to his room.

She sighed with relief. She didn't want to introduce him to Banks. She didn't know exactly why.

She washed up and cleaned the kitchen before she went to her own room to listen to music while she knitted. It was something she'd learned from her late mother. It relaxed her when she had nothing else to do. She liked to make shawls and hats, in all sorts of wild colors.

Tad and his video games, she thought amusedly. He had a space one that he was crazy about. It was good that he was, because one game was all she could afford to buy him for their used gaming console, which had belonged to Morris. The game had been on the discount shelf. It was gently used, but Tad didn't mind. Most of his electronics were second or even third hand. They couldn't afford much in the way of entertainment.

Clancey had been delighted that the benefits package she got with her new job was even better than the plan she'd had when she worked for Hollister at SAPD. Medical and dental were included. Medical expenses were the arrow in her knee. She had health problems that weren't apparent, but they could be expensive from time to time. It was nice that she didn't have to try to treat herself. She could afford to go to a doctor and be treated. There was a small co-pay, but she could manage that.

She was sorry Tad was so vehement about the military. It was probably just a wild dream anyway, she thought. They were unlikely to let her in. But on the off chance, she'd gone by the Army recruiting office before she picked up Tad at school and got some literature about joining. She'd mentioned her health issue to the soldier in charge, who grimaced, but said they did occasionally make exceptions, and she was welcome to try anyway.

She didn't want to make life even more complicated for her little brother. But when Morris got out, what were they going to do? Compared to living in a homeless shelter, the Army looked good. It looked very good.

She picked up her grandfather's guitar, sat down with it and began to play.

TWO

COLTER BANKS WAS discussing his cold case with the detective who'd worked the original case.

"Very peculiar," the detective replied, after he'd scanned the file. "The old man, Dalton Reed, didn't come home from work. There were no viable suspects, except his stepson, Morris Duffy, and we couldn't prove that he even had cause to kill the man. Reed had no enemies, unless it was someone he'd arrested during his career as a peace officer, but hardly anyone who was interviewed seemed to dislike him. Quite the opposite. His family seemed to care for him deeply. Well, there was the assault issue…"

"What assault issue?"

The detective opened the old file he'd pulled out. "Tragic case. There was a three-year-old boy who interrupted his stepbrother, who was playing some computer game. The stepbrother became enraged and started beating the child with a metal shovel, that sort that used to sit by fireplaces. Kid got a concussion and some bad bruises. His sister intervened to save him from his half brother. She took a really bad beating from the stepbrother, had two broken ribs and a lot of bruising. She was afraid of the perp and didn't want to press charges, but the officer who took her home from the emergency room saw the condition of the three-year-old, called an ambulance for the kid and promptly arrested the stepbrother. The suspect was tried on two counts of second-degree assault and battery, plus assault on a police officer and resisting arrest. He was found guilty and sent to prison for six years." He closed the file and grimaced. "The perp was on drugs and high as a kite, not that it's any sort of excuse for savaging a little kid and a nineteen-year-old girl."

"Lowlife bum," Banks muttered.

"Truly. But the assault case doesn't really pertain to your missing person."

"Where's the perp now?"

"In prison somewhere," he said. "His father's dead, victim of a hit-and-run not long after his son went to prison. No witnesses, the driver was never found."

Banks was frowning. "That's a lot of turmoil in one household," he mentioned.

"Yes, it is. They seemed well-adjusted, except for the boy on drugs, but the neighbors said a rough crowd used to hang out there during the day. The babysitter was afraid of them. She usually took the three-year-old to her house, to avoid them."

"A missing grandfather. A dead father, victim of a hit-and-run. A man sent to prison for assault on his three-year-old half brother and his stepsister." He pursed his chiseled lips. "If I wrote soap operas, this would appeal to me."

The detective laughed. "I guess it sounds that way."

"When's the boy due to get out of prison?"

"He's been a model prisoner, apparently," the detective said sarcastically. "He may get early release. It depends on the parole board. They're meeting this month."

"Can you keep me informed?"

The detective gave him an odd look. "Can't your assistant do that?" he asked.

Banks laughed. "Sure. Of course she can." He didn't question the strange wording.

"By the way, assistant DA Darrell Tarley is familiar with this case," the detective added. "He has a vested interest in it. He was the prosecuting attorney when Duffy was sentenced, and Duffy's threatened to kill him when he gets out."

"Really like a soap opera," Banks commented drolly.

"Pretty much," he chuckled. "How do you like working for the Texas Rangers?" the detective added.

"It's a hard job, but I love it," Banks replied. "It's like your job, never dull."

"You can say that again," the detective chuckled. "Never dull. Just bordering on madness."

"That's the nature of the game. Thanks for your time."

"Sure thing. Anytime."

Banks went out the door, gnawing on the old man's disappearance. He wondered if the boy on drugs knew more about Reed's disappearance than he'd let on. He also wondered if the boy might have had a motive for killing the old man. It was something he needed to check into.

His phone rang. He pulled it out of the holder on his belt and activated it. "Banks," he said.

"Hi! You free for supper?" came a pleasant female voice.

He chuckled. "I guess so. I don't really feel like cooking. Where?"

"I'm at Pete's Barbeque."

"My favorite place!"

"Mine, too! I'm tired of quick takeout," she added. "We had a full day at the clinic. Lots of emergencies."

"Mustn't let all those sick pooches and cats go without treatment," he agreed.

"Absolutely. See you in a few."

He hung up. His sister, Brenda, worked for a local veterinary practice. She loved animals. Banks was fond of cats, but he didn't like dogs. Brenda had kept one at her apartment until she moved. The new apartment didn't allow pets. It had broken her heart to give up her sheltie. She did find it a new home, though.

He had a pet of his own, a fluffy red Maine coon cat. His pet was huge, weighing over sixteen pounds. If he had to go out of town, Miss Kitty boarded at the veterinary hospital where Brenda worked.

HIS SISTER WAS in her early twenties, vivacious and cute, with short dark hair and dark brown eyes. The tips of her hair were emerald green. He made a face at that, and the small dragon tattoo on her forearm. She also liked to wear short skirts that showed off her long legs. But not at work, where she wore thick jeans and sweatshirts. Claws hurt.

"Nice tattoo," he murmured. "Not to mention the green hair." He rolled his eyes.

"I move with the times," she teased as they sat eating barbeque sandwiches and homemade French fries. "I fit right in at my office."

"The day you see me sporting a tattoo and green hair, you can commit me."

She grinned and finished her sandwich. "Have you heard the news?"

"What news?" he asked.

"Grace is coming to San Antonio for some training sessions with that missionary society she works for. Look out!" she added when his coffee cup tilted at a sharp angle. She picked up napkins and pushed them under the dripping mug.

"Grace is coming here?" he asked in a husky tone. "How do you know?"

"We're Facebook friends," she reminded him. She frowned. "You still don't have an internet presence, do you? Well, except for your email at work." She rolled her eyes. "All business."

He mopped up the spilled coffee, aware that his heart was turning cartwheels. Grace was the love of his life. She'd been engaged to his best friend, Mike Johns, a police officer in Houston, where Colter had also worked at the time. When Mike was killed in a bank holdup, Grace went a little crazy and signed on with a missionary society to go to South America.

They never told anyone, least of all Mike, but there had been an unexpected passionate kiss between them before Mike died. They were dealing with the guilt when he was gunned down. It split them apart at a time when Grace needed consolation desperately. She found it in her church work, rather than in Colter. Overseas, she'd been in an airplane crash. Colter had pulled strings to find out that she was all right, that she'd suffered only minor internal injuries. He'd written to her, but her reply had been offhand

and breezy, not the stuff of romantic fiction. Since then, years ago, he hadn't had any contact with her.

"You should get out more," Brenda said.

He raised both eyebrows. "I get out every day, chasing down criminals," he pointed out.

She gave him a mock glare. "You should date."

He made a gruff sound. "Women today," he muttered, looking her over. "Tattoos, green hair, overbearing, over-sexed…"

"Oh, for those long-ago days of women in lacy dresses, fanning themselves on the porch while they sipped lemonade," she said in a simpering tone.

He glowered at her. "You know what I mean."

Actually, she did. He'd taken out a woman who'd worked in public relations and been shocked to the back teeth when she actually tried to seduce him in a theater. She liked kinky sex.

Brenda didn't know the particulars, but she had a good idea of what had gone on. Her brother was such a prude! He didn't move with the times at all. Well, neither did Grace, who had some really radical ideas. Grace didn't believe in makeup or dancing, because her church group was one of the more radical sects. While her brother wasn't a libertine in any sense of the word, he was pretty laid-back for a lawman. He did at least take women out occasionally, because he loved to dance. She wondered if he'd really known Grace at all. She thought, privately, that the woman had been his ideal because he hadn't dated much back then, and Mike Johns idolized her. He'd only been around Grace because of Mike. They'd never been out on a real date together. Perhaps if they had, Brenda speculated, Colter's fixation on Grace might have died a natural death when he saw how rigid she really was in her belief system. But then, she decided, it was really none of her business.

She glanced at her watch. "I have to go. I don't want to miss my favorite TV show." She smiled at him. "Is Clancey still giving you fits?" she teased.

He gave a long-suffering sigh. "She threatens to quit every third day. I'd give real money if she'd actually do it."

She laughed. "She might. I saw her at the Army recruiting office a couple of days ago, getting literature."

His heart jumped for no apparent reason. He frowned. "Army?"

She nodded. "Don't knock it," she said with twinkling eyes. "She'd be out of San Antonio, for sure. And you'd be stuck with all those old files, down in the basement, all by yourself. Who'd take care of the office and handle calls while you were out? Who'd convert all those musty old files to computer files?"

He made a face and finished his coffee. "I'd find somebody. I asked for a man," he added shortly.

"She's a treasure," she chided. "She can do all that stuff and even put up with you. Don't start," she interrupted when he opened his mouth. "I'm your sister. I know you."

"I don't fly off the handle as much as I used to," he pointed out with a grin.

"Inspirational tirades, is how one of your colleagues used to put it," she mused. "He said you ran out of the usual curses in about two minutes and started making up new ones when you exploded."

He chuckled. "Well, I do have one saving grace—I don't cuss in front of women."

"I'll have to ask Clancey about that."

"Clancey's not a woman. She's just a kid," he replied.

"And please don't tell me that you're Facebook friends with her, too," he said.

"Clancey isn't on social media," she said, discouraged that he thought of his assistant as a kid. She was almost desperate to keep him away from Grace. "I don't think she even owns a computer."

"She uses ours at work."

"That's right, at work. She isn't the type who'd use work resources for personal pleasure."

"And how would you know that?" he asked.

"She goes to my church."

That was news. He knew next to nothing about Clancey's personal life. He didn't want to know. She was unsettling enough in a business sense. But he wasn't surprised that she went to church. She was mostly quiet and conscientious, she dressed conservatively, she never cussed. In fact, he'd never heard her say a bad thing about anybody, except the man who'd tried to grope her in her own office—the one who accidentally shot himself in the foot.

He laughed suddenly.

"What is it?" his sister wanted to know.

"I was thinking about the guy who groped Clancey in the office and got shot in the foot, accidentally."

She grimaced. "She should have had him arrested and prosecuted," she said hotly. "Honestly, what sort of man would do a thing like that in a public office?"

"He got shot," he reminded her.

"Pity he didn't hit anything worse than his own toe," she muttered.

He was surprised at her vehemence. She wasn't usually so passionate about things.

She caught that expression. "You're not a woman, so

you wouldn't understand," she said after a minute. "Men can be frightening when they're aggressive. I don't know Clancey well, but I overheard our minister say something to her after services one day, something about not all men being animals. That was even before she got groped on the job."

He frowned. The wording was unusual. He'd heard the terminology many times over his years in law enforcement, usually in conjunction with charges of rape or assault involving women. Now he was curious. What had happened to Clancey to provoke such a comment from her pastor?

Not that it was any of his business. She did a fairly good job and she was useful. Past that, he never noticed her.

"When is Grace coming here?" he asked.

"Next month," she said. She grinned. "She asked if you were still as straitlaced as you used to be."

"What did you tell her?"

"I told her you were even worse than you used to be."

"Gee, thanks," he teased.

She chuckled. "She said she approved." She picked up her big purse from the floor and pulled out a bill. "My turn to pay. You can do it next time," she added.

He put his wallet back up. "Okay. Fair enough. Thanks."

They got up. "Colt," she said, using the old nickname she'd given him when they were kids, "she's not the same woman she was." She continued, choosing her words, "She's very rigid in her beliefs these days. And very committed to the work she does overseas."

"That could change," he said with a wistful smile.

"It could," she agreed. "But whether it will or not is

anybody's guess. Just…well, just don't jump into anything."

"I never jump into things," he said. He hesitated. "How long have you been Facebook friends with her?" he asked suspiciously.

"Oh, not long," she lied. It wouldn't do to tell him that it had been over a year, because he'd wonder why she hadn't told him. She'd been trying to protect him. Grace spoke of Colter in fond terms, but hardly romantic ones, and she wasn't the same woman he'd known in Houston. She was very different.

She sighed. It was already too late to warn him off. He'd have to find out for himself that Grace had changed beyond his memory of her. She hoped he wouldn't break his heart all over again. And she also hoped that Grace wouldn't mention her long-standing Facebook relationship. She'd have to ask her to keep it to herself, without telling her the real reason why.

THE NEXT DAY at lunchtime, Clancey was busy converting old paper files into computer ones, in between answering the phone and wolfing down a homemade deviled ham sandwich. A thermos full of sweetened coffee with cream was sitting beside her lunch. Banks had been out of the office all morning, so she'd gotten a lot of work done. She looked up when she heard Banks close the door and come down the steps.

"The assistant district attorney on that bank robbery case last week wants to talk to you. I left his number on your desk," she said. "And one of the detectives at SAPD needs the number of the witness you spoke to about his assault case."

He picked up the paper on his desk and glowered at her

through the door to her small office. "I can't read this," he muttered.

"Look who's talking about bad handwriting," she said, exasperated. She got up from her desk in the next room and went to his. She took the paper out of his hands and printed every single word on the page. She handed it back to him. "If that's not legible enough, I can try crayons," she added blandly.

He glared at her through narrowed lids. "Isn't your coffee getting cold?"

"If we had a microwave oven in here, I wouldn't have to use a thermos," she pointed out.

"Great idea. Why don't you go talk to the lieutenant and tell him why we need one?" he asked. "Better yet, why don't you bring yours to work?"

She stared at him. "I don't own a microwave oven."

"Everybody owns a microwave oven. I even have one," he said.

"Well, I don't." She turned and went back into her office, aware of hurt pride. She didn't have a lot of things that most people did. Times were hard. She and her little brother, Tad, had to live on what she made, and even though it was a good salary for the work, it didn't cover any luxuries at all. She and Tad dressed out of thrift shops. She made her lunch and had to scrape up enough for Tad's lunches at school.

She only worked for Banks because this office was within two blocks of the house that Morris now owned, where she and Tad lived. She'd worked for Cal Hollister up until she wound up here with this infuriating lawman. She missed Cal. He was the best boss any woman could have asked for, polite and grateful for the work she did, full of praise and encouragement.

She glanced at Banks, who was on the phone now, and thought how she'd love to trade him for Cal. The problem was that the office where Cal worked was way downtown and about two miles from her home. She couldn't afford to buy even an old used car, much less afford the insurance and upkeep and gas to run it. Her legs were in great shape, even if her lungs weren't, so she could walk to work. She could also walk Tad to school every day and over to pick him up afterward at the after-school program for children of working parents. She wasn't Tad's parent, but she was responsible for him, legally responsible. Cal had helped her with that. He'd helped her with a lot of things.

"Ungrateful wretch," she muttered under her breath as she finished the last of her cooling coffee.

"Nasturtium," he countered.

"Will you stop calling me that!" she exclaimed. "I am not a nasturtium! I'll bet you don't even know what it means!" she added, throwing his own comment from the other day back at him.

He just laughed.

She put up her thermos, threw her trash into the can under her desk and went back to work on the files.

She'd never put her whole name on the employment application she'd filled out at the Department of Public Safety, under whose umbrella the Texas Rangers operated. So Banks didn't know her whole name. Wouldn't he be taken aback to know what her second given name was, and its definition? The thought amused her.

"I have to go over to the sheriff's office to see about a case I'm working," he said from the doorway. He frowned.

"What were you doing at the Army recruiting office?" he asked out of the blue.

Her fingers faltered on the computer keyboard and made a mess that she had to undo. "Who said I was there?" she asked uneasily.

"My sister, Brenda," he replied.

"Oh." She knew Brenda from church. She liked her. It wasn't Brenda's fault that she had Attila the Hun here for a brother.

"Well?" he persisted.

She looked up into curious black eyes. She averted her own. She couldn't handle meeting that glittery gaze very often. It unsettled her. "I was thinking about the benefits," she said absently.

"You have benefits here," he said shortly. "Insurance, retirement, the whole bundle, besides which, you don't have to carry a rifle and shoot people."

She flushed. She wasn't going to tell him that she'd never get in the Army, with her health problems. It had been a whim. When Morris got out, and he might very soon, she and Tad would be on the streets, because there was no way she'd agree to live under the same roof with her stepbrother. Besides being afraid of him, physically, she was afraid of what retribution he might want to exact from her and her little brother. Morris was vindictive. Clancey's testimony had put him in jail for six years. He wasn't going to forgive that, no matter how nice he'd sounded in that letter he wrote her after Ben died. Anyway, that had been years ago.

"I could learn to carry a rifle," she muttered.

"And shoot people?"

She drew in a breath and shrugged. "They have clerks and stuff in the Army," she said. "I could do that."

"Maybe you could, but what a recruiter tells you and what you actually have to do are two different things."

"Like you know," she said irritably.

"I do know," he replied. "I went into the Army at the age of eighteen. They promised me sunny California. I ended up in Afghanistan, learning to speak Farsi and shoot people."

She flushed. "Oh. Sorry."

He cocked his head and frowned. "If you don't like it here, you can always go back to work for Hollister," he pointed out. He even looked hopeful.

"I can't walk that far."

He blinked. "Are we having the same conversation?"

"I can't walk all the way downtown and back every day," she repeated. "I live two blocks from here, so I can walk to work."

"You worked for Hollister for four years," he pointed out, having read it on her employment application.

"Yes, when he was in an office the next street over, be-fore he got promoted to captain," she pointed out. "Now he works downtown."

"You can get cabs to work, or the bus."

"I can't afford cabs and the bus doesn't come near my house."

He studied her unconsciously. He noticed, for the first time, that her clothes weren't new. She was neat and clean, but she pretty much wore three different outfits to work and changed around the shirts and jeans. She had an old ratty jacket that she wore when it was cool, as it was today.

Autumn was chilly, even in San Antonio, which was far enough south that palm trees grew and thrived all over it.

"I should sign up tomorrow and let you replace me with some lazy man who can't even spell," she muttered, uneasy at his long silence and that curious stare.

He'd already tried that. There weren't any male applicants for this job. There had been four women who applied for it, three of whom were dressed like women who occupied street corners. Hence, Clancey.

"Men don't like dark basements," he said.

"I don't know why not," she said, ignoring him. "Don't men like caves?" She looked around at the dark paneling and lack of light fixtures. "This would surely qualify."

He wouldn't laugh, he wouldn't laugh… He turned the chuckle into a cough. "I'll be back in an hour or so, if anybody comes looking for me."

"If it's somebody from the mounted unit, I'll send them right along."

His high cheekbones took on a faint ruddy color. "I did not steal his horse," he said indignantly. "I appropriated it in pursuit of a fugitive!"

"I never said you stole it," she replied. Her eyes twinkled. "But he did."

"We straightened it out."

She pursed her lips. "Did you, really? I understand that he loves to park his horse right in front of your car anytime he sees you near his post."

"I'm sure it isn't deliberate."

She laughed softly. "Oh, I'm sure," she drawled.

He shoved his hat down over his thick dark brown hair. "I'm leaving."

"I noticed."

He went out and actually slammed the door behind him. Clancey fell into gales of laughter.

SHE AND TAD never went out at night. It was far too dangerous, and Clancey was nervous because there were usually men hanging around the bars that were near the theater where she and Tad occasionally had enough money for a matinee. Today, Saturday, was one of those days.

The film they went to see was *Haunted Halloween*, an animated film based on the famous R. L. Stine books that Tad loved so much. They laughed with the rest of the audience as a bevy of impossible creatures were loosed on the town by two adventurous boys in a haunted house.

They were still laughing as they went out onto the street. It was nearly Halloween. Tad had wanted a Storm Trooper costume—he was crazy about the *Star Wars* films—but they couldn't afford one. So he settled for a cobbled together Jedi Knight costume, consisting of an old hooded cloth coat that had belonged to their grandfather and a homemade lightsaber—a long stick wrapped in aluminum foil and crepe paper. It didn't look at all bad, Clancey thought.

"What are you going to dress up for at Halloween, Clancey?" Tad asked as they walked toward home in a brisk breeze that swirled dead leaves up from the sidewalk. She shivered a little. She'd only worn a sweatshirt with her jeans. She wished she'd worn her ratty old jacket. At least Tad was wearing his.

"A fairy princess," she told him facetiously.

"Come on," he persisted. "What are you going as, really?"

"A clerk for the Texas Rangers, I guess," she sighed,

looking down at her worn jeans and sneakers and gray sweatshirt, all found at a thrift store.

"We could make you a costume, too," he said.

She smiled at him. "We made you one. That's going to have to do, this year."

"Cal said he'd drive us around, if we wanted him to. Not many people where we live give out candy."

"When did he say that?" she asked curiously.

"He came by the school to give a talk on drug prevention," he told her with a grin. "It was just before lunch, so he stayed and talked to me for a little while. He wanted to know if you were doing okay."

She laughed softly. "He's a worrywart," she said with affection.

"Well, you get sick a lot when it's autumn," he replied, worried.

She drew him close to her side. "I don't go outside much," she said.

"You walk to and from work. And we're outside now, and it's windy and cold and you don't even have on a jacket," he murmured.

She grimaced. She only had a ratty old coat. It was too hot for cool days like this. Her sweatshirt wasn't quite warm enough in late afternoon. But her chest seemed okay. She had preventive medicines and she did use them—when she remembered.

"Stop worrying," she chided, planting a kiss on his blond hair. "I'm indestructible."

He drew in a long breath. "Clancey, what if he gets out soon?"

Her face tightened. "We'll figure out something."

"He owns the house. Doesn't he? I don't want to live with him. I'm afraid of him," he added in a small voice.

She stopped on the sidewalk and looked down at him. "I'm afraid of him, too," she confessed. "We'll do something before he's released. There are government apartments. I'll ask Cal if he'll help us find one."

"They won't take me away from you?" he added, frightened.

"Never," she said firmly, and prayed that she wasn't lying. "I'll never let them take you away."

He let out the breath he'd been holding. "Okay."

They turned the corner and there was Banks, talking to a uniformed officer on the sidewalk, his big black SUV parked at the curve.

Clancey hesitated. She started to nudge her little brother back the other way, but it was too late. Banks had already spotted them. He said something to the uniformed officer, who nodded and started off down the street.

"Hi, Mr. Banks," Tad said with a big smile.

Colter's eyebrows lifted in a silent question.

"I saw you on TV, on the news! Sis talks about you all the time," Tad volunteered.

Clancey went red as a beet. "I talk about work," she interjected hastily.

"I want to be a Texas Ranger when I grow up and catch criminals," Tad added.

Colter smiled down at the boy. "Do you?"

"Sis got me a book about Rangers. Do you really have to ride horses sometimes to chase bad guys?"

Colter nodded. "Yes, we do. Sometimes we're involved in cases where we have to go into the brush country in pursuit. You can't take a car in those places."

"We've been to the movies!" Tad said. "Sis saves up so we can go to one every month!"

Colter glanced at Clancey, who looked as if she wanted to go through the pavement. *Odd reaction*, he thought.

"We should get moving..." she prompted her little brother.

"It's pretty cold out here," Colter said, noting her lack of a jacket. The boy had on one that, while clean, was obviously secondhand. "Come on. I'll drive you home."

"That isn't..." Clancey began quickly, because she didn't want her boss to see the painful poverty in which they lived.

But Tad interrupted her. "That would be great! Do you have a police radio in your vehicle? And does it have one of those blue lights and a siren...?"

Colter chuckled. He liked the boy's enthusiasm. "Yes, I do, and a laptop that connects to the internet, as well."

"Wow!" Tad exclaimed, all eyes and enthusiasm.

Colter led the way to the SUV.

"You can ride shotgun," Clancey told Tad. "I'll just climb in the back."

Colter was puzzled by her behavior. At the office, she was all mouth and sarcasm. Here, out of the office, she was shy and introverted and hardly spoke. He put Tad up into the passenger seat after he'd moved his things out of it and started to reach for the seat belt. Tad already had it in place.

"Cal said I must always put on my seat belt every time I get in a car," Tad explained.

"Cal?" he asked.

"Cal Hollister. He's my friend," he said proudly.

"I know Hollister. He's a good guy," Colter agreed.

"Watch your hands." He closed the door and went around to climb in under the steering wheel. He glanced in the rearview mirror. Clancey was strapped in, also, but staring out the window as if she felt trapped.

"Okay," he said as he started the SUV. "Somebody direct me."

"It's on Oak Street," Clancey volunteered reluctantly. "Number 241. There's a 911 sign on the lawn, beside the mailbox."

He nodded and pulled out into the street. Beside him, Tad was looking at everything and plying him with questions. Clancey was grateful, because she was unsettled with her boss. She could disguise it at work, but it seemed very different outside the office, almost uncomfortable. She didn't want him to see where they lived. It wasn't just the poverty of it; there was the address. What if he remembered that from his cold case? Her grandfather had lived here, before he vanished without a trace.

She almost panicked. Then she realized that if she got Tad out of the SUV very quickly, they could thank him and rush inside. He'd probably forget the address at once. Then he wouldn't have to see what miserable conditions they endured here.

Colter drove, wondering why the address seemed so familiar. Perhaps he was remembering her job application, he thought. He'd only scanned it when she was hired, and not very closely. Strange, to have an address click in his mind. That usually only happened when he was working a case. He dismissed the thought and concentrated on Tad's questions.

THREE

BANKS SAW AT once why Clancey had tried to avoid riding here with him. It was more than apparent that her family lived in appalling poverty.

The house needed painting. The door had a torn screen. The wooden steps had a missing piece on one side, and they were bowed from long use. The shingled roof looked as if it probably leaked in heavy rain. Banks frowned as he noted the other houses nearby, most of which were in a similar dilapidated condition. It wasn't a better section of the city. He'd never thought about where Clancey lived. He wondered why her parents didn't maintain the house.

Tad unfastened his seat belt. "Come on in, Mr. Banks!" he invited. "I want to show you my meteorite that Clancey bought me! It's awesome!"

Clancey got out with the boy. "Tad, Mr. Banks is working today…" she began, her face coloring as she tried to shut down her brother.

"Oh, he's got a minute, haven't you, Mr. Banks? It's a swell meteorite!"

Colter smiled at the boy. "Is it? I like rocks myself." He glanced at Clancey, who looked devastated. He scowled at her expression.

Tad ran ahead and unlocked the door with the key he always carried in his jeans pocket.

"What do your parents do for a living?" he asked Clancey as they approached the front door.

She felt small beside him. At the office, she rarely approached him except in the line of duty, and not close up. He was tall and powerfully built and he made her very nervous.

"Mama was a clerk at a law firm," she said as they walked. "Daddy was a mechanic. He worked downtown for an automobile dealership. Ben, Tad's father, was a custodian."

Tad opened the door and motioned them inside. "Why do you refer to them in the past tense?" Colter asked, puzzled.

She drew in a breath, flushing as they walked into the living room with its sparse, dated, ragged furniture and curtains made of old sheets. "Our parents, and my stepfather, are all dead now," she said after a minute. "There's just me and Tad left."

He was shocked. He'd never considered that she might be on her own. What a responsibility! Her little brother had to be in grammar school. Was she supporting both of them by herself? He looked around, scowling at the poverty he recognized.

"How long have you been responsible for the boy?" he asked, facing her.

She spoke to his badge. She was too embarrassed to meet his eyes. "Since I was nineteen, when my stepfather, Tad's father, died," she replied. "Cal Hollister helped me get officially named Tad's guardian, so he wouldn't have to go into a foster home. He's the only family I've got left," she added softly.

Tad came running back into the awkward silence with a small black stone. He handed it to Colter. "Isn't it awesome?" he asked enthusiastically. "It's a tektite. They're one of the rarest meteorites. Clancey saved up to buy it for me. It's just small, but I'm really proud of it."

Colter swallowed, hard, as he studied the stone. He could only imagine how hard it was for the woman beside him to stretch her salary to clothing and shelter and groceries, much less luxuries like meteorites. He hadn't realized what her home situation was like. He hadn't wanted to know. He glanced down at her and noted her discomfort. She bit her lip and wouldn't look at him.

"It's really nice, son," Colter said softly, smiling as he handed the stone back to the boy.

"My name's really Terrance, but Clancey always calls me Tad," the boy volunteered, smiling back at the big man. "She doesn't use her real name, either, cause nobody can pronounce it right…"

"Shouldn't you put that up, before you lose it?" Clancey interrupted, smiling forcibly as she stared at her little brother.

"I guess so," Tad said, frowning. She looked upset. He didn't know why.

Colter wondered at her vulnerability. She didn't seem the same woman who chided him about his handwriting at work. She was so withdrawn that it was like pulling teeth to even talk to her.

"Thanks for bringing us home," she said, lifting her

eyes no higher than the neck of his spotless white shirt. "It was kind of you."

"No problem," he replied.

Tad ran back to his room, to put up his treasure. Colter stared down at Clancey until she lifted her eyes, reluctantly, to his.

"I grew up on a ranch outside Catelow, Wyoming," he said quietly. "My father had a few head of cattle. He'd been a rodeo cowboy, but he was crippled in the ring and had to give it up. He drank because he could never achieve his former glory, and when he drank, he went after me with a doubled-up belt. When Brenda was two years old, he died in an accident. Our mother sold the ranch to my father's brother and moved us down to Jacobsville, where she had a sister. She got a job waiting tables and kept us going, with Dad's Social Security check, until I was old enough to join the local police force. Her health was giving out by then. A couple of years later, I enlisted in the Army, where I got better pay and other benefits."

She sighed. "I noticed the benefits," she said wistfully.

He frowned. "And I'll remind you about what I said. They come at a cost."

She bit her lower lip.

He drew in a breath and averted his eyes. "I sent money home while I was overseas, to help Mom keep the household going. When I came home, I signed on with the Department of Public Safety in Houston and commuted. My mother died when Brenda was in grammar school. I eventually got in with the Rangers, in Houston. It's been just the two of us ever since."

"Brenda is nice," she said. "She goes to my church."

"She told me." He looked around. "You live within your

means. So did we, during lean times," he said. He moved a step closer, bringing her eyes up to his face. "There's no shame in being poor, Clancey," he said, his voice deep and soft.

Her lips parted. She hadn't known that about her boss. She'd assumed that he came from some normal, middle-class family. It was a shock that he knew about poverty firsthand. "Thanks," she said huskily, averting her eyes.

"So there's no reason to be embarrassed about where and how you live," he added softly. His lean hand moved to her short, wavy dark hair and pushed back a strand that had fallen near her eyes.

She swallowed, hard, and moved back a step, flushing because she knew he'd take it the wrong way that she'd retreated. She couldn't help it. She was afraid of men because of what Morris had done to her. It wasn't rational, and she knew Banks would never hurt her. It was instinctive. She ground her teeth together and looked tormented.

He frowned. He was remembering the overbearing man who'd shot himself in the foot trying to grope her. She had her arms wrapped around her chest and she looked as if she was being tortured to death. He also recalled what Brenda had told him, what her pastor had said to her at church.

"It's a lot of responsibility that you have here," he said after a minute, keeping his voice low.

She nodded. She drew in a long breath. At least he hadn't blown up, when she backed away. "I love my brother."

"I love my sister. She's ten years younger than me. I was responsible for her after our mother died. I know what it's like."

It was a moment of shared experience. But he didn't

know about Morris. She didn't want him to know, ever. She worked for a Texas Ranger and her brother was a convicted felon. How would that look? Worse, she hadn't mentioned it when she applied for the cold case clerk position. She could lose her job. It would be a disaster. She'd lose Tad. She'd mentioned that to Cal, who'd said it wouldn't matter. But she wasn't sure about that. She didn't trust men anymore. Well, except for Cal.

Tad came running back, with a book in his hand. "I almost never found it! This is my book about Texas Rangers!"

Colter took it from him and looked at it, smiling. It was a basic book about the Rangers and what they did; a free one.

"Sis took me to the Texas Ranger Museum one Saturday," he said. "We got a bus there and back. It was awesome, especially those pictures of the old days!"

Colter chuckled. "I know what you mean," he said, handing back the book. "Those old-timers were tough." He smiled. "The modern ones are, too," he added. "We have to be."

"I'll study real hard," Tad said, serious now. "If I get good grades and stay out of fights, maybe I can be a Ranger, too, someday."

Colter frowned. "Fights?"

The boy grimaced. "Well, not so much anymore. Cal said I had to learn to…" He glanced at his sister, who was glaring at him. He shrugged. "I don't get into fights now," he added, and smiled.

"Good man," Colter said. "Violence is rarely the answer to any problem."

He wondered why they both looked so grim. He glanced at his big watch. "I've got to get going," he said. "I'm working a robbery."

"On Saturday?" Tad asked.

He chuckled. "We work whenever we need to," he replied. "It was nice to meet you, Tad," he added.

Tad grinned from ear to ear. "It was nice to meet you, too!"

Colter glanced at Clancey, who still looked nervous. "See you Monday, kid," he said with a smile.

She forced a smile in reply. "You will," she replied.

He glanced toward a corner of the living room and saw an older classical guitar sitting in a chair. "Who plays?" he asked abruptly.

Clancey swallowed, hard. "Our grandfather used to."

He moved closer and looked at the guitar more closely. "New strings," he remarked, glancing at her with a questioning look.

"I play, too. Just a little."

He smiled. "It's a beautiful instrument."

She nodded. "Granddaddy got it when he was a boy. I miss him," she added softly.

"He's dead?"

She nodded. It was easier than telling him the truth. "Thanks again for bringing us home."

"Anytime," he replied.

He gave the guitar one last look, smiled secretively and closed the door behind him, when he left.

Clancey let out the breath she'd been holding.

"Why do you look so nervous?" Tad asked.

"I'm not comfortable around men," she confessed.

"Yeah, but Mr. Banks wouldn't hurt you. He's nice."

She managed a smile. "Yes, he is. It's a woman thing. If you grow up to be a woman, I'll explain it to you," she added wickedly.

He made a face at her. "I'm going to grow up to be a

big, strong man," he countered. He frowned. "Will I be taller than Dad, you think?"

"You might be as tall as your grandfather," she replied gently. "He was six feet tall."

"I don't remember him, much," Tad said, sadly.

"He was a sweet man," she replied. She sighed. "I miss him very much."

"I don't remember Dad so much." He shivered. "I remember Morris, though."

"We both have cause to remember him."

"They'll tell us, if he gets out early, right?" he worried aloud.

She hugged him. "They'll tell us. At least, Cal will, even if everybody else forgets."

"I like Cal. He's cool. But your boss is awesome!" he added.

She sighed. "He's not what I thought he was," she replied thoughtfully.

"Why?"

"It's a long story and I have to fix supper," she replied. "Go shoot aliens while I put something on to cook."

"You bet!"

He ran back to his room while she headed to the kitchen. If she could have afforded it, she'd have invited Banks to have coffee. But it was so expensive that she rationed it to one cup a day. Still, she could have offered. She felt cheap and mean. She was uneasy about letting him into her life—that was the real reason. She didn't want him to know about Morris. She didn't ever want him to know.

SHE LAY AWAKE that night, remembering what Banks had told her about his upbringing. He'd turned out very well, all things considered. She wasn't so ashamed of the house now. He'd been shocked that she was taking care of Tad all alone. He had no idea how much the child meant to her, how full of tragedy their lives had been. That was something she didn't intend to share.

It had been nice of him to bring them home. She'd noticed him staring at her thin sweatshirt and Tad's jacket. He must have known that she was cold.

She felt the tickle in her chest and ground her teeth together. She'd have to take some over-the-counter cough medicine and hope that it would ward off the problem she had every fall. She'd been on the job long enough to accumulate sick time, and that was a blessing, but she didn't want to have to use it. Cal had always made allowances for her. She wasn't sure that Banks would, or could. She couldn't afford to lose her job. Utilities and insurance and the mortgage had to be paid. So did heat and groceries and the medicine she couldn't do without.

Why, oh why, she wondered, was life so hard? She closed her eyes with a sigh and dreamed about having enough money to take Tad to the movies more than once a month.

MONDAY WAS A hectic day. Banks had a problem with the printer that caused him to slip and say a very bad word, after which he threatened to shoot the helpless machine.

"You shouldn't say bad words in the office," Clancey chided.

He glared at her with glittery black eyes. "I have to print out a letter to the parole board about a prisoner we put in jail. It has to go out today. It wouldn't take five minutes if this damned thing hadn't decided to be a pain in the neck!'

She looked at it curiously. She didn't own a printer or a computer, but she'd learned a lot about them when she worked for Cal. She'd worked with all sorts of office equipment. "It doesn't have any ink. See?" She pointed at the digital readout on its front. "It needs new cartridges."

"I don't have any cartridges!" he ground out. "It came like this!" He waved his big, lean hands expressively at it. "Nobody said it would run out of ink the day after we put it on the desk!"

"It was bought in August," she said in a calm voice, "and it's October. Ink doesn't last forever."

"October." He looked at the printer with a sigh. "So what do I do now?"

"You buy ink cartridges," she replied. "They have them at the office supply store two blocks over, next to the barbecue joint."

"What sort do I buy?"

She stared up at him with exasperation. "Mr. Banks, you write down the make and model of the printer and you ask for them at the store. You'll need a color one and a black ink one. In fact, you can take the print cartridges themselves and show them to the salesperson."

He stared at the printer, cocking his head. "And how do you get them out of there?" he asked heavily.

"It opens, somewhere."

"I could open it," he muttered, with his hand on his .45 automatic.

"You'll hurt its feelings and then it will shut down," she cautioned.

"Oh, come on!"

"Machines have feelings," she said, bending over to look for the switch that opened the cartridge port. "I tell my computer all the time how sweet and useful it is, and it never breaks down." She found the catch. "And I never threaten to shoot it," she added with an accusing glance.

"That doesn't mean much when you can't even shoot a gun, Clancey," he returned.

"I can shoot a .38," she said absently while she coaxed the cartridges out of the printer.

He frowned. He was watching her. She was wearing jeans and a sweatshirt. The sweatshirt was loose, but the jeans were nicely fitting, and she had long legs and a very curvy bottom. He caught himself staring and immediately averted his eyes when she stood up. She had the cartridges in her hand.

"Oh darn, they're leaking," she groaned. She went to get some paper towels off the roll she kept in the bathroom, while he stood and did math in his head to unlock his rigid body. He couldn't imagine why Clancey aroused him. He was self-conscious and a little inhibited. She was Brenda's age, much too young for him. If he'd been thinking along those lines, which he assured himself he wasn't.

He relaxed, finally, as she returned with the cartridges wrapped in paper towels in a plastic bag she'd found.

"Where did you learn to shoot a gun?" he asked curiously.

"My grandfather taught me about big guys, but Cal taught me how to shoot a pistol," she said. "He took me out to the firing range and let me practice." She winced. "It made my hands so sore. He said I had to learn to fire with either hand, like the FBI teaches you."

He scowled. "Why did he teach you?"

"It was just for fun," she stammered, and then flushed. That wasn't true. Cal had started teaching her right after Morris beat up her and Tad, while Morris was still living at home. Cal had even given her a little .32 caliber pistol. She'd assured him that she could never shoot anybody. He'd assured her that there were times when a gun might be the only way to save lives. And he added a rider about how Morris was drugged up half the time, and dangerous to both her and Tad. That was while Morris was waiting for his court case to be called. It didn't go to trial for several months after the assault that had cowed Clancey.

"Does he still take you out to the range?" he wondered aloud and could have kicked himself for asking the question.

"Not anymore," she said. There was no need, since Morris had been locked up. She handed him the bag. "The cartridges," she added.

He took the bag from her cold fingers. He noticed that she had pretty fingers, but that she wore no polish on them. He looked at her hair as well, with a frown.

"What's wrong?" she asked.

"You don't wear fancy nail polish or put green tips on your hair," he noticed. His black eyes began to twinkle. "No tattoos, either?"

"I don't like needles," she replied. One side of her pretty bow mouth pulled down. "And I can just see me trying to wear purple-tipped hair and a tattoo in this office! The first time the lieutenant saw me, I'd be standing in the unemployment line!"

He pursed his lips. "The lieutenant has a tattoo. But if you ask him where it is, he turns red and finds an excuse to leave the room."

"What?" Her eyes danced and she laughed.

Her whole face lit up when she laughed, and her pale silver eyes glimmered like sun on steel. He smiled unconsciously at the picture she made, like that.

She met those searching black eyes and her face felt suddenly tight, like her body. She moved back a step, uncomfortable and uncertain, not really understanding why she wanted to run.

"Cartridges. Right. Then if these don't work," he added, "we shoot it."

"You can't shoot equipment that's issued to us. It's a state agency," she pointed out.

"I'll shoot it in a very governmental way," he promised.

She couldn't help herself. She laughed.

"You don't do that very often," he remarked.

"Do what?"

"Laugh."

"It's not dignified."

He chuckled. "Neither am I, mostly. Okay, hold down the home fort. I'll waste half a day searching for cartridges that probably won't even fit and then try to get this persnickety piece of office equipment to cooperate with me."

"Persnickety?" she asked, eyebrows uplifted.

"It was my grandmother's word for anything she wanted to call a bad name, but wouldn't," he said. "She was one of the first female peace officers in Wyoming. She worked as a deputy sheriff."

"What a fascinating person she must have been."

He nodded. "I was ten. She was gunned down on the job, giving out a speeding ticket to a man who turned out to be a fugitive from a murder charge." His face tautened. "I think that's why I wanted to be a lawman. I couldn't save her, but I hoped I might save somebody else and pass it on."

She understood at once. "My grandfather was a deputy sheriff in a county south of here, and then in San Antonio for many years," she said. "His health failed, or he'd probably still have been doing it when…when we lost him," she said, amending what she'd started to say. "Even so, he worked as a special deputy from time to time. He loved his job."

"Tad's father, how did he die?"

"Ben was hit by a speeding car," she said simply. "It was so unexpected. He could be kind, when he wanted to."

"Any family living?"

She hesitated. Morris was a stepbrother, not family. "No," she said softly. "All my people are dead."

"So are most of mine," he replied. "I have a cousin who's a sheriff up in Wyoming. He lives in Catelow, where Brenda and I are from." He sighed. "He's had a hard life himself. His wife was a doctor. She caught a deadly virus while treating a patient. She died. Cody never got over that. He keeps to himself. He said he'd rather have her memory than half a dozen modern, man-hating women."

She sighed. "That's so sad."

He looked at her until she raised her eyes. "You don't date, do you?"

"Most men wouldn't understand why I'd have to take Tad with me if I went on a date," she said, and her eyes twinkled.

"It's a hell of a lot of responsibility," he said quietly. "You've taken care of him for how long?"

"Since I was nineteen," she said. "I love my brother," she added quietly. "I'd do anything to keep him safe."

He nodded. "I've taken care of my sister, since she was only a little older than Tad. I understand the lack of a social life." He chuckled. "I had to take her on dates, too, because I had nobody to leave her with. Odd, how it puts women off."

"I guess it would put men off, too," she mused.

His black eyes narrowed. "Don't you know?"

She grimaced. "I…sort of had a bad experience," she said hesitantly. "I don't trust men."

"It shows," he said.

She swallowed. "Sorry."

"It wasn't an accusation." He cocked his head as he stared down at her. "Was he prosecuted?"

She moved restively. "Yes."

"But you can't get past the memory."

She studied his lean, strong face. "Not really," she confessed on a sigh. "Men scare me."

"Which explains the bullet hole in the volunteer deputy's foot," he added.

"He was really aggressive." She folded her arms across her chest. "Cal taught me some martial arts moves, but he said to never confront a man I could run from. He said that no matter how well you can do those moves in a studio, it's different with a real attacker. He said that overconfidence gets a lot of women killed."

"It does," he returned. "A man on drugs or drunk on alcohol is hard to take down, even for men or women with extensive martial arts training."

"Most law enforcement agencies have women who work there. Do martial arts really work for them?"

"In desperate situations, ones where they might be killed if they can't counterattack, they usually reach for a stun gun or a pistol, or a riot gun, if other lives are in jeopardy," he replied. "A little woman is hard-pressed to subdue a man twice her size, even with ongoing instruction. We had a perp killed a few years ago for that very reason. The officer, who was female, had two broken ribs and a torn rotator cuff after she tried a stun gun, which didn't stop the perp from beating her half to death. She was barely able to get her firearm out in time to save her life. Not that male officers don't occasionally get put in the same situation." He smiled. "Not all men are six foot five and muscular," he added.

"I don't ever want to wear a badge," she said quietly.

"It's not a bad life. Certainly, not as demanding as the military."

She drew in a breath. She sounded raspy. "I guess it wouldn't be."

"You've got a good job here. Why were you thinking about the military?" he persisted.

She bit her lower lip. "Well, see, the house we live in belongs to Tad's half brother. If he ever comes back here to live, we'll have to find someplace else to go."

He scowled. "Why? Isn't he family, too?"

She swallowed. "Tad's scared of him."

He started to ask another question when his phone exploded with sound. He pulled it out of its holster, irritated at the interruption. "Banks," he said shortly.

"What? Oh! No, I hadn't forgotten," he said. "The damned printer ran out of ink just as I started to print out a letter I need to send today. So now I have to go find cartridges for the damned thing…yes, I know, I'll be there in ten minutes. No problem." He hung up.

He glared at the printer.

"If you shoot it, they'll take away your gun," she said, reading his expression.

He sighed. "They probably would. All right, I'll feed it two new cartridges when I get back." He paused at the door and looked at her over one broad shoulder. "But I'm not talking to it!"

He went out and slammed the door behind him.

Clancey went back into her own office and chided herself for almost spilling the beans about Morris.

It was a good thing that she and her grandfather didn't share the same last name as Morris and Ben Duffy. As it was, her grandfather's last name was on that police report that Banks was going by. It wasn't the same as Clancey's, either.

She felt guilty about not mentioning it. It made her feel good, that Banks was looking for her grandfather's assailant. He probably assumed that Clancey's grandfather was dead. She imagined it was true.

Morris had almost certainly killed the old man, who was trying very hard to connect Morris with a group of local drug dealers. Clancey agonized over what had really happened to him. She hoped that it was quick, at least, and that he hadn't suffered.

But she knew that he was never coming back home. She hoped that Banks could dig up enough evidence to charge Morris, even if he was never convicted. It was a shame that the kind old man was gone without a trace, and that nobody was held accountable for his disappearance.

BANKS CAME BACK much later, with two ink cartridges—the right kind—and Clancey put them in for him. But when he started the print command, the printer promptly ate two sheets of paper and jammed.

"Not a word!" he said, pointing a finger at her.

"I didn't say anything!" she said defensively.

He stood in front of the printer and his black eyes narrowed.

"It's just a paper jam," she said, easing around him to open the printer and unstick the papers inside. She fixed them in the paper holder and stepped back. "Try it now," she said.

He went to the computer, muttering to himself.

She leaned over. "You're a very nice machine," she whispered. "Come on, now, make me proud."

He pushed a button and the letter was printed and dropped into the tray.

He picked it up and studied it. "Not bad," he murmured.

"I told you," she replied, crossing her arms over her chest.

"It worked because I threatened to shoot it," he told her.

"It worked because I told it how nice it was," she retorted.

They glared at each other. Slowly, the glare became a deep, hot exchange of wordless expression that made Clancey's heart run away with her. She flushed.

Banks was feeling something similar, and it made him angry. He turned away and went back to his desk. He didn't say another word.

Clancey, shaken, went back into her office, without even a wisecrack. That look kept her awake and worried all night long.

FOUR

CLANCEY HADN'T SLEPT WELL. She dragged into the office five minutes late and worried that she was going to be in trouble. But when she arrived, Banks still hadn't come in.

With a sigh of relief, she made a pot of strong coffee. She'd been depressed for days, worrying about Morris getting out early. But she felt lighter today, happier. She couldn't decide why. Nothing in her life had really changed.

She heard footsteps on the stairs leading down into the office and her heart skipped. She knew it was Banks before he came into view. He took off his Stetson and shot it onto a hook of the coat tree. "What's up?" he asked.

"Not much, this early. Want coffee?"

"I hope it's strong," he said, yawning as he sat down at his desk. "I was called out at 2:00 a.m. to help with a manhunt down near Comanche Wells. Sheriff's department in Jacobs County asked for aid."

"Why you?" she wondered as she put a cup of black coffee in its black mug at his fingertips on the desk.

"Because I'm not married and I don't have kids," he said, glowering at her. "I'm the only single person in this unit."

"I'm single," she pointed out.

"I'm the only single Texas Ranger in this unit," he corrected. He leaned back with his coffee cup in his hand. "I'm going to end up like old Jack Holliman, holding a shotgun on visitors and hunting my teeth every morning when I try to eat breakfast."

"End up like who?" she asked, curious.

"He was one of the more famous Rangers of the twentieth century," he told her. "He lives outside the city."

"That sounds sad," she replied.

"I suppose it is. Cash Grier knew him, back when he was a Texas Ranger here."

"I've heard Cal speak of Cash Grier. He said the man is a legend in law enforcement circles."

Banks chuckled. "He is, but not for being a Texas Ranger."

She raised both eyebrows.

"Grier was a government assassin, among his other unique professions," he said, his black eyes twinkling. "Now he's married and has two kids. They say it's settled him, but not entirely."

She laughed softly. "Cal knew him overseas, in Africa."

His eyebrows arched. "Africa?"

She stopped dead. Only a handful of people knew about Cal's past. She wasn't comfortable sharing that with a relative stranger. "He said he did some classified work over there," she added with a bland smile.

"I see." He knew about those classified things Hollister had done. Things he couldn't share with a clerk.

"I'll get to work," she said, heading for her own office.

"You make good coffee," he remarked.

She chuckled. "I have to. It keeps me going."

"Me, too."

She didn't add why it kept her going. It was great for asthma attacks. If she had it soon enough, and strong enough, it could stop an attack dead. But Banks didn't need to know that.

HALLOWEEN CAME, AND CLANCEY walked the neighborhood with her little brother. He wore his costume. She went, as she'd told him she would, in her working clothes. There were still a few older people nearby who handed out candy, including the Martins, an elderly couple who were kind enough to let Clancey and Tad ride to church with them every Sunday. Tad got enough candy to last him for at least a week. Clancey only had one small chocolate bar and left the rest for him.

She was having some problems with her chest, but she kept using her medicines and taking over-the-counter stuff at night to fight the congestion. November meant colder weather, and she still didn't have a proper winter coat. Oh, if only they handed them out for twenty-five cents, she thought whimsically. At least Tad had a good coat, even if it was used. She wrote his name all over the inside of it, just in case it got lost, and he made sure that he didn't leave it behind when he went to school.

Clancey worried about Morris getting out. There hadn't been any word about it, but it was on her mind. If he got early release, he might be home by Christmas. That didn't give her long to plan. Whatever happened, she had to protect Tad.

ONE SUNDAY AT CHURCH, not too long after Banks had driven them home from the movies, Brenda stopped Clancey as she was pushing elderly Mr. Martin out to the car in his wheelchair, with Mrs. Martin and Tad at her side. The elderly couple lived two doors down and attended the same church Clancey did. They'd invited her and Tad to ride with them over two years ago, a tradition that continued into the present. They were like the grandparents Clancey and Tad no longer had.

"I just wanted to say hello," Brenda told her with a smile. "I never get time to talk to anybody at church."

"I know what you mean," Clancey said, smiling, too. "This is Rafe Martin," she introduced the old man, who smiled and shook hands with Brenda. "And this is his wife, Vera." The old lady smiled and nodded. "They're our neighbors, and they're kind enough to give us rides to church every week."

"Which is no chore at all, since this kind young lady pushes me in my wheelchair," the elderly man chuckled. "I don't know what we'd do without her. She even brings us food when we're sick."

Clancey flushed a little but didn't comment. Poor people looked out for each other.

"And this handsome young man?" Brenda asked.

Tad flushed and laughed. "I'm Tad," he said.

"It's nice to meet you all. I'm Brenda Banks," she added. "Your sister works for my brother," she told Tad.

The boy's eyes lit up and he smiled from ear to ear. "Gosh, he's so nice!" Tad said. "He drove us home from the movies just before Halloween. Sis was freezing in just her sweatshirt, and she gets sick easy in the fall…"

"Tad!" Clancey exclaimed, flushing.

"Sorry," Tad said, gritting his teeth.

"I get allergies in the fall, too," Brenda said, easing the tension. "I won't keep you—it's too cool to stand talking. I just wanted to say hi!"

"You're pretty," Tad told her, and flushed a little.

"Oh, you're going to be a heartbreaker when you grow up," Brenda said with twinkling eyes.

"That, he is," Clancey had to agree.

"See you!" Brenda said, smiling, and went to her car.

"WHAT A NICE young woman," Mrs. Martin said on the way home.

"Very nice," Mr. Martin, at her side, agreed.

Clancey, in the backseat with Tad, only nodded.

"Is her brother as good-looking as she is, Clancey?" Mrs. Martin asked with a wry smile.

Clancey took a deep breath. "Why, I don't really pay much attention, Mrs. Martin," she lied. "He's not in the office much, and I stay so busy…"

"I see." And Mrs. Martin did. But she didn't say another word about it, changing the subject abruptly to the price of bread, which she found alarmingly high.

BRENDA WATCHED THEM drive away with a sigh. Clancey was wearing a dress that very obviously came from a secondhand store, and her shoes had looked too small. Tad had on a suit that was about a size too large for him. She felt bad for them. She wondered if her brother ever noticed Clancey. She was a pretty woman. From what she'd learned by eavesdropping, it was just Clancey and her little brother at home, which meant that Clancey was obviously trying to support both of them on her paycheck. She wondered how in the world they managed.

She recalled seeing Clancey at the Army recruiting office and grimaced. The younger woman didn't look all that robust. It was painful to think of her wearing fatigues and working in some dangerous foreign country where she couldn't even speak the language.

Well, maybe Clancey would give up on that idea. She hoped so. Regardless of her brother's irritation with his clerk, Brenda liked her very much. It was a shame that Colter was still hung up on Grace. If only she could think of some way to make him notice Clancey!

CLANCEY AND TAD went through the racks at the thrift store for something that they could afford for a few dollars. It was going to be difficult, even managing that, but one of the boys at school had made a snide remark about Tad wearing the same clothes all the time. It had hurt Tad's feelings something awful, and Clancey was suffering for him. She'd planned this trip after one of their regular utility bills had been five dollars less than usual. Surely for that, they could find at least a couple of different shirts for him; assuming that one or two would fit him.

She looked around at the other people milling through the shop, elderly people on fixed incomes, young couples with three or four children, all hoping for something they could wear and afford. Her heart broke for them. It was such a hard life when you had nothing, when you couldn't get a better job or find anything part-time to supplement your full-time job.

While she was studying other people, Tad was standing beside a young boy about his size, whose shirt was torn and dirty. They were both looking at the same nice shirt that would fit them, a bargain at just a dollar.

Tad smiled. "Here," he told the other boy. "You take it. I'll find another one."

"You sure?" the boy stammered.

"I'm sure," Tad said.

"Thanks," the boy said. "I got beat up at school. This is the only shirt I had. My grandpa gave it to me for my birthday…" He choked up.

Clancey, standing behind Tad, choked up, too. Life was so hard on kids.

"I get picked on, too," Tad replied. "We'll grow up big and strong and one day, we'll pummel the tar out of them!"

The other boy chuckled. "I think…"

"Eduardo," a woman with beautiful long black hair chided as she joined them. "For shame. We forgive. We don't hold grudges, yes?"

"Yes, Mama," the boy said self-consciously.

"This is a nice shirt," she said, taking it from Eduardo. But she looked at Tad and hesitated.

"His shirt has a tear," Tad said. "Mine is okay." He gave her a big grin.

"You sweet boy," the woman said, and bit her lower lip. Her black eyes glistened.

"Life is hard," Clancey said, meeting the other woman's eyes. "But we get by." She smiled. "God loves us."

"Yes, He does," the other woman said. "Your son, he's a good boy."

"He's my brother, but, yes, he is. And so is yours," she added.

"We do our best," she replied. "He is our youngest. We have four more, over there." She indicated taller boys, standing with a man, all bent over boxes of odds and ends. "We hope for shoes. So hard to find ones that fit!"

"Tell me about it." Clancey stuck out her foot. "They're a half size too small, but they were the only ones even close to my size, so I make them fit." She grinned.

The other woman stuck out her own foot. "A size too large," she chuckled, "but I stuffed newspaper in them!"

They both laughed.

"THAT WAS REALLY nice of you," Clancey told her little brother. They'd found two other shirts that fit him, and they were on the way home with them.

"They were a nice family," he replied. He sighed. "He said his granddaddy gave him the shirt, and it was new, and some boys beat him up and tore it. Why are other kids so mean?" he asked sadly.

"I wish I knew."

He looked up at her. "Cal says I have to be less sens… sensi…"

"Sensitive," she said.

"Yeah. Sensitive. But it makes me mad when they laugh because my stuff is secondhand. I don't care. Why should they?"

"Because they don't know any better," she said simply. "If they had to live like we do, they'd understand."

"It's not so bad," he told her, and he grinned. "We got each other."

"Yes." She hugged him close. "We've got each other."

BANKS WASN'T IN the office the next Monday when she went in to work, and he didn't show up by lunchtime. She was concerned. He was always on time. In fact, he was always early, like Clancey usually was.

She phoned the other office and spoke to the lieutenant's assistant. "Have you heard anything about Banks?" she asked quickly.

"Banks? Oh." She laughed. "Are you worried about him, Clancey?"

"Shame on you!"

"Sorry. He had to go to court this morning," she said. "Didn't he tell you?"

"No." Clancey glowered.

"So you worried."

"He's always here on time."

"So are you," the other woman pointed out with a chuckle. "Well, he hasn't been shot or stabbed or carried off by Martians. Feel better?"

"Lots. I'm going to pour my thermos of coffee over his head when he gets here, though, for not telling me he had to be in court."

"Assault on a peace officer," she pointed out.

"Spoilsport," Clancey replied with a laugh. "Thanks. And, uh, don't mention that I called you, okay?"

"Your guilty secret is safe with me. Cross my heart."

"Thanks!"

BANKS WAS ALMOST strutting when he walked into the office after lunch. He tossed his Stetson onto a hook on the coat tree and grinned at her.

"So you were worried about me, were you?" he asked.

She went cherry red. "She said she crossed her heart!" she muttered.

"Maria says that when she doesn't want to promise,"

he told her. "If you want her to keep her mouth shut, you have to make her promise."

"I'll remember that next time. If there is a next time. And you didn't say you had court today," she chided.

He shrugged. "Slipped my mind. I was trying to get in touch with a parole officer in the cold case I'm working on. The old man who vanished."

Her heart stopped dead in her chest. "Oh."

He didn't notice that she'd turned pale. He wasn't looking. His attention was on his desk. "Who called?" he asked, frowning at her note.

"Lieutenant Marquez," she said, hoping her voice sounded normal. "He got a tip from one of their confidential informants about that Grayson man you're hunting in the attempted murder cold case."

"Him." He shook his head. "He's like a damned ghost. Just when you think you've got something on him, a witness leaves town or says he misremembered." He glanced at her. "How the hell do you misremember something?"

Her eyebrows arched. "You're cussing."

He sighed. "I guess I am. Ted Allen's wife miscarried this morning. He's all broken up. I'm working a case for him while he's at the hospital."

That was nice of him. She almost said so, but he turned and pinned her with curious black eyes. "Did you tell my sister that you're sweet on me?"

She looked at him as if he'd suddenly grown two heads and bat wings.

He rolled his eyes. "Never mind. I thought she was making it up." He made a face. "She's trying to set me up with anybody she can think of, before Grace gets to town."

"Grace?" It was a name she recognized from what she'd

overheard Brenda say once. Banks was carrying a torch for the woman. It hurt and she couldn't understand why.

"Grace Charles. And it's none of your business," he added shortly and with a sharp glare.

She flushed. "Well, excuse me! I was making conversation, not prying into your personal—"

"Phone," he interrupted.

She glared at him. He was closer to it than she was. With a long-suffering sigh, she went to answer it.

"Is Banks in?" a pleasant deep voice inquired. "It's Darrell Tarley."

"Yes, sir, he is." She handed him the receiver. They mostly used cell phones, but the landline was useful for business calls.

"Banks," he said, glowering at Clancey, who turned and went back into her own office.

"Darrell Tarley," the caller told Banks. "Listen, I wondered if you ever do jobs on the side. You know, after working hours?"

"Not really," he said, curious. "Why?"

"I need a bodyguard. Well, not an obvious one. But you know that I'm running for district attorney next year, right?"

"I knew that," Banks replied.

"I've had a threat. Not a direct one," he continued. "Just an indirect one, from a man I prosecuted. He's in prison, but he may get early release."

"Threats go with both our jobs." Banks chuckled.

"They do. Maybe I'm paranoid, but we had an assistant DA killed here a few years ago…"

"I remember that case very well," Banks said. "It hinged on, of all things, an expensive watch with musical chimes and a couture paisley shirt. The killer died, but his boss went to prison."

"He'll never get out, if I have any say in it," the other man replied. "The assistant DA left a wife and young children. And a politician ordered the hit to save himself from prosecution. See why I'm paranoid?"

"I do. Have you checked with Hollister, or Marquez, over at SAPD?" he asked. "There's always somebody over there looking for part-time work."

"I hadn't thought about that! Thanks!"

"You're welcome. And I'll vote for you," he added, chuckling.

"I appreciate it!"

Banks hung up the phone.

"I HOPE YOU'RE not squeamish," Clancey said from the doorway.

He glanced at her. "Why not?"

"Because the last man who volunteered Cal to look for after-hours employees for him wishes he'd never opened his mouth."

He chuckled. "I'm not afraid of Hollister."

"Brave man," she said under her breath.

"And I know what he used to do for a living, too," he added.

She shook her head and went back into her office.

"BANKS'S SISTER WON'T give me a passkey to his apartment," Cal Hollister said when she answered her cell phone that night.

"She won't?" she asked. "Why do you want one?"

"I'm going to short-sheet his bed and put salt in his sugar shaker."

"Not nice!" she chided. "And you a captain in the police department, too!"

"I told Darrell—and he spelled his first name for me, to make sure I knew that it had two *r*'s and two *l*'s—that if he wanted after-hours protection, he could come poll my officers himself."

"I'll bet that wasn't all you told him," she mused.

"There were a few invectives and some unprintable words, as well," he said with a chuckle. "I did tell him I'd put a note on the bulletin board. Hence the careful spelling of his first name that he gave me."

She laughed.

"How are you and Tad?"

"Doing well."

"Your voice sounds raspy. Are you using the preventative?" he asked.

"Don't start," she chided. "I just sound hoarse. My lungs are clear. And yes, I'm using it."

"I miss you," he sighed. "Your replacement just smiles and does her job. She never calls me names or tries to set me up on dates with streetwalkers when I ask her to work overtime."

She laughed. "I miss you, too," she said. "But I can walk to and from work, and you're too far away."

"I could drive you both."

"You're sweet, but I like being independent."

"You can be too independent," he said quietly.

She was uncomfortable at the note in his voice. "Okay, what's going on?" she asked.

There was a pause. "The parole board met today."

Her heart stopped. "And?"

"And it looks as if Morris will get out week after next."

Her whole life flashed before her eyes. She could actually see her heart beating in her eyes as she stared blankly at the other wall and felt the blood drain out of her face.

"Don't panic," he said abruptly. "It's not the end of the world."

"Banks doesn't know about Morris. He doesn't know that he's trying to find out what happened to my grandfather. He doesn't know…!"

"Why haven't you told him?"

"I could lose my job, Cal," she said. "My stepbrother is a convicted felon!"

"You won't lose your job. Many people have relatives who've been in trouble with the law."

"Most of them aren't employed by the Texas Rangers," she said. "Especially Colter Banks, who doesn't even want me to work for him in the first place! He wanted a man— he said so. But no men applied, so he got stuck with me."

"He did choose you out of a field of four women," he pointed out.

"Right. You didn't see what he had to choose from." She sighed.

He chuckled. "But I heard about it. I understand that he was of the opinion that the other three made their living at night on street corners."

"Shame!"

"So you were the best of the lot."

"He hates me."

"Probably not."

"Tad will die when I tell him," she said. "He's terrified of Morris, after all this time."

"So are you, kid," he said gently.

She drew in a breath. "What am I going to tell him?"

"Don't tell him anything, not yet."

"We can't stay where we are. I won't live with Morris. Neither will Tad."

"I'll look around for apartments."

"Can you find one for ten dollars a month, because that's what I can afford," she said, and not altogether facetiously.

"Stop that," he said. "What about the Martins? You've been wheeling old Mr. Martin to church for ages…"

"I won't put them in danger," she said solemnly. "Morris is vindictive."

"I guess I'd forgotten that," he said apologetically.

"I hadn't," she said.

"If worse comes to worst, you and Tad can move in with me," he said. "I'll have Miss Betsy and her sister move in, also, to keep people from making nasty remarks about it."

"You have a life of your own…"

"Some life," he said heavily. "The walls close in from time to time. I'm too much alone."

"You should marry again," she said.

"No, I shouldn't," he said shortly. "Once was enough."

"The world is full of nice women. What about Marquez's mother? She's wonderful."

"Fred Harris."

"I thought they were just friends."

"So did a lot of other people," he remarked. "Besides, Barbara isn't my type."

"Who is?"

He was quiet. "There was one, long ago. She did something that destroyed my faith in her. I married on the rebound, to show her I didn't give a damn about her." There was a hollow laugh. "And that backfired really well. Years of hell until my wife finally drugged herself to death, and then I lived with the guilt because she drugged herself to death."

"Love is overrated," she pointed out.

He burst out laughing. "And how would you know that?"

She sighed. "I guess I wouldn't. I've never been in love. Well, except with that dreamy guy in that movie I love," she added.

"A fairy tale. Just your style, kid. Why don't you take a good look at that tall, dark, handsome guy you work for?"

"Banks?" she exclaimed. "Are you nuts? I'd rather date a frog!"

"How odd that he said the same thing about you."

She fumed silently.

"Stings, doesn't it?" he asked.

"Only burns, just a little," she retorted.

"I'll see what I can find out about rentals and get back to you as soon as I can."

"I guess I could sneak back into my office after hours with Tad and bunk down there," she laughed.

"You'd be found out. Banks doesn't miss much. It's what makes him good at his job."

"I suppose. Well, thanks. I appreciate all you've done for Tad and me."

"I don't do anything I don't want to. You know that. I never had a kid sister until you came along."

She smiled. "That's nice. I never had a big brother until you came along." She didn't claim Morris as a big brother, despite the fact that he was her stepbrother.

"You've done a great job with Tad," he said abruptly. "He's a good kid."

"I think so, too. I've done my best. We don't have a lot, but he's never wanted for love and attention."

"Or discipline," he added with a chuckle. "Taking away his only video game for a week for fighting at school was sheer genius."

"You're only saying that because it was your idea," she pointed out.

"I have ego issues," he said. "Marquez's wife keeps upstaging me on the shooting range."

"Only by one point," she said. "And I think Gwen really tries to miss. Honest."

He sighed. "She's a sweet woman. I had a brief crush on her before Marquez waltzed off with her. I like blondes," he chuckled.

"That's because you're blond, too," she suggested.

"Who knows? Wear that ratty jacket to work tomorrow. It's going to be cold. Very cold. What are you and Tad planning to do for Thanksgiving?" he added.

Her blood froze. Morris would probably be out by then.

"Why don't you come over here for it?" he said. "I don't have family. It would be nice not to have to eat alone."

She knew he meant it. He wasn't just being kind. She smiled to herself. "We'd both like that, very much. And you do have family. You have me and Tad."

There was a hesitation. "Thanks, kid."

"The victims' service should let me know when Morris is getting out. But just in case, would you, too?"

"Of course. You take care of yourself."

"I'll be fine. You do the same."

IT MADE HER feel more secure, to have Cal looking out for her and Tad. He was a lonely man. She'd heard him speak of the woman he'd loved and lost very rarely, but she wondered why they'd broken up. His marriage had been a bad one, with no love lost on either side. If he'd married to spite his former girlfriend, it made sense. What a shame. He was a good man. She was sorry for him.

He'd been friends with a nurse at Hal Marshall Children's Hospital, a woman whose murder case he'd worked as a homicide detective several years earlier. She'd married a Texas Ranger, John Ruiz, who lived on a huge ranch outside Jacobsville, Texas, just south of San Antonio. She knew Ruiz. He had a son just a little older than Tad. He'd been in and out of the office with the boy when he was working gang-related cases with Banks, who was one of his friends. The child was nice, too. From what she'd heard of his new wife, she was just as sweet, and the boy, Tonio, loved her dearly. Ruiz's new wife had presented him with a little girl last autumn.

It must be nice, she thought wistfully, to marry and have kids. She loved Tad. She'd taken care of him since he was born, because her poor mother had always been in bad health. She'd died when Tad was still a toddler.

She often thought how it would be to have a child of her own. But just as quickly, she'd laughed at her own thoughts. She would never find anyone who wanted a ready-made family, and there was no way she was giving up custody of Tad for any man. So she'd raise him, and after he graduated from high school, she might reconsider...

Baloney, she interrupted herself. After what Morris had done to her, she'd never trust a man enough to marry him. It was just as well that she had Tad to take care of. Besides, she'd never have to risk her heart.

Poor Cal. She hoped that someday he'd find some kind-hearted woman whom he could love. He was too nice a guy to spend the rest of his life alone.

FIVE

CLANCEY FELT AS if her lungs were going to collapse as she walked to work in the first real frost of the year. She'd used her preventative, but she was hoarse and the over-the-counter cough syrup she'd used wasn't having an effect. She had to stop along the way, just to breathe. Tad had worried all the way to school that she wasn't going to make it. He tried to get her to spend money on a cab, but there was so little left until her paycheck. She smiled and assured him she was okay. But as he went into the building, she wondered how in the world she'd ever get back to pick him up after work.

Even worse, she was coughing up something brown, always a worry this time of year. She hadn't slept well and she'd woken up sweating, ironic considering that the house was icy cold because they had to conserve so tightly on the gas heat they could ill afford for the rickety old house. The sweating indicated fever. The colored sputum went with pneumonia. She knew the symptoms all too well.

Well, she had to hope that she could wear it out. She'd

managed that once before, by drinking lots of water and filling herself full of cough syrup and exercising to keep fluid from accumulating in her lungs. The only thing was that she'd had a prescription cough syrup and antibiotics that a nurse practitioner at her pharmacy had prescribed for her. She couldn't afford the hospital emergency room or a private physician because the co-pay on her insurance often was more than she had available. The pharmacy had the nurse practitioner come in once a week for the poorer clientele. She guessed she'd have to stop by there after work and pray that she could get credit, because she couldn't afford the medicine any other way. The added monthly cost of prescription medicine, even with her insurance policy's help, was too much for her frail budget. The pharmacist knew her, though. She always paid off the bill, even though it sometimes took her a few months. He was never impatient.

She was dragging by the time she got downstairs and into her office. She was going to avoid Banks at all costs. She had to pretend to feel fine. Hopefully he'd be out of the office most of the week. He usually was, and he was filling in for another Ranger right now, which would keep him busy.

She pulled out another old file folder and started typing the contents into the computer. She wished she felt better. She had a thermos of soup, having forgone her usual coffee—she only had the one thermos. But there was coffee in the office. She'd put a quarter in the kitty and hope it was enough. Banks never fussed when she got it out of the office coffeepot anyway. She supposed that he considered that her making it entitled her to drink it.

She was reminded that Joceline Blackhawk, the administrative assistant for her husband, Jon Blackhawk, over at the local FBI office, refused to make coffee at all. That chore fell to agent Murdock. There had been some very inventive threats about ways to stop him from making it, one of which was a shovel and a pickup truck…

She laughed out loud, picturing FBI agents from Jon's office in ninja gear carrying agent Murdock out to the truck in a big sack.

The door snapped shut and Banks came down the steps. "What are you laughing about?" he asked.

"Agent Murdock," she said, and laughed some more.

"God!" he snorted. "If I ever have to speak to Jon Blackhawk on a case, I take my own coffee. Once, he even tried to buy it from me!"

"I am not surprised," she returned.

He stuck his head in her door and frowned. "What's wrong with you?" he asked suddenly.

Her eyebrows arched. "What do you mean?" she asked innocently, and ruined the pose by coughing so hard that she hurt her chest.

"You're sick," he said.

She swallowed. "I am…not," she argued. "It's just a cough."

He moved closer. "It's not. What's wrong with you?"

"I got chilled," she said stubbornly.

He put his big, lean hand out and felt her forehead. The frown got worse. "Clancey, you're burning up with fever. Let's go."

"No!"

"Yes. Do you want me pick you up and carry you out of here?" he added.

"You wouldn't dare!" she said haughtily.

"STOP STRUGGLING OR I'll drop you," he muttered as he reached his SUV. He balanced her on one upraised thigh while he opened the door. He put her inside and closed the door on her furious muttering.

He got in beside her. "Fasten your—" He glanced at her. "Good girl." He cranked the SUV. "Who's your doctor?"

She swallowed, hard. "I go to the nurse practitioner on Saturdays at Fred's Pharmacy."

He looked at her, shocked. "You don't have a doctor?"

She bit her lower lip and fought tears.

He recalled where she lived, how she lived. Stupid question, he chided himself. He turned the truck toward Hal Marshall Memorial Hospital.

"I CAN'T AFFORD THIS," she exclaimed as he marched her slowly into the emergency room.

"I can't afford to have you die," he returned. "They won't give me anybody to replace you. I'll have to teach your ghost how to type."

"Mr. Banks..." she protested.

He signed her in. The clerk, who knew him, raised her eyebrows, glanced past him at a red-faced, sickly Clancey, and nodded. "Bring her over and let's get some information. Then we'll get her right in."

Clancey gave the clerk the information and her insurance card. They did have great insurance at work, and maybe she could take Tad and flee to another country before the bill came due for what the insurance wouldn't pay.

The form was filled out, and a nurse came for Clancey. She was escorted back to a room where, a few minutes later, a smiling technician came to draw blood. The doctor came in long enough to ask her a couple of questions and listen to her chest. He grimaced and ordered a chest X-ray, then went back out again.

It was almost an hour later when she was diagnosed with pneumonia, given two prescriptions, and sent back out to the waiting room.

She was wondering how she'd get back to the office when she saw Banks still sitting there, patiently waiting for her.

She burst into tears. He'd been impatient, irritable, insulting, all sorts of things over the months she'd worked for him. But when she was sick, here he was, taking care of her when nobody would have faulted him for leaving her and going back to work.

He got up and went to her. "What's wrong?" he asked in the softest deep, gentle tone she'd ever heard from him.

She swallowed a sob. "It's so kind… I thought you'd go…back to work," she sobbed.

"And leave you here alone, to find your own way home?" he asked.

She looked up at him with wet cheeks and glistening pale silver eyes. And she fell in love. Just that quickly.

It was a long walk down the hospital corridor to the exit. She had to stop and breathe twice before they got to the door.

Once outside, he swung her up into his arms and curled her up against his broad, muscular chest.

"Sorry," she managed. "I'm so heavy…"

"You aren't heavy." His chin was resting on her dark hair. She closed her eyes, sick and vulnerable, and curved one arm hesitantly around his neck. She nestled close with a sigh.

Banks felt that movement all the way to his boots. She was overly warm, but her temperature wasn't what he was noticing. She smelled of wildflowers. She was immaculate, even with her scruffy clothes. He liked the way she felt in his arms. Her firm little breasts were pressed close to him, her whole body trusting as she let him carry her. It was a new sensation, like walking on clouds or something. He didn't understand the warm glow that washed over him as he carried her out to the SUV. He didn't like it or trust it. He was getting soft, he told himself.

He put her down beside the vehicle and unlocked the door. He guided her hand to the handle inside that she could use to pull herself up, but he grimaced when he noticed that it hurt her to lift her arm.

"Here," he said softly, and he lifted her up into the seat. "Chest hurt?"

"Just…a little." She drew in a painful breath. "Thanks," she added shyly.

"You're welcome."

HE DROVE HER to the pharmacy and went inside with her to wait while the prescriptions were filled. She gave the clerk her insurance information and her debit card. She prayed there was enough left in her account to cover what the insurance didn't pay.

When she had her prescriptions, Banks drove her home.

"But I need to go to work," she protested when he pulled up in front of her house.

"You need to go to bed," he said shortly. "You'll never get well if you don't."

She tried to protest, but it did no good.

He lifted her down and carried her to the front door. She got out her key and put it into the lock.

"It's okay," she said nervously. "I can walk. It's just a few steps."

"If you need anything, you call me, okay?" he asked quietly.

She looked up at him with all the turmoil inside her making silver lights in her eyes. "Thanks for taking me to the hospital, and all," she said huskily.

He tilted up her rounded chin and studied her fever-flushed face. "Why didn't you tell me you had asthma?" he asked suddenly.

"How...how did you know?" she faltered.

"One of the techs was discussing your X-ray with the doctor. I overheard them." He scowled. "He said there was evidence of two broken ribs, as well."

"Oh, those," she said quickly. "I had a...a fall."

"Recently?"

"Several years ago." She didn't want to elaborate on how her ribs had been broken. That would lead to Morris and questions she didn't want to answer.

"You shouldn't be walking to work with your lungs in that sort of shape," he said sternly.

She managed a shallow breath. "Well, the limousine service won't transport me with a Ferrari sitting in my driveway."

He burst out laughing.

She grinned. "I can't afford a car. They break down. They have to have gas. It's not feasible."

"Cabs run," he reminded her.

"So do limousines. Same difference."

She was making a point that he understood. She couldn't afford cabs.

"Cal offered to bring me back and forth to work when his office moved, but I wouldn't let him. It's an imposition," she explained.

The idea of Hollister wanting to protect her made him uncomfortable, and he didn't know why. Her predicament seemed to be without any sort of resolution. He scowled, because it bothered him. She looked so fragile.

"I'll be fine. I'll come to work tomorrow…"

"You will not," he said. "Or I'll set fire to your desk and let you explain it to the lieutenant."

"You wouldn't dare," she returned indignantly.

He pursed his chiseled lips and his black eyes twinkled. "You don't know me, kid," he replied. "There isn't much I won't dare."

"I'll stay home for two days. The medicine will be working by then."

"Your lungs will be dicey for a few weeks. That's a bacterial pneumonia, not walking pneumonia." He'd had that from the doctor himself.

"How do you know that they'll be dicey?" she wanted to know.

"I had pneumonia once, a few years ago," he said solemnly. "It laid me flat out for a week. I was even in the hospital for a few days. I haven't forgotten the recovery period."

One side of her pretty bow mouth pulled down. "I have it every year. Believe me, I know about the recovery period."

"Every year?" he asked, surprised.

"Nobody knows why. I avoid sick people, I take vitamin C, I do all I can to stay healthy. Nothing seems to work." She stared at his spotless white shirt. "Cal protected me, when I worked for him. I was out a lot before I got the new medicines. He wouldn't let them fire me. They probably should have." She sighed, wincing when it hurt. "I'm not...robust."

"No. But you're efficient. You don't goof off, you don't complain about working overtime if you have to, you don't even fuss when I make coffee."

She looked up into soft black eyes. "You make terrible coffee."

He smiled. "I know."

She clutched the bag of medicine. "Well..."

"What about your brother?" he asked suddenly. "Don't you walk by the school to pick him up?"

She nodded. "I'll ask Cal," she said. "He won't mind dropping Tad off. Where we live is on his way home anyway. He has a ranch down near Comanche Wells," she said.

"I know. I live in Jacobs County, too."

She hadn't known that. "Cal runs purebred Angus cattle."

He cocked his head and his eyes narrowed. "You know a lot about him."

"He was my boss for four years," she pointed out.

He made a sound in his throat. She didn't know what it meant.

"All right, then, I'll get back to work."

"Call me if you need to know about any files I'm working on," she said. "I'll keep the phone with me."

"I'll do that. Go to bed."

She smiled. "Yes, sir."

He chuckled as he went out the door.

SHE TOOK THE first doses of her medicines, got into her pajamas and went to bed. She phoned Cal.

"I hate to ask," she began.

"But can I bring Tad home for you," he finished for her with a chuckle. "Sure. No problem."

"How...?" she stammered.

"Banks mentioned that you were sick. He was in the office to see Marquez," he added.

"He took me to the hospital. I didn't want to go," she sighed.

"He said that, too. I imagine there will be some gossip at the hospital, considering the way you arrived," he added, tongue in cheek.

"Well, I refused to go," she said defensively.

"So he carried you in." He chuckled. "Leave it to Banks. He said you showed up at work sick as a dog and never said a word about it. I told him that's the way you always were. You came to work, regardless."

"I didn't want to get fired." Her voice was getting more hoarse by the minute.

"Stop talking and take a nap," he told her gently. "I'll pick up Tad and bring him home. What do you want for supper and I'll bring that, too."

"Cal!" she fussed.

"Just tell me, or I'll ask Tad."

That would mean pizza and she couldn't stand it. "Soup," she murmured.

"What sort?"

"I don't care."

He chuckled. "Okay. Soup it is. Want one of those Greek parfaits with yogurt and fruit and granola?"

"That sounds heavenly!"

"Thought I remembered those preferences. I'll bring them. Get better." He hung up.

SHE LAY STARING at the ceiling, propped up on two pillows with a third pillow she could hold to her chest when she had to cough. She remembered Banks carrying her in and out of the hospital, the way it felt, the tenderness in his black eyes, and her heart raced. She'd never thought of Colter Banks as anything except a grumpy boss before, but it was suddenly difficult to put him back into that perspective.

She was recalling spicy aftershave and strong arms, a muscular chest pressed hard against her breasts, a square chin resting on top of her short, wavy dark hair. It had been a moment out of time when she felt safe and warm and…cared for. She caught her breath as those sensations she'd felt washed over her even in memory. She moved restlessly in the bed. She had to get her feelings under control before she went back to work. It wouldn't do to have Banks notice how she felt about him. She had to be careful. He thought of her as a kid. He even called her that. He was a kind man, but his kindness had been impartial. She had to try to remember that.

SHE WAS DOZING when the front door unlocked and Tad burst in just ahead of tall, handsome, blond Cal Hollister.

"I've got soup and parfait," he called. "Putting them into dishes as we speak."

"Thanks," she called hoarsely.

"Gosh, I'm sorry you're sick, sis," Tad said, patting

her hand on the coverlet. "I was afraid you wouldn't even make it to work. Can I get you anything?"

"No, thanks, honey. I'm good." She gave him a wan smile. Her chest was still giving her fits.

"Cal and I had supper already, but we brought yours home. Can I go play my video game?"

"Sure."

"Okay. Thanks!"

"Do you have homework?" she called after him.

"Just math. I'll do it before I go to bed. Honest."

"You'd better," she chided.

Cal came walking in with a bowl of soup and a packaged Greek parfait. "Can you sit up?"

"Yes." She propped herself up, keeping the covers up to her collarbone. "This was so sweet of you. Thanks a million. I'll pay you back…"

"I'll paste you one," he threatened. "Well, I won't hit you. I'm an officer of the court and a gentleman, so I never strike a woman. But you won't pay me back. Period."

"You were the nicest boss I ever had," she said as she started to ladle the delicious chicken soup into her mouth.

"I was the only boss you'd ever had until you deserted me to work for the Texas Rangers," he said, chuckling as he pulled out a chair and dropped down into it. "God, I'm tired," he mused. "Police commissioner called a meeting and we sat around the table for the better part of two hours listening to a boring speech about something."

"About something?" she teased.

"Well, I wasn't really listening," he said. "I didn't sleep last night. I was trying not to drift off. It might have been a career-ending move."

"You should see one of those sleep specialists."

"Oh, that would help," he said sarcastically. He ran a hand through his short, straight, blond hair. "The memories get to me sometimes."

"You have to try to look ahead, not behind," she said quietly. "I know it's hard. I don't manage it very well, either."

"Banks mentioned those broken ribs. He was fishing, but I didn't bite," he added quietly. "That's your business."

"Thanks."

"You need a car. Or a car pool," he added when she gave him a sardonic look over her soupspoon. "Doesn't anyone around here work near you? Somebody you could ride with?"

"The Martins live two doors down. They're both disabled. I go with them to church on Sundays so I can push Mr. Martin in his wheelchair," she said. "Of the other close neighbors, one grows marijuana in his bathtub and the other entertains men at night."

He whistled.

"I know, you're a lawman and marijuana is..."

"I was thinking of the smell."

Her eyebrows arched.

"If he grows it in his tub, he must stink like crazy."

She burst out laughing, almost spilled her soup and had to put it down to hold the pillow to her chest in a burst of coughing.

"Damn. Sorry," he said through gritted teeth.

Tears were rolling down her cheeks. "It was...worth it," she choked. "He probably does, too. Stink, I mean."

He grinned.

She finished her soup. "I'm so tired. I felt sorry for Mr.

Banks. He stayed at the hospital the whole time, until I was ready to leave. I didn't expect him to wait for me."

"Oh, Banks is a gentleman," he said with a lazy smile. "His mother was very old-fashioned. She took both the kids to church and took privileges away from them for cussing or talking back or being rude."

"She must have been a nice woman."

"She was," he replied. "She lived with her sister on a ranch near mine. The old lady died last year, so Banks and his sister own the place now. It's not too far from Comanche Wells. He commutes, like I do."

"Does he have cattle?" she asked, curious.

He nodded. "A few head of black baldies and some horses," he said. "He doesn't plan on ranching as a profession, but he likes animals. There's a big cat, too. She lives indoors."

"Mr. Banks has a cat?" she asked.

"A big, red Maine Coon cat," he chuckled, "that he calls Miss Kitty."

"Well!"

He smiled. "His sister dates one of my detectives," he said. "She loves her brother. Talks about him all the time."

"She's nice. We go to the same church. I guess she lives with her brother."

"She has an apartment in town," he corrected. "Banks is hard going as a housemate, to hear her tell it. She did most of the cleaning because he kept threatening to shoot the vacuum cleaner."

She laughed. "He threatens to shoot the printer at work, too."

He shook his head. "She convinced him to hire a couple to live in the foreman's cabin. The wife cooks and cleans for him. The husband oversees the livestock and keeps an eye on the place, along with a couple of part-time cowboys. It's not a big spread."

She recalled that Cal's was. He ran purebred black Angus cattle and he had a lot of cowboys, some of whom were rumored to be old comrades from his former line of work.

"I wouldn't mind having a ranch," she sighed. "At least Tad and I would always have beef on the table."

"Of course you would," he chided. "You'd name the beef steers and dare anyone to carry them off to the abattoir."

She made a face. "I guess I'd plant a garden and grow vegetables," she conceded. "I'd plant lots of fruit trees and shrubs, though. I like fruit."

"Me, too. I have pear, apple, cherry and peach trees for the birds, and three pecan trees for the squirrels."

"For the squirrels?" she probed.

"The damned things strip the pecans off the tree green," he muttered. "I have to buy pecans."

She chuckled.

He sighed and stood up. "I'll come by first thing and drop Tad off at school," he said, "and bring him home tomorrow afternoon."

"I wouldn't have asked..." she said softly.

"No. You got a double dose of pride when they handed it out. You don't like being obliged to people. But you'd do the same thing for me without being asked, if our situations were reversed."

She sighed. "I guess so. Thanks."

"Friends help each other out," he reminded her, and he smiled. "Can I get you anything before I leave?"

She shook her head. "Tad will check on me. He's a good kid."

"He really is. Bighearted." He hesitated. "Have you told him about Morris getting early release?"

She grimaced. "I didn't have the heart," she said. "He's even more afraid of Morris than I am." She studied his hard face. "There's a rumor that Morris made threats against the assistant DA who prosecuted him, the one who's running for district attorney next year."

"Yes. Darrell Tarley—Darrell being spelled with two *r*'s and two *l*'s, as he constantly reminds us," he returned, shaking his head. "God help us if he gets elected. The man can't find his feet when he's looking down. How he ever got into law is a question a sage couldn't answer. He's got the worst record of convictions of any officer of the court in the history of San Antonio. His only successful prosecution was your stepbrother," he added with a laugh.

"He has a reputation for making deals," she said simply. "He's very politically astute. Of course, he's also politically correct, to a fault."

"I will never be politically correct," he said shortly. "If they force it on me, I'll retire and raise herd sires."

"You'd be bored out of your mind in a week," she returned.

One side of his chiseled mouth pulled down. "I guess I would. So far I've managed to avoid offending more than ten people a week."

"That's an improvement," she pointed out. "When I worked for you, it was fifteen a week."

He laughed. "True enough. I'll get home. You call if you need anything. And I'll let you know if I hear any more about Morris's release."

"Thanks, Cal."

"And I haven't forgotten about looking into apartments for you."

"I appreciate that more than you know," she said softly.

He smiled. "Tell Tad I said goodbye and I'll see him first thing tomorrow."

"Will do."

SHE LAY AWAKE long after Tad went to sleep, worrying about the future. It wasn't just herself she was concerned for. If Morris was willing to make threats against a candidate for DA even before he got parole, it didn't do to think about what he might have planned for Clancey. It was she, after all, whose testimony had put him in prison in the first place. He'd be after revenge. And who held the key to Clancey's heart? Tad. She'd do anything to protect her brother, and Morris knew it.

She kept thinking about that cold case of Banks, the inquiry into her late grandfather's disappearance. She was certain that Morris had done something to the old gentleman. If only there was some way to prove it. But it was five years ago. Witnesses moved away or died. Evidence, undiscovered, was lost. Morris would never confess. So that was that.

She prayed that she could manage a way to protect her little brother if Morris did come back. A bigger problem was, where would they live? She knew Tad would never agree to live with Morris, any more than Clancey would. Morris legally owned the house.

"I guess we'll end up in a homeless shelter," she murmured to herself, "hiding in corners and hoping Morris won't find us."

It wasn't a problem she could solve by worrying about

it. There was one bright spot in her misery; perhaps Morris would do himself in by threatening the candidate for DA. Threats of violence were punishable. He'd have to watch his step, if he was on parole, wouldn't he?

The thought gave her a little peace. She closed her eyes, propped up on two pillows, and finally slept.

SIX

CLANCEY FELT A little better the next morning. Cal had driven Tad to school, leaving Clancey with a cup of hot cappuccino from a coffee shop and a bagel with cream cheese—favorites he recalled from when she'd worked for him. She'd savored every bite, every sip. She couldn't afford the expensive coffee these days, with Tad's growing necessities for school. She didn't begrudge him a penny, but money was always tight. Luxuries like coffee shop treats were out.

Unexpectedly, Banks showed up at her door at noon, with a burger and fries and a strawberry milk shake.

To say that she was surprised was an understatement.

He went straight into the kitchen, pulled out a plate and emptied the contents of his sack into it. He carried that, and the milk shake, in to Clancey.

She was sitting up in bed in her blue satin pajamas with the worn sheet and ancient quilt pulled up over her breasts. Her heart was racing like mad. She hoped that he wouldn't notice.

"That's so sweet of you…" she began.

"I was out this way on a case," he said, pulling up a chair. He sailed his Stetson onto the foot of her bed and leaned forward. "Is the medicine working?"

She nodded. "I feel a little better today." Her eyes were full of worry. "I can barely get down the hall to the bathroom," she began.

"I cleared it with the lieutenant," he said easily. "He said for you to stay out until you feel like coming back to work. You haven't claimed a single sick day yet, and you've done more overtime than you're paid for. The lieutenant keeps up with all the employees through his assistants," he added with a chuckle. "Including me."

"Oh thank goodness," she said. "I was so scared you might fire me."

"For being sick?" he chided gently, and he smiled. "Shame on you."

She smiled back shyly and picked up the milk shake. She sipped it and let out a heartfelt sigh. "This is so good! How did you know I like strawberry best?" she added.

He shrugged. "I didn't. But some people are allergic to chocolate, and not a lot like vanilla, so strawberry seemed like a safe bet."

She laughed. "It is. Heavenly!" She sipped more of it and nibbled on a French fry.

"Do you remember anything about Dalton Reed being a member of any clubs or organizations?" he asked suddenly.

She jumped, almost tumbling the plate she was holding. "Dalton Reed?" she asked.

He scowled at her reaction. "It's the cold case. The elderly man who went missing and was never found."

"Oh, that one," she said, hoping she sounded more composed than she felt. She drew in a breath. "He was a Sunday school teacher at the Meadow Methodist Church," she said.

"The one you and my sister attend?" he asked, taking notes on his cell phone absently as they spoke.

"Yes."

"What else?"

She sipped the milk shake slowly. "He was a member of the Texas Sheriffs' Association."

He glanced at her. "What?" He pulled up another field and studied it. "That isn't in the file."

"I knew about him from church," she blurted out. "He was a deputy sheriff for several years in Bexar County."

"I can't believe they left that out of his files," he muttered as he copied down what she was telling him. "That's the problem with cold cases. A lot of times the evidence is missing, vital information is missing. Over the years, things get misplaced."

"He played piano," she added quietly. "And classical guitar." She still had his guitar, the one that Banks had noticed in her house. It was a treasure.

Banks was studying her with narrowed eyes. "You knew him."

She forced herself not to react visibly. "Well, yes. He used to sit in the pew in front of us at church. I went with my mother to church until she died. Our stepfather wasn't much on religion, and Tad was just a baby."

Things were swirling in Banks's mind. He was making connections, but not consciously. "You never said you had a stepfather."

"Yes, I did," she corrected, "when you brought Tad and me home that Saturday."

He glanced at her. "So you did. Was your stepfather Tad's father?"

She nodded. She smiled. "But I couldn't love him more if he was a blood relation to me. Tad is my whole world."

He frowned slightly. "Don't you want to get married, have kids?" he probed.

"When Tad's out of high school," she returned.

"That's a long time from now."

"Not so long," she said. "I'll only be thirty-two. Lots of women have kids at that age."

He didn't say anything. He was remembering the statistics on motherhood. For a woman in her thirties having a child for the first time there were risks.

She got a look at his face and she sighed. "I know about the risks," she said abruptly. "And I might never marry. I don't mind. I love my brother."

"He's a sweet kid," he agreed.

"Tomorrow's Saturday," she said. "And you're going to be out of town Monday on that case you're working up. So how about if I come back to work Tuesday?"

"If you're up to it, okay," he said. "But you stay home until you're well."

She knew his attitude was impersonal, but it was still nice to have somebody who was concerned for her welfare, even impartially. "Thanks for lunch, and for being so nice about letting me stay home."

"Walking to work in the cold and wet," he said quietly, studying her wan face. "Honest to God, Clancey, there's got to be a bus or a car pool, some way you can get to work without having to walk!"

"Walking is great exercise, and except for having pneumonia every autumn, I do very well."

He sighed heavily. He was concerned. She was so young to have health problems and a very young dependent. "I thought you lived at home with your parents and had all the support you needed. It was a shock to find you solely responsible for a young child in school, with no one else in your family."

"I do okay," she said easily, smiling.

"You do better than that," he said with evident admiration. "Most young women your age would have put Tad in foster care."

"A few might," she conceded. "But I don't really have a social life to worry about, and Tad's a joy to have around." Her pale gray eyes sparkled like silver in candlelight. "I love kids."

His heart jumped, for no discernible reason. "I've never thought about kids. Well, I did once, before Grace went off on a mission to South America." His face was drawn and sad. "After the one she worked for in Africa."

"Brenda says she's very religious."

"Yes."

"And she goes to villages way back in the Amazon jungle with her church's mission program. She must be very brave."

He smiled with delight. "Yes, she is. Her boyfriend was my best friend. We were together a lot." His eyes dulled. "When Mike was killed, we both went a little off the rails. He was a great guy."

"Wasn't he a policeman?"

He nodded. "He took his mother to the bank. He was off duty at the time. There was a robbery and he was shot and killed, along with his mother. His sister is married to one of the Hart boys, down in Jacobsville," he added. "I see her from time to time."

"That's a shame about him and his mother both dying. Did they catch the robbers?"

"They did. They're serving life sentences for felony murder." His eyes were cold. "I go to every parole hearing."

She could guess why. "I had a best friend in high school, but she moved to California with her family." She grimaced. "I don't get close to people anymore."

"Neither do I," he replied gruffly. His black eyes searched her silver ones in a silence that grew intimate, dangerous.

She felt her heart beating in her throat at the intensity of that stare. It made her uneasy. It was violent, passionate. Images filled her mind. She fought them. This wouldn't do, not at all. She dragged her eyes away from his with an effort.

He was feeling something similar and fighting it for all he was worth. Grace was coming home. He had to keep that in mind. Clancey was too young, too burdened, too everything.

He got up from the chair. "Can I get you anything before I go?"

"No. Thanks for everything, Mr. Banks."

It rankled that she was so formal with him. Of course, it was better that way. Good idea not to be intimate, even in speech.

He picked up his hat and slanted it over his right eye. "If you need anything, call the office."

"I will."

He nodded. He looked around at the sparse furnishings and back to the colorful quilt that covered her. He noted the different colors and cloths. "Is that a memory quilt?" he asked suddenly.

She laughed. "Yes, it is. My mother made it long ago, from scraps of cloth that came from her great-grandmother and all the kids, down to me and Tad. It's comforting, in a way. She's gone, but echoes of her live on in the house."

"Echoes." He nodded. "We have a memory quilt that our grandmother made for Brenda when she was a kid. She still sleeps with it. She says it's like our grandmother cuddles her in it."

She smiled up at him. "That's how I feel, when I sleep under mine."

"You women and your fantasies," he teased. "I have a plain comforter. Keeps me warm. No sentiment attached."

"I like sentiment."

"Of course you do. You're a woman."

She just shook her head.

AFTER HE LEFT, she recalled that long, hot look they'd exchanged and her whole body throbbed. She had to get herself together. Banks was not for her. He was already hung up on Grace Charles, and they had a history. It made her sad to consider the other woman. Banks was sexy and responsible and he had a nurturing nature, although he rarely let it show. She was never going to forget how kind he'd been to her when she got sick.

But along with those memories was the fear of having him find out that Morris Duffy was related to her, even just as a stepbrother. He was working on a case involving her grandfather and he didn't know it. She was grateful that he'd never connected her address with that of Dalton Reed, her grandfather. She hoped that one day she could work up the courage to tell him the truth.

CAL BROUGHT TAD home and presented her with a fish platter from the local fish place.

"Oh, I love fish! Thank you so much!" she exclaimed.

"I like fish myself, and Tad is crazy for it," he chuckled.

"I sure am! Thanks, Cal!" Tad called as he ran down the hall toward his room. "Video game time!"

Clancey just shook her head. "If we could just bottle that energy," she said of her brother.

Cal laughed. "Dream on." He checked his watch. "Well, I'll see you later. I'm going down to the restaurant."

She knew the one he was talking about. It had flamenco dancers and a super band. She'd gone there with him once, to watch people do the tango. Cal had tried unsuccessfully to teach her how to do it. But she had two left feet.

"What are you thinking so hard about?" he wondered.

"Tango," she returned.

He rolled his eyes and shook his head. "I have never in my life met anyone who couldn't even do a simple two-step before. You're a lost cause, Clancey."

She grinned. "I know! I love music. Granddaddy played classical guitar. He could make the instrument wail."

"You do pretty well with that yourself," he recalled, having heard her play.

"I took lessons, while Mama was still alive. I love the guitar."

"Do you still play?"

"Not so much," she said quietly. "But I still can."

"I used to play piano," he recalled. "But I can't even remember the scales anymore. We lose what we don't use."

"So true." She sighed. "Thanks so much for all you've done for us this week," she said.

"It's no problem. You going to try to go back to work Monday?"

She shook her head. "Mr. Banks said to come in Tuesday. He'll be out of town all day Monday on a case."

"You should be on the way to recovery by then," he replied.

She glanced toward the doorway and lowered her voice. "Have you heard any more about Morris?"

"Not yet. I'll keep checking. There are some new apartments over by the hospital," he said. "They're low-rent. I'm going to check on them early next week."

"I appreciate that." She sighed. "I love this house, but I can't live with Morris. I won't even try. I know Tad won't."

"Your stepbrother is fooling the parole board," he said coldly. "He's ingratiated himself to the warden with favors. I'm not sure exactly what they are, but the man went to bat for him at his hearing. It carried weight. He's been on his best behavior. No infractions. He hasn't even gotten into a fight in five years."

"That doesn't sound like Morris," she said flatly. "He had a black temper."

"I think he probably still does," he replied. "He's putting on an act. But when he gets out…"

"I know. The old gang he ran with is still around," she said. "They cow the merchants nearby and extort money from them."

"We've tried to catch them in the act," he replied, "but

without much success. There's so much crime and so few of us who try to prevent it."

"You do a great job," she told him.

He chuckled. "Thanks. I've got a good crew." He cocked his head. "You going to be okay over the weekend?"

"Yes. We've got plenty of food in the freezer, and I'll feel like cooking by tomorrow. The fish is wonderful," she added.

"I'm glad you like it. I'll be in touch."

"Thanks again."

He threw up his hand on the way out.

WHEN SHE WOKE up the next morning, it was to the sound of voices in her kitchen. One was Tad's, excited and talkative. The other was deep and slow and amused. Banks!

She sat up in bed, delighted to note that it didn't hurt anymore. She could even take a deep breath without a coughing fit. *The wonder of modern medicine*, she thought warmly.

She started to get up just as Banks walked into the room with Tad. He was carrying a plate with a pecan waffle and bacon.

She caught her breath. "Oh my goodness," she exclaimed, fighting tears. "It's my very favorite…!"

"So Tad said. Don't stand on ceremony. Dig in!" He handed her the plate and a syrup bottle.

"You angel," she said to Banks, and flushed a little at the way he smiled.

His black eyes had lowered to her blue pajama jacket. She flushed and turned away quickly, putting her plate on the end table before she climbed quickly into bed and pulled up the covers.

"Heavens, you and Cal are spoiling us!" she exclaimed with a grin as she dug into her treat. She closed her eyes and moaned with delight. "I love waffles!"

He was studying her with a faint frown, his eyes narrow and thoughtful. She was joyful at the simplest things, like a child. It always seemed to surprise her when people were kind to her. He wondered suddenly what her life had been like, before she ended up being Tad's only support. Those broken ribs he'd learned about in the hospital worried him. She'd never spoken of being in an accident. Clancey was mysterious, in her way.

"Mr. Banks says that Texas Rangers go all over the world on cases, Clancey!" Tad said, breaking the silence.

"Yes, we do," Colter chuckled. "It's an interesting job."

"Dangerous, though," Clancey said involuntarily.

"Most jobs that involve guns are dangerous," he said easily. "However, my sister counters that anybody who works with dogs and cats is in a dangerous profession. She's got scars."

"Scars?" Tad asked, all ears.

He chuckled. "She's been bitten, clawed, climbed, knocked down, dragged and otherwise abused by a succession of unwilling patients at the vet clinic where she works," he explained. "But she loves it. We always had pets at home, when we were young."

"Do you have pets?" Tad asked.

He nodded. "A big red Maine Coon cat named Miss Kitty. She sleeps on my shoulder every night."

"I'd love to have a cat," Tad sighed. "But we can't on account of Clancey's got asthma."

"I'm not allergic to all cats. Just certain ones," she clarified. "It depends on the dander, not the fur." She laughed involuntarily. "One man suggested that if I rubbed a cat with a dryer sheet, it might help. I asked if he'd be willing to hold the cat while I rubbed it."

Banks chuckled. "I saw this video once, about how to bathe a cat. It seems to involve rubber boots, a rain slicker, a scuba helmet and thick rubber gloves. Convinced me that Miss Kitty was never going to need a bath, I might add."

"I'll bet she's pretty," Clancey said. "There was a show about cats a few weeks ago that Tad and I watched. There was a big black-and-brown Maine Coon cat who was taught to play fetch. His owner walked him on a leash."

"They're smart," he agreed. "My housekeeper fusses because she can't use the sink until I come home and remove the cat."

"What?" she asked.

"Miss Kitty loves sinks and bathtubs," he explained. "And water of any kind. She likes to play in it." He shook his head. "On hot days, she curls up in the kitchen sink and goes to sleep."

Clancey smiled. "She sounds very sweet."

"She is, until you want her to do something that she doesn't want to do," he replied with a sigh. "Then it's all teeth and claws and hissing. She weighs sixteen pounds, so she can be formidable."

"I didn't know that cats got so big," Clancey remarked as she put her empty plate on the bedside table.

"Only a few breeds do." He smiled at the picture she made, sitting up in bed with her wavy hair faintly tousled and those pale gray eyes that reminded him of sterling silver.

He glanced at his watch and grimaced. "I have to go. I'm meeting an informant."

"He won't hurt you, will he?" Tad worried.

"Mr. Banks has a gun, Tad," she returned with a wry smile.

"Oh." Tad studied it in its hand-tooled leather holster. "It's a big gun."

"A .45 caliber Colt 1911 ACP," Banks said. "But I hardly ever have to use it. That's a good thing."

"I don't think I could shoot people," Tad said worriedly.

"Has somebody asked you to?" Banks asked with an indulgent smile.

"Well, I want to be a Texas Ranger when I grow up, just like you," Tad explained, while Banks's high cheekbones took on the faintest ruddy tint.

"I wouldn't worry about it," Colter told him gently. "It's a few years in the future, right?"

Tad smiled. "I reckon."

"If you need anything, you call me," he told both of them.

"Thanks," Clancey said. "I'll see you Tuesday. And thanks again for the treat. There is nothing more wonderful than a pecan waffle," she added with a grin.

He smiled back at her, his black eyes assessing, curious, searching. She flushed and dragged her eyes away. He chuckled deeply.

"Lock the door after me," Colter told Tad, ruffling his hair affectionately. "Can't be too careful with an invalid in the house."

"I am not an invalid," Clancey said with mock hauteur.

"Yes, you are, nasturtium."

"I am not a…!"

"Good night." Banks closed the door.

Tad was still laughing as he put on the chain latch.

IN SPITE OF all her arguments, Cal Hollister came by for Tad Monday morning and took him to and from school. He was back the next morning to drop off Tad and Clancey at school and work, respectively.

"This is out of your way," she complained gently.

He just laughed. "Not really. I have to go by your house on my way to and from work." He glanced at her with affection. "Besides, I don't want you trying to walk to work in the cold wind. You'll end up back in the emergency room."

She sighed. "I wish I had good lungs."

"Wishing doesn't do much for us."

"I guess," she agreed. "Anyway, this is very nice of you."

"If you had a car, you'd do the same for me." He glanced at her and grimaced. "I really wish you wouldn't walk to work. Frankly, when Morris gets out, it will be more dangerous than you think. He's sworn vengeance on our DA candidate. You're on the firing line, as well."

"I wouldn't mind if he'd just leave Tad alone," she sighed. "I don't think Morris has changed, either, Cal," she added. "He could always put on a good act, when he wasn't high."

"We'll do what we can, within the limits of the law, to keep him from hurting any of you. But we can't watch him all the time," he added.

"How about that apartment?" she asked suddenly.

He sighed. "No vacancies," he said. "I'm looking into

rentals in family homes. It might be better than an apartment anyway."

"I wouldn't mind that," she said. "Neither would Tad." She wondered how she'd ever manage rent when she and Tad lived right up to her salary. She looked out the window. "I wish they'd kept Morris another year or two."

"So do I," he replied.

"At least he's not out yet," she said. "I have a little time to do something."

"Pack a bugout bag."

"A what?"

"A bugout bag," he replied. "It's a bag with a few essentials that you can grab and run with, in case of an emergency. I always used to keep one."

"Oh, I see." She laughed. "If Tad packed one, he'd put in comic books and fruit bars."

"Keepsakes and photos you can't replace," he continued as if she hadn't spoken. "A little money, your bank book, your birth certificates, any other important paperwork, and at least a change of clothes and an extra pair of shoes."

"I can do that." She wrapped her arms around herself. "If only Mama had lived longer," she said softly. "Or Dad or even Granddaddy."

"It's hard to lose parents."

"You don't have yours, either, do you?" she asked.

He shook his head. "Not for many years." He pulled up at her office. "I'll pick you up at five and we'll swing by and get Tad."

"Thanks so much," she said.

He waved away her thanks. "Friends help each other out," he said simply.

She nodded. She climbed out of the car, closed the door and waved as he drove off.

She went down the steps slowly. Banks was at his desk, on the phone, clearly annoyed at something or someone. He looked up when she walked into the room and smiled with soft black eyes. Her heart melted. She turned away and hung up her ratty jacket, trying to still her pulse.

She mouthed "coffee?" and he nodded. She went to make it while he growled at someone on the other end of the line.

She was just pouring it into two mugs when he came up behind her, so close that she could feel the heat and power of his tall body.

"Thanks," he said, reaching around her to take one of the cups.

"You're welcome."

He didn't move for a few seconds. Her heart felt as if it were trying to break through her rib cage. He moved away before she had time to wonder if it was deliberate.

"I've got SAPD helping on the Reed case," he said, turning away so that he didn't see her almost spill her coffee on the floor.

"Have you?" she asked in a tone that was a little high.

"Marquez said that they kept paper files on some cases that hadn't been transferred to digital media. He was going to have one of his people check it out and see if they had anything they could scan and email to me."

"That was nice."

"Marquez has his moments." He sat back in the chair. "You're still having trouble breathing," he added.

She smiled. "It's hard to get over pneumonia," she said

simply. "I'm much better, but I still get winded when I move around."

"How the hell did you walk to work this morning?"

"I didn't. Cal drove us." She shook her head. "He's like a bulldozer. You can't say no to him."

He glared at her when she didn't see him. He grimaced. "I guess he's like family."

"He really is," she agreed. "He doesn't have any family, either. He's been kind to Tad and me. So have you," she added shyly. "I don't know how we'll ever pay either of you back for all you've done."

The depression lifted when she said that. "I like Tad," he said.

She smiled. "He's crazy about you. He really wants to be a Texas Ranger now."

He chuckled. "He'll probably grow out of it."

"Did you always want to work for the Rangers?" she asked.

"No. I wanted to be a pilot."

She frowned. "You were in the military, you said."

"Sure. But to be a pilot, there's a height limit. I was way, way over it," he added with twinkling eyes.

"Oh."

"Besides, I had a pal who flew F-22 Raptors," he said. "He told me that when those babies took off, your stomach tried to exit through your spine. Plus, there's the 'Raptor Cough.'"

"The what?"

"The Raptor Cough," he said. "All the Raptor pilots get it—nobody knows why. It's one of the mysteries of life."

"Oooh," she said. "It's aliens, isn't it?" she asked with

a grin. "They get into the cockpit when you aren't looking and blow smoke in your face."

He burst out laughing.

She loved it when he did that. He had a wonderful laugh, deep and genuine.

"Aliens," he sighed, shaking his head.

"You never know," she returned.

The phone rang. He held his hand out, palm up, waiting for her to answer it.

She was still laughing when she picked up the receiver.

It was Cal. "I'm sorry. I have to be out of town for a few days. Some damned seminar in Denver," he muttered. "Listen, I've hired a cab company to take you and Tad to school and work and home again. Don't argue," he added when she tried to. "You know it won't do any good."

She sighed. "Okay. Thanks," she added.

He chuckled. "I have to look out for my adopted family," he said simply. "Watch your back."

"Have you heard anything?" she added quickly while Banks was on his cell phone, answering another call.

"About Morris, you mean? Actually, I have," he added, and he sounded pleased. "There's been a slight hitch. It's going to be a few weeks before they turn him loose. One last evaluation, or some such thing."

"That's a relief," she whispered. "A reprieve."

"Yes, and we have to find someplace for you and Tad to go. When I get back, that will be my priority."

"Thanks," she said.

"No problem. I'll talk to you soon."

"Okay."

SEVEN

A THOUSAND WILD thoughts ran through Clancey's mind all at once. A few weeks. Well, it wasn't the end of the world. She had time. Not a lot, but time to look for apartments at least.

Banks put down his cell phone. "Who was that?" he asked.

She just smiled. "They changed my dental appointment," she replied, forcing herself to look nonchalant. "It's just for a cleaning."

He was already nose deep into a new computer file. He just nodded idly and went back to work.

Clancey went into her office, out of his sight, and ground her teeth together. Morris wasn't coming home soon, but he was definitely coming home. She and Tad would have to leave the house. She was going to have to do something. She didn't dare involve Banks and she didn't want to obligate Cal any further. She'd have to play her cards close to her chest. Meanwhile, she had to start searching want ads. She picked up the telephone directory and started looking up numbers.

SHE FOUND TWO promising leads on family apartments. She had a little money saved. She spent some of it that weekend, going to inquire about the apartment with Tad in tow.

The first was a no-frills basement apartment that smelled of mold. It was in a house with several apartments, and the tenants weren't friendly or welcoming. The landlord had a shifty look.

"Thanks for letting us look around," she told him with a determined smile.

"Going to take it?" he asked quickly. "I've got three other parties interested."

In a pig's eye, she thought, but she kept smiling. "I have others to see. Don't hold it for me, though."

He shrugged. "Your choice. Hard to find an apartment with winter coming on." He smiled, too, but it wasn't a nice smile.

She just nodded.

"I DON'T LIKE HIM," Tad said when they were back in the cab en route to the next place, still hopeful.

"Me, neither," she said. "And the basement smelled full of mold." She took out her rescue inhaler and took a puff. She'd been coughing since they left the apartment.

"You okay?" he asked worriedly.

"Don't fuss," she said softly. "I'm fine. I'm just sensitive to mold."

"Where's the next place?" he asked.

She pulled out the want ads. She didn't have a smart phone or she could have used an app to look for rentals. She'd circled the two most promising, and one of those was already a no-go. She hoped against hope that the next one would suit them.

IT WAS IN a large, Victorian house right near the Texas Rangers office and Tad's school, within easy walking distance. The owners were an elderly couple, and Clancey noted the religious paintings on the wall and a Bible on the coffee table. It relaxed her.

The apartment had two twin beds, which meant that she and Tad would have to share a room. But it had a nice view. It was well lit and airy and very clean.

"I love this," she said softly.

"Me, too!" Tad agreed.

The landlady smiled complacently. "You and your son will like it here."

"Oh, Clancey's not my mom," Tad piped up. "She's my sister."

The landlady looked taken aback. "Your parents?" she asked gently.

Clancey grimaced. "All dead," she said quietly. "It's just Tad and me. I work for the Texas Rangers, the cold case unit," she added. "Tad and I go to the Methodist church."

"We're Baptist," the landlady said, and looked not so pleased.

"Church is church," Clancey said gently.

The woman shrugged. "Well?" she asked. "Are you going to take it?"

Clancey glanced at the paper. "The ad said you were asking…"

"We had to have the roof replaced, so we've had to add to the rental price to help us pay for it," she said.

She named a figure that was four hundred dollars more a month than the quoted price.

Clancey's face mirrored her disappointment.

"Are you going to take it?" the landlady asked again.

Clancey sighed. "I'm sorry," she said gently. "But it's way over my budget…"

The landlady turned and walked out, leaving Clancey and Tad to follow, muttering about cheap people who didn't know a bargain when they saw it.

Tad exchanged a long look with his sister. Now that they weren't prospective tenants, the landlady dropped her sweetness and reverted to type. This would not have been a good place to live. Clancey, oddly, felt relieved.

"Thank you for letting us look at the apartment," Clancey said politely at the door. "I'm sorry we can't take it."

"No problem," the woman returned curtly. "We had five other queries from the ad already. Good day."

She shut the door in their faces.

Clancey turned to Tad as they walked toward the waiting cab. "By the skin of our teeth," she whispered.

Tad chuckled. "Yeah," he agreed. "I didn't want to live there anyway." He looked up at her. "Why can't we ask the Martins if they'll rent us a room? They could use the money, I know."

Her heart jumped, but just as quickly calmed. "We wouldn't dare," she said. "What if Morris came after us there and hurt them?"

He ground his teeth together. "I didn't think about that."

"I work for the Texas Rangers," she said. "It rubs off." She flashed a grin at him as they got into the cab. "I'm developing incredible deductive skills."

The cab driver, a patient soul who had turned the meter off while they were in the house, laughed with them. "I have a brother who's a deputy sheriff," he told them.

"Really?" Clancey said. "My grandfather was one, also!"

"Where does he work?"

Clancey sighed. "He's been missing for over five years," she said sadly. "We think he's probably dead. They never found a—" she hesitated "—a body."

"That would be worse than finding him," he agreed.

"At least we still got each other, Clancey," Tad reminded her softly.

She hugged him. "Yes, we do!"

"Family," the cab driver mused, "is the most important thing on earth. Fame and glory are fleeting. Family prevails."

"Very nice," she said.

"I have a degree in philosophy," he replied. "Graduated with honors." He indicated the cab. "So this is the great job I found with all my years of study."

Clancey just shook her head. "I know a pizza joint owner who has a PhD in psychology."

"Some professions don't offer the opportunities that others do," he said with a sigh. "In retrospect, I should have become a bricklayer. Not much chance for advancement, but the pay is really nice!"

They all laughed.

BANKS WAS RESTLESS. He didn't know why. He found himself watching Clancey from time to time, observing how nice she looked in those formfitting jeans and that perky yellow sweater that outlined her small breasts. He was paying far too much attention to her, and it bothered him. There was Grace Charles in the background, on her way to San Antonio soon. He hadn't seen her in years. But he'd grieved for her, ached for her, wanted her more than life. So why was he staring at Clancey?

She was fragile. It had been a couple of weeks since she'd had pneumonia. She still got winded easily, although she'd bounced back fast. Cal Hollister was still transporting her and Tad to school and work, respectively. She said Hollister was just a friend, but the man was close to her. Very close. And he wasn't.

He wasn't jealous. Of course he wasn't…

"Do you like flamenco?" he asked Clancey abruptly late the next Thursday.

She dropped a file folder and flushed as she bent over to pick it up, grinding her teeth at what her clumsiness betrayed. "Well, yes, I like… I like the music. I can't dance," she blurted out, flushing.

That vulnerability made him feel protective. He leaned back in his chair with his big booted feet on his desk and smiled at her, black eyes twinkling. "Suppose you and Tad go to dinner with me tomorrow night and we'll watch the dancers?"

Oh my gosh, she was thinking, her heart racing. Was that like a date, or was he thinking of giving the kid a treat?

She just stared at him, her cheeks rosy and almost glowing. Her pale silver eyes were soft. "Well…well, I love to watch dancing," she said, flustered. "So does Tad. It's so nice of you. And you've done so much for us already…" She was floundering.

"I don't do anything I don't want to," he said simply. He smiled. "Well?"

"We'd love to go," she said at once.

He grinned at her. "Okay. I'll pick you both up about six. That okay?"

She nodded. "Six."

"Don't dress up," he added. He scowled. "You know that I carry the gun everywhere I go, right?" he asked suddenly.

"Well, yes," she said.

"It won't bother you?" he persisted.

She moved closer to the desk, file folders pressed to her breasts. "My grandfather was a lawman," she reminded him softly. "He always wore a sidearm. We never thought anything about it." She smiled. "My great-grandfather was a lawman, too."

"A lawman." He smiled. "What sort?"

She drew in a breath. It was safe to tell him. He didn't know about her family. "He was a deputy United States Marshal," she said. "His son, my grandfather, was a sheriff's deputy. It sort of runs in my family."

"Not in mine," Banks said wistfully. "I was the first. My mother was scared to death that I was going to get killed. She tried to talk me out of it, but it wasn't possible. I love what I do."

She smiled. "I used to think I'd like to go through the police academy, when I first went to work for Cal Hollister."

His eyebrows arched. "What changed your mind?"

"Cal gave us a ride home one afternoon," she said very quietly, her hands holding the file folder even tighter as the memory invaded her mind. "There was a bank robbery in progress. Cal stopped at the scene, said for us to stay in the car. He pulled out his service revolver and walked right into the shotgun one of the perps was holding. He should have been killed. The robber actually missed. Cal didn't." She swallowed, hard. "There was so much blood," she whispered, her eyes blank as she relived the incident in her mind. "When Cal finally came back, to drive us home, his eyes were terrible. He didn't speak the whole way. Tad and I just sat quietly. Both of us were shaken. We'd never seen anyone killed." She stared at the wall behind Banks. "Cal said that you never got used to having to shoot somebody. It was like giving up a piece of your soul that you could never get back. He was on administrative leave for a few days and he got stinking drunk. Lieutenant Marquez went out to his ranch and talked him down." She shook her head. "After that, I knew I wasn't cut out for a career in law enforcement."

"But you didn't stop working for him," he said.

She shook her head. "There was a case, a criminal case, some years ago. Cal had just made lieutenant. He helped investigate the case, and he offered me a job. I owe him a lot."

"A criminal case?" he prodded.

She hesitated, wary of giving anything else away. She'd already said too much.

The phone rang. Banks made a face and answered it. He spoke to someone on the other end, said he was on his way and hung up.

"Another kidnapping," he said. "They've requested us and the FBI. I'll be late. And I'll be out of the office on another case tomorrow. But you remember. I'll pick you and Tad up tomorrow at six."

She smiled. "At six," she agreed, and her heart lifted out of the tortured memory she'd relived.

He pursed his lips. "Maybe I'll teach you to dance."

"Maybe you'll teach cows to fly," she countered.

He was still laughing when he went out the door.

CLANCEY WAS A nervous wreck at the end of the day, when the cab deposited her and Tad at home.

"What's wrong with you?" Tad asked when they were inside the house.

"Mr. Banks wants to take us out to eat at Fernando's, that flamenco restaurant, tomorrow night."

"He does?" Tad was all eyes. "What did you say? You said yes, right? Right?"

She laughed at his enthusiasm. "I said yes."

"Whoopee!" he exclaimed. "Tacos and enchiladas and flan!"

"Leave it to you to think of the food first," she teased.

"Well, the dancing's nice, too. You going to dance with Mr. Banks?"

She flushed. "I might."

He grinned.

SHE WENT THROUGH her meager stock of clothes and found one nice blouse that was sort of fancy to go with her best jeans and boots. It was a button-up blouse in shades of green and brown and gray that complemented her olive complexion and brought out the pale silver of her eyes. She couldn't do anything about her mop of hair that set itself into thick waves when the humidity was high. It was easy to keep as long as she had it cut infrequently. She used the lightest touch of makeup, just some powder and a gloss lipstick. But she looked presentable, if not overly pretty.

She had some cologne, but she hesitated to use it. Sometimes even the floral fragrances she liked caused asthma attacks. She used a light deodorant instead and hoped for the best.

Tad whistled when she came into the living room. "You look nice," he said.

She grinned. "Thanks." She picked up her ratty old jacket with a sigh. "Maybe they won't mistake us for vagrants when we walk in the door," she said.

"Nobody's going to be looking at what we wear," Tad protested gently. "I mean, they have a live band and they have people who dance the tango. That's what everybody will be watching. Not us. Remember when Cal took us there? The food was great! Anyway, nobody will care what you're wearing. Honest."

She laughed. "Leave it to you to reduce my greatest fears into feathers."

He grinned. "I like Mr. Banks," he said. "It's really nice of him to take us out."

"Cal goes there to eat most Friday nights," she commented. "We'll probably see him, too."

"I like Cal a lot," Tad said. He looked up at her. "Clancey, when is Morris coming back?"

She drew in a breath, worried and unable to hide it. "Cal said he's getting early release," she said, grimacing as she told him. He lost a shade of color, but his chin went up.

"Do you know when?" he asked sadly.

"No. I don't know exactly when."

"We won't live with him, will we?" he asked uneasily.

"Silly boy." She hugged him close. "No way."

"Thanks. I was worried." He looked up at her. "Do you think he's changed?"

"No," she said flatly. "Very few people change what they actually are. Some of them put on a really convincing act. Morris was good at that, even before he went to jail."

"He'll be on parole, though, right?" he added. "I mean, they'll keep an eye on him. He made threats."

"Nobody heard him make them," she replied quietly. "It's only gossip that he threatened the man who's running for district attorney. It's only gossip that he threatened me, because I sent him to jail." She bit her lower lip. "He wrote me that nice letter, after your father died. He thanked me for all I did for Ben."

"I still don't trust him."

"Neither do I, Tad," she replied. "He ran with a bad crowd before he was sentenced, and they're still around. Granddaddy thought he was dealing drugs as well as using them. He said he was going to prove it…" She hesitated, because that was a secret she'd never shared with Tad.

The boy looked up at her with sad eyes. "I thought there might be a reason that Morris would want to hurt him."

She nodded. "There was. I didn't tell you before. I'm sorry."

"It's okay."

She pushed back an unruly lock of his hair. "I'm sorry our apartment hunting didn't do us any good. We'll try again Monday, okay?"

"Cal would let us live with him," Tad said.

"I know he would, but I don't want to get dependent on other people," she told him. "It's never wise to do that. We have to try and take care of ourselves."

"It's you who's doing most of the taking care of us," Tad pointed out.

She smiled. "I'm getting pretty good at it, yeah?" she teased.

"Really good," he agreed. He looked around at their meager furnishings. "We don't have much. Well, except for your guitar," he added.

"Which Morris would smash in a fit of anger if he had the opportunity." She set her lips firmly. "I'm taking it over to the Martins when we go to church day after tomorrow. They'll keep it for me, just in case we have to pick up and leave in a hurry."

His heart jumped. "Where would we go?" he asked worriedly.

"There's a nice homeless shelter," she said with wounded pride. "It isn't much, but it has a good reputation. I've already talked to the woman who runs it, just in case." She bit her lower lip. "I don't make enough money for a really good apartment. Not yet. That's why I was thinking about the military…"

Tad hugged her close. "No way are you going to go and get shot trying to take care of me," he said firmly. "We'll live on the streets if we have to. I can't lose you, too, Clancey. I've lost everybody else."

"Me, too," she said on a sigh. She hugged him back. "We'll do whatever we have to do."

"If we have to go to the shelter, Cal won't like it."

"Cal won't know," she returned. "It's closer than the house to your school and my work." She drew back and forced a smile. "Not so far to walk," she added.

He grimaced. "I guess."

"I wish I was a better provider," she began.

"You just hush," Tad told her. "You're the best sister in the whole world and I wouldn't trade you for worlds."

She flushed a little. "Thanks."

He grinned up at her. "You're welcome."

Outside, a big SUV was just pulling in at the front walk. Clancey's heart jumped. She told herself, and not for the first time, that this wasn't a good idea. She and Banks worked together. It was dangerous, in more ways than one, to get involved with a coworker. There was probably a regulation somewhere about it.

Banks was thinking something similar. This had seemed like a good idea at the time, taking the kids out for a meal and some good music at a family restaurant. But he was getting cold feet. Clancey was a coworker. He shouldn't have made the invitation in the first place.

He rapped on the door. Clancey opened it.

He just stared at her. She wasn't really pretty, but she had a nice figure and a pretty mouth. She was abrasive, but she had a sweet nature.

"This is probably a bad idea," he began.

"I was just thinking the same thing," she blurted out. "Maybe we should…"

"Mr. Banks!" Tad exclaimed, running back down the hall from his room, pulling on his jacket as he came. "Gosh, this is nice of you! I love flan!"

Banks laughed in spite of his misgivings. "I have to admit, so do I," he replied.

Clancey was noting the blue chambray shirt that covered his broad, muscular chest, the way his slacks clung to the hard muscles of his legs. He was wearing hand-tooled tan boots that matched the belt that held his service revolver in its holster. On the handle of the weapon was the famous Cinco Peso design of the Texas Rangers.

"That looks so cool," Tad remarked, staring at the automatic pistol in its holster.

"What, the gun?" Banks asked.

Tad chuckled. "No. The star."

"It's a new gun. I had the handle modified," Banks told him.

"It looks nice," Tad said. He studied Banks. "Have you ever had to shoot anybody?"

Banks nodded solemnly. "Not often, though."

"Clancey can't really shoot a pistol," Tad said solemnly. "Cal tried to teach her, but he said she's just hopeless."

"My hands aren't strong enough," she replied with a laugh. "I couldn't even cock the darn thing."

"Wheel guns don't require cocking," Banks pointed out.

She glared at him. "I am not using a sissy wheel gun when everybody who works in law enforcement carries a cannon."

Banks's eyebrows arched under his creamy Stetson. "I don't carry a cannon."

"Those things sound like a cannon going off," she pointed out. "No wonder you guys have to wear earplugs on the firing range."

Banks just chuckled. "Half the old-timers were deaf from that noise. Modern accessories reduce the damage."

"Good thing," Clancey said with a nod.

BANKS PUT THEM both in the big SUV and climbed in beside them. "I don't know about you two, but I'm starving."

"I could eat a horse!" Tad exclaimed.

"I'll tell them," Banks said with a grin.

Tad blushed. Then he laughed.

Clancey listened to the two of them talk without saying much. She kept thinking about the threats Morris had made. Banks didn't know about her family, about her very dangerous stepbrother. Somehow, she was going to have to find the courage to come clean about it, before he found out the hard way. She didn't want him to think she'd lied about it, or worse, covered it up. She'd done those things, of course. She couldn't afford to lose her job. Banks was, in many ways, a by-the-book lawman. He could bend the rules when he needed to, but he never broke them. He wouldn't like having to find out from somebody else what Clancey didn't trust him enough to tell him.

Besides that, he was investigating her grandfather's disappearance, and he didn't know a thing about the man except the sketchy information in the old case files. She could tell him many things that might help him find the truth.

"You're quiet," Banks remarked to her when he pulled into a space in the restaurant parking lot.

"I'm enjoying the ride," she lied, forcing a smile. "I'm used to walking everywhere."

"It's raining!" Tad exclaimed.

Banks glanced at Clancey. "Think she'll melt?" he wondered aloud with twinkling eyes.

Clancey glared at him. "I will not!" she exclaimed. "I don't even own a pointy black hat!"

Tad grinned. "And we live in the wrong state," he pointed out. "That was Kansas, not Texas."

"Exactly," Clancey said smugly.

Banks chuckled. "Before they married, Wolf Patterson used to accuse Sara Brandon of having flying monkeys."

"Do they live in San Antonio?" Clancey asked as they got out of the SUV.

"They alternate between his Jacobs County ranch and the Wyoming ranch Sara owns jointly with her brother, Gabriel," he said. "He used to be with the FBI, but most recently, he was a merc."

"A who?" she asked, dashing for the awning with her little brother and Banks before the rain soaked her jacket.

"A merc. A professional soldier," he explained.

"Oh," she said, nodding. "That's like a sell sword in *Game of Thrones*, right?"

His eyebrows arched. "You watch it?"

She flushed. "Oh no. I just got the books from the library and read them. One of my coworkers watched it on cable and said it was really, well, explicit. I couldn't watch a show like that with Tad around," she added. Plus, she couldn't afford anything except basic cable. No pay-per-view channels at all, but she wasn't telling him that.

He pursed his lips. He was a fan of the series as well, but he understood what she was saying. The language and adult situations in the television program were not suitable for a small boy.

"We can't afford cable anyway, though, so it doesn't matter," Tad laughed, while Clancey cringed inside at the blow to her pride. "We watch movies on this old DVD player we have. Granddaddy loved movies. He had almost every Western movie ever made."

Clancey gave him a look that silenced him abruptly. "We don't watch much television anyway," she said.

"She used to practice all the time," Tad sighed. "Not so much lately."

"Practice what?" Banks asked as he opened the door for them.

"Guitar," Tad said. "She plays guitar."

"Well," Banks said softly as she passed him.

She didn't look up. If she had, she'd have seen a whimsical smile on his chiseled mouth.

"THIS IS SO GOOD!" Tad said, closing his eyes as he munched on an enchilada.

"Yes, it is." Banks sipped the strong, cinnamon-flavored coffee the restaurant was famous for.

"I've never tasted coffee like this," Clancey said, sipping it with obvious enjoyment.

"They make it like this in Mexico," he told her with a smile. "I was on a case there early this year. I had to fly down to Cancun."

"I've read about it," Clancey told him. "They have books on it with beautiful color prints." Her expression was dreamy. "It must be a fascinating place, with all the ruins."

"It is. I made time to walk around Chichen Itza. It's one of the oldest Mayan ruins. The ball court and the pyramid are still standing after all the centuries, including an observatory."

She nodded. "They were a brilliant civilization, before they disappeared. Nobody seems to know why they vanished."

"Climate, most likely. There were cycles of drought and flooding. They've found evidence of violent fluctuation in temperatures in ice cores in the Antarctic."

"They say climate change is because of human civilization," she said.

"Were there factories twelve thousand years ago, when the ice caps melted?" he wondered aloud, and his twinkling black eyes met Clancey's pale silver ones.

Her heart jumped. She stared back helplessly. What had he been saying? Something about ice cores in the Antarctic?

"Climate change goes back hundreds of thousands of years," he continued. "There are cycles. Long before men built cities, drought decimated ancient civilizations. It put an end to many of them."

"How do you know so much about that?" she asked.

"I minored in anthropology in college," he said simply. "It was one of my favorite subjects. We spent a lot of time digging up things."

"Oh. I didn't know you went to college."

"I have an undergraduate degree in criminal justice," he said. "Since I planned a career in law enforcement, I thought it was a good idea. I worked with the Department of Public Safety in the daytime and went to school at night."

"That must have been hard," she said.

He smiled. "It was interesting," he agreed.

"I've often wondered..." She stopped in midsentence and looked up. Cal Hollister had just walked in and was being seated on the other side of the restaurant.

Banks saw him at the same time that Clancey did, and his black eyes glittered. He had a sudden, mean urge to go over and throw Hollister through the nice picture window beside the booth where he was seated...

EIGHT

"CAL'S HERE," TAD remarked with a grin.

Clancey smiled. "Yes, he likes the flamenco dancers," she said. She glanced at Banks, who had the oddest expression on his face. "He's a wonderful dancer. Sadly, he could never manage to teach me. I have two left feet," she confessed sheepishly.

"Can you dance, Mr. Banks?" Tad wondered aloud.

Banks chuckled. "Yes, I can."

"You should teach her," Tad suggested, nodding toward his sister. "She can't even do a two-step."

"I could if I wanted to," she told her little brother stubbornly. "I just don't want to give other women an inferiority complex with my fancy footwork, that's all."

Banks laughed softly. He couldn't remember a woman who made him laugh so often. Grace had been somber, like Mike Johns. In fact, so had Banks. In recent years, he was more taciturn than outgoing. He hadn't realized just what an influence Clancey had on him. It was surprising.

"Cal can do the tango," Tad said, staring over at Cal, who was sitting all alone.

"Doesn't he date anybody?" Banks asked curtly.

"No," Clancey said. "He really is a loner. I don't think he likes women very much, actually."

"He seems to like you," Banks said, with a bite in his deep voice.

Clancey looked at him, surprised. "Of course he likes me—I'm his kid sister. Well, adopted, sort of," she clarified. "Me and Tad. He's way older than me," she added, flustered at Banks's somber expression.

He scowled. "He's thirty-five," he said.

She just stared at him, uncomprehending.

"That's not way older than you."

"It's twelve years," she pointed out, still all at sea.

He scowled. His black eyes averted. Hollister wasn't that much older than his own thirty-two years, but Clancey thought of the other man as too old to interest her. Did she feel that way about any man on the wrong side of thirty?

"It wouldn't matter anyway," she added, fumbling with her water glass while her little brother stared raptly at a man playing the guitar while a woman in a beautiful red-and-black flamenco dress stomped her feet to the Spanish music while the dance band rested. "I have too many obligations."

She said it softly, so that Tad didn't hear her. He wasn't an obligation. She loved him to distraction. She smiled at him, her eyes soft and loving.

Banks drew in a breath as the waitress stopped by their table to see if they wanted dessert.

"Yes," Tad said at once, diverted. He grinned. "Flan!"

"Make that three," Banks added with a smile.

The waitress jotted it down, nodded and went to fetch it.

"They have great desserts here," Tad piped up.

"They do, indeed," she murmured.

The dancer and the guitarist finished, and the crowd applauded. The master of ceremonies announced that the band was taking a brief break but would be back shortly to provide music for dancing.

"They're so good," Clancey said, indicating the couple. "Cal said they've been married for over…" She stopped, because the guitarist was coming toward them, smiling.

"You guys are great!" Tad enthused.

The man, tall and dignified and very Latin, made him a bow. *"Mil gracias,"* he said softly.

"De nada," Tad returned, grinning.

The guitarist pulled out a chair and handed Clancey the guitar. "Your friend the police captain over there," he indicated Cal, "says that you play like an angel. May I presume upon you?"

She flushed scarlet, although nobody nearby was paying them any attention. "Well…"

"Go on," Banks said gently.

She drew in a breath, turned sideways and gently took the guitar that the man offered. "It's exquisite," she whispered, running her long fingers along the sounding board and onto the frets.

"It belonged to my father," the guitarist said. "He was magnificent."

She smiled. "I'm not magnificent," she said shyly. "But I love to play."

He extended a hand, palm up. "Please."

She drew in a breath, drew the guitar close, and began

to play "Recuerdos de la Alhambra," by Francisco Tárrega, one of the most beautiful pieces for guitar ever written.

Banks had been expecting something Western or country, and nothing fancy. A lot of people played guitar in a standard sort of way. But when Clancey's long fingers touched those strings, the sound they produced was incredible. He just stared at her, his lips faintly open on a breath of surprise. Her eyes were closed as she played. Her fingers moved faultlessly along the frets, her other hand delicately strumming the nylon strings with the longer fingernails that acted as a pick. She didn't notice that Banks wasn't the only person drinking in her performance. Diners at nearby tables had stopped eating to listen.

She finished, the last chord dying away to an odd, profound silence. She opened her eyes to a sudden burst of applause from the people around her. She flushed like a beet and laughed softly, bowing her head at the other diners in gratitude.

She handed back the guitar. The man just shook his head, still smiling. "A rare gift, young lady," he said gently. "Were you taught?"

She nodded. "My grandfather played. I still have his guitar. He taught me to play when I was in grammar school."

"Well, if you ever need a job, you can come and work with us," he chuckled.

She grinned. "Thanks. But it's too embarrassing to play for other people," she added, still red faced as she glanced shyly around her.

"You could play professionally," Banks said quietly. "You really are talented."

"Thanks. But I just do it for my own amusement. Mostly when I'm worried or sad. It calms me."

He nodded, as if he understood.

Cal Hollister stopped by their table on his way out.

"You told him," she accused.

He shrugged, his hands in his pockets. "People who can play like that should play."

"I'll get even," she said with a wicked grin.

"I superglued my hood shut," he said blithely.

She burst out laughing while Banks sat frowning at the byplay.

"She knows how to take out a rotor," he told the Texas Ranger. "I couldn't figure out why the hell my old ranch truck wouldn't start up. My car was in the shop, so I'd driven the truck to work. I started to go home and the truck wouldn't crank. I was cussing and Clancey was standing at the back door of the building laughing her head off." He glared at her. "I didn't even make a sarcastic comment. I just said you needed to learn to change the cartridges in the printer before we all got fired. The police commissioner himself sent us a note about the faded documents we were forwarding to him."

"Wasn't my fault," she said haughtily. "It was a stupid printer."

"Well, it was, but no printer is going to work without having its ink cartridges changed periodically."

"He tried to shoot ours," she indicated Banks.

"It wouldn't work," he replied defensively.

"She dropped ours accidentally," Cal sighed. He glared at her. "Three times in a row."

"My hands slipped," she said. "And when the stupid thing couldn't be fixed, we got a new one that worked just fine and did a much better job. Besides that, you could actually get the cartridges in it without using bad words."

"She knows a lot of bad words," Tad interrupted.

She glared at him. "Bad Spanish words that you aren't supposed to understand."

"My best friend is from Guatemala," he returned, "and he taught me all of them."

She flushed.

"Corrupting an innocent child," Cal said, clicking his tongue. "For shame."

"If you arrest her, can I put the handcuffs on?" Tad asked with a grin.

"Bad idea," Banks told Cal. "You'll put her in a holding cell and two winos and a prostitute will try to overpower a jailer to get away from her."

Cal chuckled at Clancey's look of indignation. He glanced at his watch. "Well, time to go home. Have a good evening."

"You, too," Clancey said.

He threw up a hand and walked out the front door.

BANKS WAS CURIOUS about the rapport Clancey had with Hollister. He had to admit that he saw no romantic attachment there. Hollister did, indeed, treat her like a little sister.

"Isn't it early for him to go home?" Banks asked, glancing at his watch.

"He never stays long," she said. "Actually, the gossip is that he keeps coming in here looking for somebody?"

His eyebrows arched. "Somebody?"

She nodded. "A woman from his past. Apparently she used to come here for the music, too, a long time ago."

He drew in a breath. "I guess hope springs eternal," he said, and he was thinking about Grace Charles, who was coming to San Antonio soon.

Clancey knew about Grace. It was painfully obvious that Banks was carrying a torch for her. If only she could convince her heart, stupid organ, that he was committed to someone else.

"Nobody makes flan like they do," Tad said with a heartfelt sigh as he swallowed the last tiny bite of his dessert.

Clancey grinned as she finished her own. "Nobody in the world," she agreed.

The band tuned up and started playing again, a lazy two-step. Banks stood up and held out his hand.

"Shall we?" he asked with twinkling black eyes.

"I'll trip over my feet and put my head through the bass drum, or I'll knock some poor unsuspecting soul into a bowl of hot soup," she sighed. "I'm absolutely graceless."

"Grace can be taught," he said softly. "We'll be back, Tad."

"I'll watch!" the boy laughed. "The music is just great!"

"It really is," Clancey said when Banks pulled her onto the dance floor and slid a big, warm hand around her waist. He curled her hand into his and moved lazily to the music. She stumbled once, but he righted her.

"Don't look at your feet," he said softly.

"They won't know where to go unless I tell them," she protested.

He chuckled. "Not true. Come on. Close your eyes and listen to the rhythm. Move to it. Dancing is more instinct than exercise. It's art."

"No, actually, art is what you go to museums to see."

"A lot of that isn't art at all. It's insanity."

She grinned. "That's exactly what I told Tad when we went to the traveling art exhibit from Europe. Honestly, some of those paintings could have gotten the artists arrested only twenty years ago."

"I know what you mean." He turned her easily as the lazy tune played. "I don't move with the times much, either. Our mother was old-fashioned. So are Brenda and I."

"Brenda's so nice," she said.

"She loves dogs and cats," he pointed out. "Animal people are usually nice. Besides, she gardens."

"That's almost a character reference," Clancey laughed. "People who plant things and work in gardens are some of the nicest folks on earth."

"They are." He lifted his head and looked down into her pale eyes. "Now, see, you're dancing very well indeed."

She flushed. "Better than I used to. Thanks. For being patient, I mean."

His fingers slid in between hers. "I'm always patient," he murmured at her temple. His voice sounded like rich, smooth velvet and her heart ran wild in her chest.

"You...are not," she returned, trying to regain her equilibrium. "You threaten to shoot printers."

"I need to find that cop from Palo Verde and bring him up to our office."

She looked up at him. "Hmm?"

"They had a soft drink machine that ate dollar bills and didn't return money or soft drinks. So this officer accidentally hit it with a baseball bat several times."

Her eyes twinkled. "Did they catch him?"

He nodded. "He told them it was a muscle spasm, but

the judge didn't buy it. The policeman had to replace the machine."

"I hope the replacement was a better machine."

He sighed. "Well, that's the problem."

"What is?"

"It was a better machine. It came with all these instructions about how to put the money in, and how to press the appropriate button. The same officer kept pushing the button for a chocolate bar and getting peanuts in return. After the sixth time, he pulled his service revolver and shot the machine."

She burst out laughing. "Oh dear."

"He lost his job and had to find something else to do with his life. I'm not sure his career choice is much better."

"What's he doing now?"

He pursed his lips. "Servicing soft drink machines."

She laughed until tears stung her eyes. "Oh, the poor man!"

"He holds the record for the number of drink machines destroyed in south Texas." He cocked his head and studied her. "I'm thinking of challenging his record on the subject of printers."

"You can't. They'll think I did it."

"Damn."

"I did sort of total the stupid machine at Cal's office. A second one will look very bad on my record."

"I'll drop it off at the local landfill and tell people it's been kidnapped," he said lazily. "I'll even forge a ransom note."

"You'll end up in Leavenworth," she pointed out.

He grinned. "You can come visit me on weekends and bring nail files."

She chuckled.

"How long did it take you to learn that trill you do with your right hand on the guitar?"

"Not long, really," she said. "I can't use a pick. My fingers don't work right. But I keep my fingernails just a little longer on my right hand, and they work very well. Especially in flamenco."

"I've never heard anyone play like that who wasn't on a stage."

"You should have heard my grandfather play," she said, her voice soft with memories. "He could play country, Western, pop, folk, flamenco, even jazz. He did an arrangement of 'San Antonio Rose' that won him an award, in fact. He'd studied music for years, under a fairly famous guitarist who came from Spain."

"I'll bet you have calluses as hard as plastic on the fingertips of your left hands," he mused.

"I do. I could set a match to them and I'd never feel it. But I can only play nylon strings. I can't manage steel strings. My hands aren't strong enough."

His fingers smoothed over them sensuously. "Mine are. It takes a good bit of hand strength to shoot a pistol, especially a .45 auto. We learn to do it with both hands, too."

"I remember," she said. "I don't mind guns. I just hate it when angry people think they're the answer to all life's problems."

"All too true."

She was wheezing, just a little. He stopped in the middle of the dance floor. "Need to sit down?" he asked gently.

She looked up at him and would have chewed her tongue off before she'd have agreed with him. It was sheer heaven to stand close to him, to feel his strong arm at her back, his fingers linked into hers, curled into his chest while they moved to the music.

"Oh no," she blurted out. "I'm fine."

His lean hand reached out and pushed a strand of soft, wavy dark hair off her forehead. His black eyes were intent on hers. "You're not what you seem, Clancey."

"What do you mean?" she asked, concerned that he might have learned something about her that she didn't want known.

"You're not the snippy clerk I thought you were when I gave you the job."

"Actually, I am snippy," she confessed. "I got picked on a lot when I was younger."

"By other kids, I gather."

Not by other kids. By her stepbrother and her stepfather and her stepbrother's friends. But she wasn't going to open that can of worms. "Something like that," she said after a minute.

He glanced behind them at Tad, who'd struck up a conversation with a couple at the next table and was speaking animatedly.

"He mixes well," he said.

She nodded. "He never meets a stranger," she said with obvious affection. "I'm the opposite. I had to learn to bluff when I went to work for Cal. I'm not used to people and I don't mix well. I'm an introvert."

"So am I," he replied easily, smiling at her surprise. "We're taught to put people at ease during questioning and to behave in a professional manner. But I had to work at sounding pleasant and interesting. I just wanted to chase bad guys."

"I love detective shows," she said. "Especially Sherlock Holmes."

He laughed. "I grew up watching him. I think it had something to do with why I chose a life in law enforcement. I like solving crimes, too."

"There are all these books about the Locard's Exchange Principle, and how you can take just a seed and find out where a perp was from," she said excitedly.

"You read true crime," he guessed.

"Oh yes. I love forensics."

"You should have studied it."

She made a face. "I really wanted to, when I was twelve."

"What happened?"

"There was this vet. He had a book on pathology he was going to lend me, so he took me back to his office to get it." She sighed. "He was like an octopus. I made an excuse and got out. When I told Mama, we never went back there again."

His black eyes flashed. "Twelve years old," he said gruffly. "Damn him!"

"He left town years ago. I understand there was at least one death threat."

He searched her pale silver eyes. "You don't really like being touched by men," he said.

She looked up at him with vulnerable pale eyes. "I had sort of a bad experience in my teens. After the overbearing vet."

"What was it?"

She hesitated.

He brushed his knuckles over her soft mouth, staring at it intently. "Tell me."

"There was this boy," she said, choosing her words carefully. "He hit a relative of mine and I rushed in to save him." She swallowed. "I got two broken ribs. My friend got a concussion."

"What happened to the boy?" he asked curtly.

"He was arrested and prosecuted. He went to jail."

He stopped dancing and stared down at her. "For how long?"

"He's still there," she said. She couldn't admit that it was her stepbrother. "He won't get out for a long time, they say," she lied with a smile.

"I should hope not." He touched her rounded chin gently. "Your life has been no bed of roses, has it?"

"Everybody has problems," she said easily, and she smiled. "Mine are no worse than anyone else's."

"There it is again," he murmured.

"What is?" she asked, curious.

"That incredible optimism," he replied. He smiled quizzically. "The only other person I've ever known who had it was Grace. She lost her fiancé in a bank holdup, got shot down on a missionary plane in South America and spent years ministering to poor people in the jungles. She was always smiling, downplaying her own tragedies."

"She must be very kind," Clancey said noncommittally.

"Kind, and loving." His eyes held a faraway, dreamy look. "I haven't seen her in years. I'm looking forward to it."

"When is she coming back?"

"In a couple of weeks, I believe," he said. "We've got a lot of catching up to do."

"I imagine so."

IT WAS LATE when the band wrapped up and started packing its instruments. Banks drove a sleepy Tad and a subdued Clancey home.

Tad woke up when they reached the house. He yawned as he went ahead of them to the front door and leaned against the wall while Clancey unlocked it.

"Thanks for supper, Mr. Banks," Tad said, smiling. "It was great!"

"We'll do it again," he promised.

"Swell! Well, good night!" He went down the hall to his bedroom, leaving Clancey and Banks on the front porch, with the door standing open.

"It was a lovely night. Thanks very much," Clancey told him.

He moved a step closer. His heart was hammering in his chest. Being close to her all night had provoked some odd sensations in his tall, fit body. It had been a long time since he'd had a woman. Clancey made him hungry. He had to remember how young she was, how sheltered.

He toyed with a short strand of her hair as he looked down at her. "This was fun. I don't get out much, except on business. I guess I've forgotten how to enjoy a night out."

She smiled. "We enjoyed it, too. We don't go out at night much." She grimaced. "It's pretty dangerous for wimps like Tad and me."

"Just as well to be cautious." He glanced at his watch and made a face. "I'd better get home. I'm off tomorrow, so I'll be overrun with ranch chores that don't get done when I'm working in town."

"It's supposed to rain."

He smiled. "I get wet all the time. I never get sick."

"I wish I could say that," she replied ruefully.

He stepped closer, watching her blouse move with her increased breathing. This was wrong. It was a bad idea. It was a very bad idea.

Even as he thought it, he pulled her close and bent his head to hers. She grasped his arms, her nails biting in. This was new territory, and she wasn't sure about it.

"Just relax," he whispered as his mouth hovered over hers. "We all start out as novices."

Her breath was racing, like her heart. "I guess…we do."

"Life is all lessons," he whispered as his tall head bent. His lips touched hers, softly, slowly, with a sensuous brushing motion that made her mouth follow his helplessly as he began to increase the contact.

Those nails were digging in, he mused. She had no idea what to do, and she was nervous. It was so earthshaking that he forgot her age and his caution. An innocent, with no idea about men and women and how they interacted. It was like rich, heady wine.

He drew her even closer and framed her head in his big, warm hands. "It's like falling into fire," he whispered.

"It's…what?"

He smiled as his lips began to part hers. "You'll see."

She wasn't sure that she wanted to see. Her life was complicated enough. This was going to be a major complication. But while she was thinking it, she was moving even closer, lifting her mouth, going on tiptoe to tempt him into something more satisfying than these brief little brushing contacts that made her ache all over.

His hands moved to her waist and pulled her against his powerful body, so that she could feel his long legs pressed to hers. Her heart jumped. She'd never been so close to a man. Her eyes were faintly worried as they met his.

"Softly," he whispered, brushing his mouth slowly across hers. "Very softly." He nibbled her upper lip and then her lower one, but her lips stayed primly together. He laughed, deep in his throat.

He bit at her full lower lip, not enough to hurt. "Open your mouth."

"Wh…what?" she whispered, shocked.

His hands lifted her closer. His nose nuzzled hers. "Open your mouth. Let me taste you…"

She gasped, giving him the opening he'd been looking for. He twisted her completely against his powerful body, holding her there when she instinctively tried to jerk away. One lean hand smoothed her hips against his, much too close. He was aroused and she knew it. Even as she thought of pulling back, his tongue teased inside her mouth and began to arouse her in ways she'd never imagined. While he was invading her soft lips, his hands were sliding up her rib cage until they came to rest just under her small breasts, not quite touching, but so evocative that she found herself lifting helplessly toward them, reaching up to plead for something harder, more intimate, more fulfilling.

She moaned under the crush of his mouth. He half lifted her against him, grinding her body into his while his mouth absolutely devoured hers. He forgot about her age and his, all the differences between them, and just gave in to the mindless hunger that made him feel as if he could fly.

Her arms tightened around his neck while she gave in to the first real adult kiss she'd ever had in her life. She'd been kissed a time or two by boys when she was in high school. She'd never liked it much, and kissing had been pleasant but not really appealing to her.

This was different. This was, as he'd said, falling into fire. She didn't recognize the woman who clung to Banks's neck as if in panic that he might stop kissing her. She opened her mouth for him, pressed as close as she could get to all that warm, muscular strength that was making her as weak as a kitten. His mouth was hard and tender and insistent, all at once. She'd never felt anything remotely like the anguished longing he was arousing in her.

She felt his breath jerk as he lifted his lips just a breath away from hers. He was trying to get back the control he'd almost lost. Clancey's pale silver eyes were half-closed. She looked dazed, yielding, completely his. The snippy office clerk was melting in his arms, hungry and sweet and soft as silk.

"This is a mistake," he managed gruffly.

She nodded. "It's a terrible mistake," she whispered, lifting her face. "Please do it again…?"

His mouth settled back on hers. His arms slid around her, bringing her intimately close as the devouring kiss went on and on and on. He groaned, because the need was suddenly painful. He had to stop or lay her down on the front porch in view of the whole world.

He drew back breath by breath, his big hands firm on her shoulders as she tried to get close again.

"We have to stop. Now," he said in a voice so husky that it didn't even sound like his.

Clancey looked up at him with her mouth swollen, her silver eyes wide and full of dreams, her face flushed from the torment of emotions he'd awoken in her.

His hands were almost bruising, but she didn't feel them. She was lost in new knowledge of him.

"I'm nine years older than you. We work together. Grace is coming home soon." He began reciting all the reasons he should never have touched Clancey.

"Nobody ever kissed me like that," she said, sounding dazed.

He scowled. "Never?"

"I didn't like boys in school," she said unsteadily. "I never...felt anything. I thought there was something wrong with me."

"There's nothing wrong with you," he said gruffly, his eyes helplessly going to the little points on the tips of her firm young breasts that revealed how attracted she was to him.

Her eyes sketched his hard face. She knew how he felt about Grace. She couldn't fight a ghost. Not that she wasn't tempted. But she had too much baggage to get involved with a lawman who was working, unknowingly, on a cold case that concerned her.

"It was all the tequila," she said. "You know, it makes people act out of character."

He stared down at her. "We didn't have any tequila."

"I know, but the fumes were everywhere," she continued blithely and with a wicked little smile. "I'm sure that's what caused it."

He chuckled in spite of himself. "Tequila fumes. Now I've heard everything."

She reached up a hand and touched his hard cheek gently. "Everybody gets lonely sometimes," she said softly. "It's not a big deal. Honest."

He sighed heavily, scowling. "It was still a bad idea, Clancey," he said quietly.

She shrugged and smiled, pulling her hand away. "But it was fun."

He shook his head. "It was fun," he had to agree.

"On Monday I'll threaten you with old case files and phone calls you don't want to take, and we won't even remember tonight."

"You think so?" He looked at her in a new way, a different way. "You play like an angel."

Play? "Oh, the guitar," she said, belatedly. "My grandfather was a good tutor. I miss him very much."

"I miss my mother," Banks said quietly. "It's hard to give up family."

"Very hard."

He tweaked her hair. "I'll see you Monday, kid. You and Tad have a good weekend."

She grinned. "You, too. Thanks for dinner. It was great."

"You're welcome."

He turned and got into the SUV, but he didn't move it until Clancey was in the house with the door closed and locked. She liked that protectiveness of his. She liked kissing him, too, and that was something she was going to have to forget. There were a million reasons that she couldn't get mixed up with Colter Banks. Morris was the main one.

She went to bed and finally slept. Her dreams were wild and erotic, and all about Banks.

NINE

SEVERAL DAYS WENT BY, during which Clancey looked for apartments with no luck. She and Banks were getting along well, but they never discussed anything personal. She was determined to forget what had happened when he took her and Tad to the restaurant. She had to, for her own peace of mind. Kissing Banks could become very addictive.

Banks was thinking the same thing. He caught himself glancing at Clancey when she didn't see him. She always looked nice, even in old clothes with faded patterns. She was neat and clean, and she never shirked work. He remembered all too well the feel of her in his arms when he took her home and kissed her to within an inch of her life. It had been a long time since he'd kissed a woman. Perhaps that was why it had affected him so deeply. It had to be that. Clancey was too young, and she worked for him. If he could just keep that in mind, he might manage to get his mind off her.

Something was niggling at the back of his mind, something about the way she played guitar. He couldn't quite place it. But he remembered a man, an older man, playing the song she'd played at the restaurant. If he could only remember who, and where.

His phone rang, interrupting his thoughts. He answered it, his mind still on the guitar. "Banks."

"Hello, Ranger. This is Darrell Tarley. I was wondering if you'd had any word about Morris Duffy getting out of prison? I spoke to the parole board and they said they'd cut him loose, but they weren't sure when he'd be arriving in San Antonio. He made death threats against me."

It took Banks a few seconds to remember who Tarley was—the assistant district attorney who'd prosecuted Morris Duffy. "I'm aware of the death threats. But why call me…?"

"Well, you're working the cold case that involves him, aren't you?"

"What cold case?" he asked blankly.

"The disappearance of Dalton Reed," the assistant DA replied. "Morris Duffy was named a person of interest in the investigation. There were rumors that Reed was trying to prove that Duffy was dealing drugs."

"Why would he have involved himself in that?" Banks asked curiously.

"He was a former deputy sheriff," he was told. "He retired, but he never quite gave it up. He still worked as a special deputy to help with crowd control at ball games, that sort of thing."

"I've heard about that." Banks recalled Clancey telling him; she'd gone to church with Reed. He was frowning. "Do you know anything else about him?"

"Not really. One of the men who works in my office

used to be a special deputy. He worked with Reed. He said the other deputies revered him. He had quite a history with the department. Not only that, he worked down in Jacobs County with their sheriff's department for a while, as well."

Banks sat up in his chair. "It might not be a bad idea to have somebody tail Duffy when he gets home. He'll be assigned a parole officer. I'll make it my business to see that he never misses a meeting," Banks added curtly. "Meanwhile, you might see if Lieutenant Marquez can spare an officer to watch your back."

Clancey, overhearing the statement, felt her heart jump. Morris was on his way home? No! He couldn't be. She stayed where she was, still and quiet, and waited for any more snippets of news about her stepbrother.

"Word is that he'll be here within the week," Darrell told him. "I've already asked Lieutenant Marquez about having somebody shadow me. He's assigning one of his officers to follow me around, just in case. I've had death threats before, of course—we all get them. But this is one I pay attention to. If Duffy actually killed his grandfather, a second murder isn't going to ruffle him one bit. After all, he got away with the first one—assuming he did kill the gentleman in question."

"I'll keep an eye out. I'll talk to victim services. They should know when he's due home. Does he have a place to live?"

"Yes. He owns a house. Some relatives have been living in it."

"Ask Marquez to double the patrols around it. They might see something interesting."

"I'll do that. If you hear anything, please call me."

"I certainly will."

He hung up, checked information for the number and called victim services. "Is that Melody?" he asked when a familiar voice came on the line.

"It is. Hi, Banks, long time no see!"

"Same here," he chuckled. "Listen, do you have any information on Morris Duffy yet?"

"Let me check." There was a pause. "Yes, I do. He's being released Friday. He should be here within a day or two of that. Why?"

"Darrell Tarley is worried. The man made death threats."

"I'd be more concerned about Morris's stepsister and stepbrother. It was his stepsister's testimony that sent him to prison. If he's out for revenge, she'll be first on his list."

"I'll have to track them down," he said.

"You won't have to look far," she began, and got interrupted. "I have to go. If you need anything else, call me back, okay?"

"Okay. Thanks."

He put up the phone and scowled. What an odd statement. Why wouldn't he have to look far for Duffy's family?

"What was that all about?" Clancey asked with pretended unconcern.

"What? Oh. The assistant district attorney's worried about Morris Duffy being released. He's made death threats."

"Duffy's in prison," she began.

"Not anymore. He's being released Friday." He started to get to his feet, oblivious to Clancey's white face and trembling hands. "I don't think he'll do anything to Darrell. He's sure as hell not going to want to go back to jail…"

He was cut off by the front door opening and the sound of high-heeled feet coming down the stairs. Banks looked up in time to see a woman with chestnut hair in a bun, wearing a dark blue concealing dress and a lightweight coat coming into the office.

"Colter?" she called.

He stepped around the pillar, bareheaded, breathless. "Grace!"

Before she could speak again, he had her up in his arms and he was hugging the life out of her. "Grace!" he whispered into her throat. "Oh God, it's been so long!"

She laughed and held him back, smiling. "Years and years and years. Oh, it's so good to see you!"

Clancey felt as if her world had suddenly fallen apart. Morris was coming home, and Colter Banks's true love was in his arms. She thought she might strangle on her own misery.

Thoughts rushed through her head. She had to get herself and Tad out of the house. She had to collect all their treasures, including her grandfather's guitar, and put them someplace safe. With the Martins? No. Too risky. Morris knew them. He could find out that Clancey and Tad went to church with them every Sunday. She grimaced. They'd have to give up going to services for the time being. They had to be someplace Morris couldn't get to them easily.

She didn't want to involve Cal Hollister. He'd done so much for them already. She didn't want to make him a target for Morris. But she could trust her guitar and her most precious items—photographs and scraps of memory in an album—and the quilts her grandmother had made for her and Tad to him. She'd have to come up with some good lie about why she couldn't take those things to her new apartment. Something about being afraid of theft because the apartment was in a low-rent district. She could tell him they were going to the Brandiff Apartments. They were near her job, full up, but Cal was unlikely to check it out. He trusted Clancey to always be truthful with him. She ground her teeth together. She was going to have to deceive a lot of people, and if Banks checked out Morris, it was inevitable that the trail would lead to her. She'd barely escaped detection when she applied for the job, by not putting any relatives except Tad on her application. But Morris was coming home, and she was in terrible danger.

"Clancey!"

"What?" She jumped. "Oh. Sorry. I was thinking about a case file I misplaced," she said quickly, and forced a smile to her face as Banks brought Grace around to her desk.

"This is Grace Charles. Grace, this is Clancey. She holds down the office when I'm not here and keeps the files in order."

"It's nice to meet you," Clancey said, smiling. "I've heard a lot about you from Mr. Banks's sister. I go to church with her."

"Yes, I know Brenda," Grace said with a sigh. "It's easy to go to church, you know. It's a lot harder to live by the tenets we learn there."

Banks bristled just a little, but quickly erased the irritation from his expression. "I'm taking Grace to lunch. I'll be back late, if anybody calls. If it's important, tell them to call my cell phone."

"Do you have to wear that firearm everywhere you

go?" Grace asked Banks worriedly. "It's an instrument of violence, you know, Colt."

"I carry it so that other instruments of violence won't triumph over innocent lives," he returned with a faint smile.

"Yes, but—" Grace began.

"Lunch," he interrupted her, taking her elbow in his big hand. "Let's go."

Clancey looked after them with a sinking heart. Grace didn't like what Banks did for a living and made it clear. She hated guns. She thought Brenda Banks wasn't living a truly good life, when Brenda was one of the kindest, most religious people Clancey knew.

She felt rather sorry for Banks. It was obvious that he'd idealized the woman for years and was caught up in a helpless passion for her. Clancey remembered how sweetly he'd kissed her, remembered the feel of his strong arms around her, the scent of his spicy cologne in her nostrils, the taste of him as his mouth ground into hers.

She'd never felt so hungry for a man in her whole life, and it had to be a man who was in love with someone else. It seemed unfair, somehow. Her whole young life had been one of violence and terror. She was facing the worst terror right now. Morris was on his way home and she was scared to death. She had to get Tad and her precious few things out of that house today. In fact, they'd have to go directly to the homeless shelter after work, after they took a cab to Cal's office and left their treasures with him. She groaned at the thought of how much the cab would cost. But it had to be done. She had no time left for apartment hunting. She had to get somewhere that Morris wouldn't look for them.

She phoned Cal a minute or two later.

"Hi," she said. "I'm sorry to bother you, but Tad and I got an apartment and we don't have room for my guitar and some quilts. Can I get you to take them to the ranch with you and keep them for us?"

"Your guitar?" he exclaimed. "Why can't you take it with you? That's the most precious thing you own!"

She drew in a breath and apologized in her mind for the lies. "It's sort of a low-rent place. I mean, it's safe, but I don't know anybody there yet. I don't want anything to happen to the few treasures Tad and I have. So, you know, just in case...?"

"I see. I wish you both would come stay with me," he replied.

"That's very kind of you. But we need our own place," she told him gently. "Thanks for the offer. It means more than you know."

He sighed. "Okay. I'll hold on to your stuff. Want me to meet you at the house after work?"

"I'll take a cab and meet you at your office."

"No sweat. I can drive you to your new apartment, if you like."

"That's sweet, too, but we can't move in for a few days. They're repainting the bedrooms."

"I see. Okay, then. I'll see you after work. Lungs still doing okay?"

"They're doing great. And I wear the mask when I go outside, just in case," she laughed.

"Good girl. See you later."

"Thanks, Cal."

"Anytime."

She hung up. That was one problem solved. Now for

the next. She called victim services and spoke to Melody. "What about Morris?" she asked when she'd identified herself.

"Oh, you poor thing," Melody said with genuine sympathy. "I should have called you days ago! I'm so sorry…!"

"It's okay. I overheard Mr. Banks talking to you just now."

"I know you're dreading this. Morris will be in San Antonio late tomorrow, if our information is correct. He still owns the house, yes?"

"Yes," Clancey said miserably. "Ben, my stepfather, left it to him. He left nothing to his other son, Tad."

"That's the way it goes sometimes. Listen, if Morris gives you any trouble at all, you call me. He'll be on parole, and there will be strict rules. You can take out a restraining order if you have to."

"If Morris wants me dead, it won't do any good," she said quietly. "I just worry about Tad. I don't think Morris would go after him—he was only three years old when it happened—but he might target Tad to get even with me."

"He had a good record in prison. He even attended church services," Melody said.

"He sent me a nice letter when Ben died. I had to handle the funeral and all. But Morris could always be polite when he needed to be. It didn't stop him from hanging out with drug dealers and criminals. My grandfather was certain that he was involved with a drug lord. I think that was why he disappeared, and I still think Morris was responsible. I just have no way to prove it."

"Haven't you talked to Banks about that? After all, he's working the cold case as I understand it."

"He doesn't know about me and Tad and Morris," she

said miserably. "I was afraid to tell anyone. I have a step-brother in prison for assault, and I work for a law enforcement agency. I was afraid they'd fire me and I'd lose custody of Tad."

"I don't think there's any chance that Banks would fire you, Clancey. He's not that sort of person."

"I was afraid to take the chance. I guess he'll know soon. He'll have me dig out the file on Morris. It's all in there."

"Don't take it so hard," the other woman said gently. "You have friends who'll go to bat for you. Besides that, Morris has made threats against Darrell Tarley since he got out. They'll be on his tail wherever he goes."

"That helps." Clancey sighed.

"You aren't going to try to live in the same house with Morris, are you?" Melody added.

"No chance of that. Tad and I have a new apartment. We're moving in tomorrow."

"Okay. If you'll give me the address…"

"You can have my cell phone number," Clancey interrupted. "It's much better than an address for snail mail. I can even get email and texts on it," she laughed. "Got a pen?" She gave Melody the number.

"That's great," Melody said. "If I hear anything, I'll call you."

"Thanks so much."

"No problem. It's what we're here for. You take care."

"You, too."

Clancey hung up. She laid her head on her desk and groaned silently. Why was life so hard? she wondered. It would have been easy to just sink into the misery she felt, but she had Tad to consider. She'd have to tell him tonight, before Cal came to the house, and she'd have to swear her little brother to secrecy about what they were going to do. She knew from past experience how dangerous Morris could be. She had the memory of two broken ribs and Tad's concussion to remind her.

BANKS HAD A long lunch with Grace, during which she spoke at length about her devotion to her faith and the adventures she'd had in South America. She spoke of Mike Johns, as well.

"I thought I'd never get over him," she confided with a long sigh. "My faith saved me. I was almost suicidal when Mike died. I loved him, so much."

"I know." His own heart was breaking, not only at the thought of his late best friend, but of Grace and how much she meant to him.

She stared at her bottle of water. She'd refused anything with caffeine, which ruled out tea and coffee. "Do you ever think about what happened with us, just before Mike died?"

His heart leaped. "Of course," he said. The memory of that long, sweet kiss they'd exchanged had haunted him for years. He'd felt guilty for betraying his best friend, even more so when Mike was killed just shortly after that.

"So do I," she confessed. "The guilt ate me alive. I couldn't stand to think about it, so I ran, all the way to South America."

He slid a big hand over hers. "We're all human, Grace," he began.

She sighed and met his black eyes evenly. "Of course we are. But it was a betrayal of the vows I made to Mike.

That was hard to live with. I almost went insane when he died."

"I remember." His hand tightened on hers. "He was the best friend I ever had."

"Those were good times that we shared," she said softly.

He smiled. "Very good times. How long are you going to be in town?"

"Just for two weeks," she said easily, smiling. "I'm attending a seminar for our sect, learning things about intervention and mission work."

"It sounds interesting."

"It's my life now," she said simply. "I've learned so much about giving, about being a person of faith in a faithless world. I'm doing my part to fight the evil around us and bring people back into the church."

"A noble goal," he agreed.

She pursed her lips. "Do you go to services with your sister?"

He cleared his throat. "My job takes up a good bit of my life."

"Do you shoot people?"

His face hardened. "When I have to."

"Can't you just reason with them?" she asked.

He took a breath. "Grace, you can't reason with a man so high on drugs that he's just killed one of his kids and is trying to knife two police officers in a frenzy."

"Oh." She opened the water bottle and took a sip. She put the lid back on, staring at it instead of Banks. "Isn't there some way to keep people from using drugs?" she asked. "Outreach programs, that sort of thing?"

He'd found that nothing in his profession was more

dangerous than an angry human being saturated with illegal drugs, and the only way to stop them from harming people was to shoot them. But he wasn't going to mention this to her. That would've sounded harsh. He'd actually seen a police officer empty a .45 automatic into a lunatic who'd broken his wife's arm and thrown one of his kids off a balcony. The man reached the police officer and killed him before he died. It had been a life-changing experience. But he hesitated to relate it to Grace, who seemed out of touch with the realities of the world. She was sheltered and secure in her religion, apparently having seen little violence in the places where she worked.

"Weren't you exposed to violent people where you worked overseas?" he asked delicately.

"Well, not really. I lived in a small native village far back in the Amazon in South America. The men hunted, the women cooked and made clothing and necessary items and raised their children. The only real violence was when children fought," she added with a soft laugh.

He began to understand. "Life in America is a little rougher than that, these days," he said. "We've had a drug epidemic and a gang epidemic coexisting, especially here where I work. We've had shootings and murders, gang warfare…"

"There should be more churches involved in the community," she said with a smile. "It all goes back to families and how children are raised. Attitudes can be changed while children are young."

"That may be," he conceded. "But we have to deal with the result of bad parenting and peer pressure."

"I imagine it's not easy. Mike hated the part of his job that required using firearms. I almost had him convinced to try for a supervisory position, where he wouldn't have to be involved in actual police work."

Banks was shocked. He hadn't realized that Grace was so averse to Mike's job. In fact, Mike loved being on the streets, interacting with people, helping people. It was what he was best at. Through no fault of his own, he'd walked in on a bank robbery on his day off and been killed outright without getting off a single shot.

"Mike didn't have his service revolver on at the bank holdup," Grace recalled. "I'd made him promise that he wouldn't wear it off duty, although he said it would get him into trouble if he got found out." She bit her lip, unaware of Banks's shocked expression. "I suppose that might have been a mistake on my part. But at least he died without a death on his conscience. That was important."

It was more important that Mike might have lived if he'd had his service revolver on him. He was irritated, despite his feelings for Grace.

He remembered what Clancey had said about his carrying a weapon all the time; that her grandfather had always worn one, and she had no issues with it. He compared that with Grace's attitude. She seemed to live in a world of her own, where violence and danger didn't exist, and career criminals could be turned around with soft words and counseling.

"Well, enough about Mike. I've moved on. I think about him from time to time, but I'm sure he's in a better place," she said with a soft smile. "It's so good to see you again, Colt."

"It's good to see you, too, Grace," he replied huskily, his black eyes sketching her pretty face. "I hope you'll have a little time to spend with me, while you're in town," he added.

"I'm sure I can manage a few hours," she replied. "We could go to a movie."

"I'd like that."

"Me, too. I miss movies most of all. I saw this incredibly sweet religious movie when I first got to the States. Of course, it was in a small, independent theater," she added irritably. "Religious movies don't appeal to most people in this country, do they? There's so much sex and violence. And the language!"

Banks ground his teeth together. "It's the culture."

"It's a sick culture," she replied with obvious distaste. "I prefer the area our mission works in, over in South America." She shook her head. "It's so different from here."

"No theaters, obviously," he mused as they got to their feet.

"No. We have storytellers. We sit around fire pits at night and the old people tell tales of the way the culture was when they were young. It's quite fascinating. We even have films of it. You might like to watch one with me."

His expression lightened. "I'd enjoy that."

"Great! We're showing it at the mission house here in San Antonio on Friday night! It would be great to have you there!"

He almost swallowed his tongue. He'd thought of being alone with Grace to watch it.

She was looking in her purse, oblivious to his disappointed expression. "Want a mint?" she asked. "I always carry them."

"No, thanks," he said. He smiled at her. She smiled back, but without any real feeling. He'd expected so much more.

He turned and went to pay the bill.

HE WAS OUT of sorts when he got back to the office, after a meeting with Marquez at police headquarters on a kidnapping they were both working. It was almost quitting time. He didn't notice Clancey's restlessness, her worried face. He was too concerned with his own situation, with Grace's lack of involvement with him. He'd missed her, hungered for her, for so many years. Now, here she was, back in Texas, and she was a stranger.

Perhaps it was guilt, he pondered. She'd said how guilty she felt when she and Banks had kissed so passionately just before Mike Johns was killed. Yes, that had to be it. She was still working through the guilt.

All he had to do was be persistent, he told himself. Maybe he could get her down to the ranch on the weekend and have her to himself. That was going to be his next move. He didn't have much time, so he was going to have to be quick. In two short weeks, she'd be back on her way to South America. The thought was depressing.

CLANCEY COULD ALMOST see the thoughts in his mind. Grace didn't like firearms and he worked in law enforcement. There were probably other issues as well, since Grace didn't apparently approve of Banks's sister, Brenda.

She hated herself for being glad about that. She chided herself for it. She wanted Banks to be happy. It wasn't kind to wish him ill. He was crazy about Grace. She'd seen his face when they embraced. It had wounded her. He was still involved with the woman, after all the years she'd been away. Clancey had hoped… Well, she had to face reality. Her stepbrother was coming home to kill her. She hoped her death wouldn't inconvenience Banks too much.

She had to fight hysterical laughter at the thought. She took a deep breath and turned off her computer. She went into the bathroom and called a cab, so that Banks wouldn't hear her do it. She didn't want him to know where she was going.

It was going to be a difficult couple of days. She wished Morris would decide to go and live somewhere a thousand miles away. That was unrealistic. Why would he, when he had a house right here in San Antonio that Clancey had been keeping up.

She paid the utilities, including the heat. Everything was current, including the mortgage payment. Lucky Morris. He wouldn't have to worry about power or heat or water and garbage pickup for a month, at least.

She groaned inwardly. The homeless shelter was nice. But it wasn't home. At least, it was unlikely that Morris would look for her and Tad there. She recalled that there was also a battered women's shelter, but she hesitated to go there with Tad. It might be the first place Morris would look.

She put on her ragged coat and picked up her purse. "I'm leaving," she told Banks.

He looked up, surprised, as if he hadn't registered the time.

"Is it quitting time already?" he asked.

She nodded. "I have to pick up Tad at school."

He frowned, remembering her recent lung infection. "It's cold and it's raining out. I can drive you…"

"Thanks," she said quickly, forcing a smile, "but I've got a cab coming. I don't want to get sick again."

"Oh. Well, see you tomorrow."

She nodded. "Have a good evening."

"You, too."

She started up the steps.

"Tomorrow, I want you to pull out all the files you've got on Morris Duffy and any that are related to that cold case that might involve him," he said.

Her heart skipped. "Of course," she said, without turning.

"You've read the file, haven't you?"

She half turned. "Yes."

"His grandfather's body was never found. Were neighbors questioned about any unusual activity?"

"Yes," she said. "But the neighborhood was run-down and most people who lived there avoided any contact with the police. Besides, there was a violent drug gang whose leader lived there. People were afraid to talk."

He pursed his chiseled lips. "It might not be a bad idea to canvass the neighborhood again. If there are any elderly people in the vicinity who knew the missing man, they might be less afraid to talk about the case now."

She nodded. "That's a good idea." Inwardly she was cringing. If he looked at that file, the address might ring a bell. A big one. "Well, I'll get going. See you tomorrow, boss."

"Sure."

He was deep in thought. The case worried him. There was something so familiar about it, about the people involved. It irritated him that he couldn't drag the details out of his mind.

He was probably just tired, he told himself. It had been a long week. At least tomorrow was Friday, something to look forward to. He might talk Grace into coming to the ranch or going out to dance with him. He smiled to himself.

CLANCEY WASN'T SMILING. She sat rigidly in the back of the cab as it pulled up at the curb where Tad's after-school program was held. She ran to get him, and ran back with him. The meter was still running. She had the cab stop by their house so that she could pick up their few prized possessions. Then it was off to take them to Cal.

The cab dropped them off at Cal Hollister's office building. She phoned him on the way, so that she wouldn't have any trouble getting into the building with Tad. He shepherded them into his office and closed the door.

His eyes were sad as he surveyed the few things Clancey had brought and registered the misery on her face.

"He won't hurt either of you," Cal said, cutting to the heart of the matter. "I promise you he won't."

She drew in a breath and fought tears. "Thanks."

She handed him the quilts and her guitar case, along with a grocery bag full of small treasures, carefully wrapped in paper towels. "Be careful with those," she said, indicating the bag. "Some are Christmas ornaments that our grandparents had..." She bit her lip.

"Damn, Clancey." He put the things down and pulled her into his arms. He rocked her gently. "Come on, kid, it's not the end of the world."

"Yes, it is," Tad said, moving close to Cal to be hugged, too. "Morris will kill us...!"

"He will not," Cal said firmly. "Whatever it takes. You'll be safe. Why don't you come home with me?"

Clancey took a deep breath and pulled back, forcing a smile as she wiped her eyes and Tad's with a paper towel wadded up in her jean pocket. "Thanks. But we've got a nice place to stay. Or we will have, tomorrow. I'll give you the address when we move in, but you've got my cell phone number."

He nodded and grimaced. "Damned bad luck, having him get out just before Christmas."

"It's his house," she said simply. "We can't live there. Not when he's home. He'll go right back with the same gang he used to run with, I guarantee it. He may have managed to fool the jailers, but I know him. He's a good actor. He should have gone on the stage," she added with faint bitterness.

"He'll make one mistake, and he'll go right back in," Cal said with steely eyes.

"He'll have to be caught doing something wrong, first," she sighed. "If he really killed Granddaddy, and I think he did, he got away with murder."

He rammed his hands into his pockets. "He wasn't being watched, at the time." He smiled coldly. "He'll be watched, this time."

"I know about law enforcement budgets," she began.

"I have friends," he said simply.

She knew the friends he meant. People he'd been in combat with, overseas. Mercs. She smiled. "Okay. Thanks."

He shrugged. "I have to look out for the only family I've got left," he said with a smile and a sigh.

She fought tears.

"Stop that," he muttered. "My assistant's right outside the door. Imagine if he looks in here and sees me bawling…!"

"There would be such terrible gossip," she returned with twinkling eyes.

"You can't even imagine." He glanced at his watch. "I have to go to a meeting with some local civic leaders in thirty minutes. I'll drop you two off on the way. How about that?"

"That would be very nice of you." She glanced at the guitar sadly. "You'll take care of…?"

"I'll lock the door while I'm in the meeting, and I'll have two trusted associates sitting on the hood and the trunk."

She burst out laughing.

He grinned. "Let's go."

TEN

"TELL BANKS," CAL said firmly when he let them out at their front door.

She sighed. "I don't know how. I've kept it a secret for so long now that he'll never trust me again if I tell him."

"He's going to know when we start shadowing Morris and looking for witnesses in the disappearance of your grandfather, Clancey," he replied. "Our department's cold case unit is going to assist him. You can't hide it any longer."

"I guess not. Okay. I'll tell him."

"His old flame's back in town, I hear," he remarked.

She nodded. She forced a smile. "She's really nice. Her name's Grace. I like her."

He studied her for a minute and just shrugged. "Have a good night."

"You, too. Thanks again, for everything."

"Call me when you're in the apartment and give me the address."

"I'll do that," she lied.

He drove off. Clancey went inside with Tad, feeling empty as she looked around at bare tables and a lonely corner where the guitar had rested.

"It will be okay," Tad said, hugging her. "We'll be all right."

"Of course we will," she replied, with thorns stabbing her in the throat as she fought tears. It was hard to be the oldest person in her family. For the time being. Morris was older.

She sighed. "We have to go to the shelter. Make sure you've got all your books, everything else you need for school. Clothes and stuff."

"I've already packed them in my duffel bag."

"I've done the same. We'll make one last look around and I'll call the cab."

He looked up at her sadly. "It's been my home my whole life," he said.

She hugged him close. "We'll get another house when Morris is taken care of," she promised.

"Okay."

SHE LOCKED UP the door and put the key under the mat, where it had been kept when Morris was living at home. She and Tad would have no reason to come back here, maybe not for a long time.

She'd phoned the Martins and told them that she and Tad would be missing church for a couple of weeks, and she was sorry. She didn't explain why. They told her not to worry—they could watch services on television temporarily. Mrs. Martin asked if there was anything they could do for her. She almost cried at that kind question. She said no and told them to call her if they needed anything. Then she and Tad got into the cab and had it take them to the nearby homeless shelter.

IT WAS A closer walk than the house to Tad's school and her office. She dropped him off, and then had a talk with the principal to tell him about Morris and make sure that nobody could get Tad out of school for any reason except his legal guardian—herself. The principal promised that he'd watch out for the boy and have the staff made aware of the situation.

Then she went to work, feeling a closeness with people who'd once walked up the steps to the guillotine. Banks was going to be mad. She hated having to tell him the truth.

She put up her coat and purse and started pulling out files. One of them, the one she'd kept hidden, had photos of the victims of Morris's violent assault—Tad and Clancey.

Banks came in looking out of sorts. He'd phoned Grace last night and invited her to the ranch. She'd said sorry, but she had too many obligations in town for that. She added that she didn't like the idea of cattle. Animals deserved better treatment than to be eaten. She was a vegetarian herself.

He tossed his hat onto the coat tree and hung up his shepherd's coat. He sat down behind his desk with a glowering look at Clancey.

"What's up?" he asked, frowning as he noticed her uneasy look and the file folders she was clutching to her chest.

"Something to confess," she said quietly. She moved

forward and put the files on his desk, moving back to stand with her hands folded at her waist, her heart racing.

"I remember. I asked you for the file on Morris Duffy yesterday," he recalled as he opened the file folder. "He's coming home today. I assume he'll be staying at the house he…inherited…"

His voice slowed and then stopped, dead. Clancey looked younger in the photos that documented her injuries, but she was still recognizable. She saw Banks wince as his black eyes went from the crime photos of her injuries to those of little Tad, who'd only been three years old at the time.

So many odd observations fell into place. Her idea to go into the military, the way she spoke of her grandfather. The missing man. Dalton Reed.

He looked up at her miserable, sad face. "Why didn't you tell me?" he asked.

"I work for the Texas Rangers and my stepbrother is a violent, convicted criminal," she said simply. "Tad is all I have. I couldn't bear the thought of losing custody of him, if I got fired…"

"You idiot," he said softly. "I'd never fire you. You can't help who you're related to."

She bit her lower lip. "He's coming home today."

"Home." His chiseled lips parted. "Home. To your home. No wonder the address sounded so familiar. I'd seen it in Morris Duffy's file."

She nodded.

"And your grandfather was Dalton Reed," he added.

She drew in a breath. "He was certain that Morris was dealing drugs. He was going to a friend of his at the sheriff's department, to tell him what he'd found out. He went missing that night. He never came home."

"He taught you the guitar." As she nodded, another memory fell into place. "He was at a retirement party for another sheriff's deputy who'd worked in San Antonio but moved to Houston. I was there. Your grandfather sat in with the band. I heard him play. That's where I remember him from. No wonder you're so good. He was memorable."

"Yes. He was a good, kind man. I can't prove it, but I'm almost certain that Morris did something to him. It was terrifying, going back to that house after what Morris did to Tad and me. Ben, Morris's father, was still alive then. He hated me because I told the police what Morris did. Morris was arrested and prosecuted, and Ben spent every dime he had on a lawyer. It didn't do any good. When the case came up, I had to testify. So did the arresting officer. Morris was convicted." She sighed. "Ben hated me. He loved Morris so much. He was forever getting him out of trouble, making excuses for him. He didn't pay any attention at all to Tad."

"What about after Morris went to prison?"

"Ben was killed by a hit-and-run driver soon afterward. I had to handle the services and get custody of Tad, so he didn't go into foster care. Cal Hollister helped me. I worked for him."

He didn't understand why he felt so much anger at Hollister, who'd tried to help her. He put it to the back of his mind. "You aren't going to try to live with Duffy?"

"Not on your life. Tad and I already have another place to live."

"Where?"

"In the Brandiff Apartments," she lied with a straight

face. "It's low-rent, but there are nice people there. We have a door that locks. We'll be fine."

He drew in a rough breath. "Fine," he muttered. He was thumbing through the file. "Nobody in the neighborhood would talk. Police went door to door, asking about your grandfather. Nobody knew anything."

"They were too afraid of Morris to talk," she said simply.

"It might be a different story today," he said. "I'll talk to Marquez and see if he can spare a few people to help canvass the area. Some of the elderly people might still remember something helpful."

"Pigs might fly," she said solemnly.

"Pessimist," he mused, smiling at her.

That smile made her toes tingle, but she forced herself not to react. She couldn't compete with Grace. She wasn't even going to try. "My whole life has been a study in pessimism," she said simply.

"You lost your mother years ago, didn't you?"

She nodded. "It was just Ben and Morris and Granddaddy and Tad and me. Granddaddy protected us. After he died, it was just Tad and me against Morris and Ben. I didn't have anywhere else to go, and I couldn't take Tad because Ben wouldn't let me. I had to stay to protect Tad from Morris."

"What a hell of a way to grow up," he murmured.

"I love my little brother," she said softly. "I'd do anything to keep him safe."

He felt sick to his stomach. He'd been so wrapped up in Grace's homecoming that he'd ignored all the signs that Clancey was going through some sort of turmoil. He could have helped, if he'd known.

"It isn't nice to keep things from the boss," he said firmly. "Don't do it again."

"Okay." She hesitated. "You don't want to fire me...?"

"Who else could I get to work down here?" he returned. "I told you, not a single man applied for the job."

"Several women did," she pointed out.

He grimaced. "Women who were looking more at attracting the boss than doing the job," he pointed out. He pursed his lips. "Imagine if I'd hired one of them and Grace had come down here to see me. My, my."

She hid a laugh.

He chuckled. "She has a pretty low opinion of modern society."

"So do most people of faith," she replied simply. "It doesn't mean she's wrong."

He glowered at her. "Don't you start."

She held up both hands. "Forgive me. I wouldn't dare offend you, now that you've promised me I still have a job. Miserable though it is. Working in a dungeon, hardly any time off, a boss who threatens to shoot helpless printers..."

"Stop right there while you're ahead," he said firmly.

She grinned.

He grinned back. His black eyes fell to her soft bow of a mouth and he had a sudden, inconvenient ache as he remembered, vividly, the feel of it under his on her porch. It seemed like a lifetime ago, now.

He stood up. "I'm going to talk to Marquez. I'll see if he can spare somebody to help keep tabs on you and Tad..."

"Cal already did," she interrupted gently. "He has some old...friends," she said after a second, "who owe him favors. He said they'd keep a watch over us."

He moved closer, so that she had to look up at him.

"Hollister is only a couple of years older than I am, and he doesn't go out with anybody."

He was insinuating something. "He's my big brother," she said quietly. "And not one like Morris, who hated sharing the house with me and Tad and Granddaddy. You don't know about Cal, and I can't tell you, but he's had a tragic life. He wasn't always a policeman," she added.

His black eyes narrowed. "There are rumors."

She nodded. "Lots of them."

"He's friends with a priest who sent six violent gang members with automatic weapons to the emergency room, and he wasn't even armed."

She laughed softly. "The priest converted some of them. The others made sure they never encroached on his turf again. He's good friends with the leaders of the Serpientes gang." She held up a hand when he started to speak. "Gangs are bad. But the Serpientes take care of the elderly and the very young, and they go looking for people who try to hurt the helpless. As gangs go, they're far and away better than the Little Devil Wolves were."

"Were, is right. Their leaders were put in prison and the gang disintegrated. No loss."

She nodded. "I totally agree."

He studied her somber face. "You're damned young to have lived through the things you've endured."

She shrugged. "Everybody has problems."

"Now I understand the broken ribs on your X-ray," he added.

"There was a steel shovel by the fireplace—one of those things you use to scoop up ashes." She grimaced. "Tad interrupted his video game and caused him to lose a battle. Morris picked up the shovel and knocked Tad off the chair he was in. I stepped in to save Tad, and he turned on me with the shovel. Ben was furious because he had to call an ambulance. I wasn't going to tell what happened, but the doctor in the emergency room knew that a fall couldn't have produced the damage he saw. He asked a policeman to take me home. The officer dragged it all out of me. We went home. Morris was waiting outside, but he couldn't keep the officer out of the house when he had probable cause. When the policeman saw Tad, who was still bawling from his injuries, he called another ambulance and arrested Morris on the spot. Morris tried to escape. He got in a couple of licks, but the policeman wasn't under the influence of drugs and alcohol and it was a short fight. All Morris accomplished was to have resisting arrest and assault on a police officer added to his charges. Ben was furious at me because Morris got arrested."

"You're afraid of Morris," he said, studying her pale face.

She drew in a breath. "I'm terrified of him," she confessed. "Not because of what he did to me, but what he could do to Tad, to get even with me. It's the way he thinks. He doesn't come at people head-on. He got mad at a neighbor and killed his dog."

Banks's eyes narrowed angrily. "What a piece of work," he muttered.

"I worry about the Martins," she blurted out. "Tad and I have been going with them to our church every Sunday, so I can push Mr. Martin's wheelchair. If he's after me, even they aren't safe. Tad and I thought about leaving some of our few treasures with them, because we didn't want to take them to an unfamiliar place and risk having them stolen. But I was afraid that Morris might hear about it and go after them."

"You should have told me all this, Clancey," he said somberly.

Her eyes, wide and bright with unshed tears, met his. "It's my burden, not yours," she said.

His heart jumped. He wondered if she was protective like that about other people. Certainly, she was about her little brother. She loved Tad.

"You know, there is a chance—a small one—that Morris really has changed," he said. "Men find religion and give up bad habits."

"Have you?"

His eyebrows arched. "Have I what?"

"Found religion and given up your bad habits."

He looked uncomfortable. "Don't you start," he said curtly.

Meaning, she assumed, that Grace had been after him about that. The woman, while sweet and pleasant, was committed to her faith. So was Clancey, but not to that extreme.

"What did you do with the guitar?" he asked suddenly.

"Cal took it home with him," she replied. "It's the most precious thing I own."

He didn't like that. It bothered him that he didn't like that. He could have taken it home as easily as Hollister could have. The difference was that Clancey had known Hollister for years. She'd only known Banks for a year and she didn't trust him as much. He wondered if she really trusted any man very far.

"What sort of apartment is it?" he asked suddenly.

She hesitated while she searched for an answer that

wouldn't make him suspicious. "It's bare bones. Furnished, but barely, two small bedrooms with twin beds and dressers. A worn sofa in the living room. Nothing fancy. It's just as well. It's only a place to sleep."

"Do you have a portable television?" he asked.

Her heart jumped. She'd forgotten Tad's video console and his two games. She didn't dare go back and get them.

"What is it?" he asked, because she looked wounded.

"The television, the gaming console, everything belongs to Morris," she said. "Even the furniture. He wouldn't have wanted the guitar. He'd probably have smashed it because he knew it was something I loved. He didn't like my grandfather."

"He may have changed," Banks repeated.

"He threatened to kill Darrell Tarley for prosecuting him," she said simply. "If he's reformed, why did he tell that to his cellmate? He also told him that I was on his retribution list. That isn't surprising. He's spent five years in prison on my testimony. He gets even with people."

"He's not getting even with you," he said shortly. "No matter what it takes." He went back to his desk, unlocked a side drawer and pulled out an automatic weapon in a holster. He locked the drawer back and handed the gun to Clancey. "Can you shoot one of these?"

She drew in a breath. The gun was heavy and she hated the whole idea of it. "I can't shoot anybody, Mr. Banks. Not even to save my own life."

"How about to save Tad's life?" he returned curtly.

She looked up at him with terror in her silver eyes.

He grimaced. "I didn't mean to put it that brutally. You can call the police. But there are times when you don't get the opportunity. A good many men who attack will do it in a blitz style, to circumvent any self-defense. In that case, a pistol might make the difference between living and dying."

She looked at the gun blankly.

"Grace hates the very idea of weapons," he remarked heavily.

She lifted her eyes to his. "It's a tool of your trade," she said simply. "Part of your uniform. You use it to protect the helpless. Why should it be hateful to anyone?"

He felt those soft words to the soles of his boots. She made things sound so simple. She wasn't judgmental. She wasn't overbearing about her attitudes. The contrast with Grace, with his long-lost love, was painful.

She averted her gaze. He was looking at her in an odd, intent way that made her heart race. She stared at the gun. "I don't have a concealed carry permit," she said.

"Go down to the sheriff's department and get one," he returned.

She sighed. There was no arguing with him. "What am I supposed to do with it in the meantime, strap it around my waist?" she asked out loud.

He chuckled in spite of himself. "Wouldn't that look interesting? People would think working in this office was dangerous if the administrative assistant had to go armed."

She smiled back.

He frowned. "Our special deputy who shot himself in the foot," he said, recalling an incident from weeks ago. "What did he do?"

She flushed and drew in a long breath. "He backed me into the wall and…" She moved restlessly. "Scared me to death. After what Morris did, anything roughly physical was frightening. I guess he was practicing his Tarzan routine—me Tarzan, you Jane, go make sandwich." She chuckled.

He didn't. He was furious, after the fact. "The sheriff fired him."

Her lips parted. "I didn't know."

"Our sheriff doesn't tolerate sexual harassment in any form. He said so."

"He had to go to the hospital. I felt bad about it. I just panicked. I'm not sure he meant to be that aggressive. Maybe it was the way he thought women liked to be treated," she added.

"Don't, for God's sake, make excuses for him," he said curtly. "If the gun hadn't gone off…" He ground his teeth together, "You've never been with a man, have you, Clancey?" he asked bluntly.

She fumbled with the gun, shocked at the question. He took the pistol out of her cold hands.

"Never mind," he mused. "I knew the answer before I asked the question."

"I'm out of step with the world."

"So is my sister." What Grace had said about Brenda irritated him. Brenda was a good, kind woman with a loving heart.

"I know. I like Brenda," she added with a warm smile.

"She likes you, too." In fact, his sister had several things to say about Grace and Clancey. Mostly about Grace, who'd seen her at lunch one day and given her a lecture about the way she dressed.

Clancey cocked her head and looked up at him. He was brooding. "There's nothing wrong with the way your sister dresses," she said abruptly. "It isn't as if she's going around in a thong."

His thick eyebrows lifted. "And how do you know what a thong is?" he asked with twinkling eyes.

She gave him a glowering look. "Watch crime shows, learn about life."

He sighed and shook his head. "She dresses very conservatively at the vet, when she's working," he said. "If she wants to wear short skirts after hours, it's nobody's business except hers. She has nice legs, even if she is my sister."

"Yes, she does. And she has a very smart boyfriend who works for Edward Jones, the investment company."

He smiled. "She takes him to church, I hear."

"Yes, and they aren't shacked up together," she added shortly.

He pursed his lips. "Grace accused her of it. How did you hear about that?"

"Somebody at church mentioned it Sunday." She winced. "I feel so bad, not going with the Martins. They can't manage if they don't have somebody to push his wheelchair. But I don't want to be anywhere with Tad that Morris might be able to get to him, and I can't justify putting the Martins in harm's way, even to get to church. It's like walking on the rim of a volcano."

"It will be all right," he said in a deep, soft tone. "We'll keep you and Tad safe. And we'll find out what happened to your grandfather. I promise you, we will."

She nodded. "Thanks," she added huskily.

Her hair smelled of wildflowers. She looked very pretty in that red-checked cotton shirt with her jeans and loafers. She made him feel useful. Strange word, he thought as he stared at her.

"I'll go by the sheriff's office on my way back from lunch," she said abruptly, moving back a step.

"Don't stop at the Army recruiting office," he said abruptly.

She gasped.

He nodded. "I thought you might be considering it again."

She ground her teeth together. "I was. But I have asthma. The recruiting officer wasn't certain that I could get in," she confessed.

"They might not send you into combat, but you could still be stationed as support troops for men who are," he said shortly. "You're much too young to have the memories combat produces."

She searched his black eyes. "Cal has nightmares from his."

He drew in a rough breath. "So do I," he returned curtly.

Her lips parted. She didn't really know him at all. He seemed perfectly in control of himself, of the world around him. But perhaps he had insecurities, just as she did.

He'd never told anyone except Brenda about the nightmares; not even Grace. Funny, but Clancey invited confidences, despite her sometimes acerbic comments.

"Tad has nightmares, too," she said after a minute. "His school psychologist said he needed therapy." She laughed softly. "As if. We can barely make the utility payments every month."

"There are social programs that provide that sort of help," he replied, watching her expression change. "Call up the county health department and explain Tad's issues. They'll find someone for you."

"That would be really nice. If they could help him, I mean."

He nodded. "There are plenty of free services. You just have to look for them."

"I see." She knew about free services. She and Tad were living at a free homeless shelter, although there was a nominal charge—nothing outside Clancey's budget—to help with the expense.

"Okay, I'll wander over to Marquez's office," he said after a taut silence. "You can go to lunch when I get back."

"That's fine."

He locked the extra pistol back in his desk for the time being, pulled his Stetson's wide brim down over one narrow eye and walked up the steps.

Clancey watched him go with relief. At least she still had a job. Maybe things wouldn't be so bad after all.

She wondered if Banks was right and Morris really had changed. It would be a blessing if he had. But she was going to reserve judgment, for the time being at least. Thank goodness Cal was having Tad watched, just in case.

SHE AND TAD had a light supper in a fast-food joint and went on to the homeless shelter for the night.

"I wish we had my gaming console," Tad said. He grimaced at Clancey's expression. "I'm sorry," he said quickly. "I shouldn't have…"

"I'm sorry, too," she said. "We could have sent it home with Cal. I'll make it up to you at Christmas, somehow."

"It's okay, sis," he said, smiling at her. "We got the really important stuff."

"I guess so." She pulled up her knees, where they were

sitting on the cold floor, and rested her chin on them. "TV would be nice, but we can live without it."

"Maybe we could get a Monopoly game," Tad said. "We could look for one at the Goodwill store."

"So we could," she replied, smiling. "We'll go look tomorrow."

He moved a step closer. "Clancey, is that a gun in your pocketbook?" he blurted out, indicating the open purse with stiff leather visible in the opening.

She ground her teeth together. "Oh gosh," she muttered, and got up to close the purse. "You didn't see that," she emphasized.

"Who gave it to you? Cal?" he persisted.

"Mr. Banks did. He made me go get a concealed carry permit at lunch today."

"He's nice, your boss. I like him."

"I like him, too." She didn't want to, but she did.

"I wish we had your guitar. You could play us some music."

She smiled. "When all this is over, and we have a proper place to live, I'll do that. I promise."

He smiled back. "Okay, Clancey."

"Get on to bed. You have school and I have work tomorrow."

He nodded. "You sleep good."

"You, too."

SHE SAT UP LATER, her mind jumping from subject to subject, leaving her no peace. She couldn't close her eyes for worrying about what was going to happen next.

Her cell phone vibrated madly. She picked it up. She

didn't recognize the number. It wasn't one she knew. She hesitated. It didn't stop ringing.

"Hello?" she said, answering it at last.

"Well, well, if it isn't my dear, sweet stepsister," came a curt, sarcastic voice over the line.

"Morris," she stammered. "How did you get this number?"

"You never changed it, did you?" he returned.

"So you're home."

"If you can call it that. What a dump! Was this the best you could do?"

"I don't make a lot of money," she returned. "Tad and I have to live within our means."

"Nice stores of food in the kitchen," he said. "Beds made up, floors swept, all that domestic stuff taken care of. Where are you?"

"Tad and I have an apartment," she lied.

"Try again," he drawled.

She didn't speak.

He laughed coldly. "I can find you, or Tad, anytime I want. I still have friends on the outside, so don't think you can hide the kid."

"I won't let you hurt him," she said icily.

"Now why would I want to hurt a little kid, Clancey?" he asked in a seemingly sincere tone. "You shouldn't make accusations like that. You could be arrested for charging me with crimes I haven't committed."

She sat down on the ragged couch and let out a sigh. "What do you want?"

"The last five years of my life back, you little snitch," he said in a soft, furious tone. "You sent me to prison!"

"You beat up a three-year-old child. What did you expect would happen?" she demanded.

"I expected you to keep your damned mouth shut," he shot back. "You were part of my family. Your duty was to protect me."

"It was to protect Tad. I did."

"You didn't protect your old granddad, did you?" he asked in a husky tone. "You don't even know where he is. And you never will. Where's that guitar he used to play?" he added angrily. "It's worth a small fortune."

"Your father sold it to help pay your defense attorney, when you were convicted," she lied. There was no way he could check that out and she bluffed well.

There was a long pause. "So that's where the money came from," he mused out loud. "Resourceful."

"Ben loved you more than anybody else. He always did."

"Yeah, he loved me, for all the good it did. You got me sent to prison."

"You beat up Tad. You broke my ribs."

"I was high as a kite. I don't remember any of that," he returned. "Nobody should have to serve time for something they don't even remember doing!"

"That's not how the law works," she said stiffly.

"And you'd know, wouldn't you, kid?" he drawled. "You worked for a cop for four years, now you're working for a stinking Ranger."

"Is there some reason you called me?" she interrupted.

"Well, yes, there is," he replied. There was a smile in his voice. "I'm going to pay you back for those five years. You and the assistant DA who put me away."

"They'll send you back to prison in a heartbeat if you hurt anyone…!"

"They'd have to prove it. Where's your granddaddy, Clancey?" he asked with a cold laugh. "I didn't serve time for his disappearance. You don't even know where he is."

"He was the sweetest man I ever knew," she said sadly. "He was unselfish and kind and brave. All the things you're not," she finished angrily.

"And he's still missing."

"They'll find him."

"Maybe. But I doubt it. Watch your back, baby sister," he added quietly. "Watch it carefully. I don't get mad. I get even. As for going back, I'm not going to. Even death is preferable to several more years in that hell behind bars. I've got nothing to lose. Nothing at all."

He hung up. Clancey sat on the floor with her heart hammering at her chest, wondering if the Army would really be such a bad choice.

ELEVEN

CLANCEY WAS GOING to tell Banks about her phone call of the night before, to ask him what to do next. But circumstances put an end to that.

Banks came in on time, but he wasn't alone. He had Grace with him. He was almost glowing. She'd agreed to let him take her down to the ranch. He'd taken a day off—a very unusual thing for him—to do it.

He was smiling as he and Grace paused in the office.

"Hi, Clancey," Grace said with a smile. "You look very nice."

Clancey flushed. She was wearing old jeans with a blue checked cotton shirt, buttoned all the way up with a long sweater-vest worn over it. "Thanks."

"I don't approve of the way most young women dress these days. Honestly, it's as if they were advertising everything they've got!"

Banks was too happy to bristle at Grace's unexpected riposte at his sister, Brenda. "Got the weapon and the permit with you?" he asked Clancey.

She nodded. "They're both in my purse."

"Keep the gun close."

She started to tell him about her phone call, but he was quite obviously impatient to leave.

"You're giving her a gun?" Grace asked, aghast. "What are you thinking, Colt?"

He gave her a long, steady look. "Sorry. That's privileged information. I can't share it."

Grace just stared at him. Clancey stared at him, too, confused. He ignored both of the speculative glances.

"Come on, Grace. It's not a long drive," he added when he saw her looking at her watch.

"I hope not. I have a meeting with one of the mission elders in two hours."

"I'll have you back before then," he promised. His heart sank. She'd hardly have any time to spend with him. Well, there was always tomorrow, he told himself.

He glanced at Clancey. "If anyone calls who can't get me, take down the name and number and say I'll get back to them tomorrow, okay?"

"Okay, Mr. Banks," she said with a big grin.

He hated having her address him so formally. He frowned, wondering why. Grace put her hand around his arm and smiled up at him and he forgot everything.

"I won't be back in today," he added.

"No problem," Clancey replied. "Have a good time."

"We're going to see a ranch where they slaughter poor calves," Grace sighed. "I'm afraid it isn't my idea of a good time at all."

"I love cattle," Clancey replied with a smile. "I wish I lived in a place where I could have some. I'd have two milk cows, so that I could always afford milk."

"It's cruel to milk them," Grace said sadly. "It oppresses them."

"Excuse me," Clancey said earnestly, "but have you ever seen a cow who hasn't been milked? They actually cry because the pain is so bad. Sometimes a calf can't take all the milk. If they're beef cattle, you can't milk them because it's too dangerous. But if they're dairy cattle, or a cow you keep for milk, you can. It's a lot crueler not to milk them. Honest."

"How would you know that?" Grace said, and not in a truly friendly way.

"My ex-boss has a cattle ranch in Jacobs County," Clancey said. "He keeps two milk cows."

Grace just stared at her without speaking.

"We'd better go," Banks said shortly. He tugged Grace along with him. "I'll be here in the morning. If there's anything urgent, you can text me."

Before she could tell him that she didn't know his cell phone number, he was up the steps and gone.

Clancey hoped the number was somewhere accessible, because if an emergency came up, she'd have to be able to contact him. It shocked her that she hadn't asked for it before. He always called in when he was out of the office, so she'd never had to track him down. Yet, at least.

Then she remembered. Even if she didn't have his cell phone number, Cal would have it. She could call him, for the number or for help, if she needed it.

She sat down at her desk with a long sigh. It looked as if Banks was head over heels in love with Grace. She didn't blame him. He'd known her a long time, cared for her a long time, been alone for a long time. She wanted him to be happy. He'd been kind to her, and to Tad.

It was sad that Grace had such a bad opinion about guns and cattle. But then, she was really religious. It made sense that she'd have firm attitudes. Clancey was religious, too, but she wasn't rigid in her beliefs. She simply thought that the way people chose to live was between them and God, and it wasn't her place to judge them.

She went back to work, hoping that the daily routine would keep Morris out of her thoughts, even temporarily.

GRACE WENT OUT to look at the cattle with Banks, her arms folded tight over the simple dark coat she was wearing.

"I have about a hundred head of Santa Gertrudis," he told her. "I have two full-time cowboys who keep them safe from predators and help me around the place."

"It smells terrible," she murmured.

He was faintly offended. "We keep the lots clean," he said defensively. "But cattle do function, and when it's fresh, it smells."

She turned away, looking over at the big barn. "What do you have in there?"

"The milk cows and a couple of Australian shepherds that we use to help us herd cattle."

She made a face. "I don't like dogs. There weren't any in the village where I lived overseas."

He'd already driven her around the ranch, showing her the newly painted fences and the pastures and the cattle. He'd given her a tour of the house, as well. To say that she hadn't been impressed was an understatement. Probably the collection of guns in his gun case had something to do with that.

He drew in a quiet breath and sank his big hands into his pockets. "Coffee?" he asked.

She glanced at her watch again. "Heavens, I'm going to be late for my meeting! Can we go now?" she asked, looking up at him.

There was no joy in her eyes, no interest, no nothing. He wondered absently where she'd gone, that passionate young woman who'd kissed him so hungrily just before her fiancé was killed. She was a different person altogether now.

"Certainly we can," he said politely.

They walked to the SUV.

"It's so lonely here," she said, glancing around. "No close neighbors at all. How do you stand it?"

"I like the solitude," he said simply.

"Well, to each his own," she sighed.

Which was, if anything, an understatement.

HE DROPPED GRACE off at her church and left her with a smile. She gave him one, too, an impersonal one that she might have given a stranger.

He hadn't planned to, but he stopped by the office. Clancey was having a quick lunch at her desk while she keyed old files into the computer. She looked up, surprised, when he came down the steps.

He scowled. "What the hell are you eating?" he asked shortly.

"Grits," she said. "Why?"

He made a terrible face. "Grits? For lunch?"

"I like grits," she said. "And just what have you got against corn?"

"They make grits out of it," he returned.

"Well, you're in a sweet mood today," she muttered as

she scraped out the last little bit of grits and spooned it into her mouth.

"The cattle being oppressed has soured me," he retorted.

She looked up, curious. "What sort of cattle do you have?" she wondered.

"Santa Gertrudis."

She smiled. "I like them. Cal runs black baldies, just beef cattle, but Cy Parks has purebred Santa Gertrudis that are famous all over the world."

He scowled. "How would you know that?"

"He and Cal are friends. Cal took Tad and me with him one Saturday when he had to talk to Mr. Parks about something. Harley Fowler took us on a tour of the place while Cal was busy. It was fascinating. I didn't even know that the foundation herd of Santa Gertrudis was at the King Ranch, up in Kingsville!"

He was staring at her. It was actually painful to compare her attitude about cattle with Grace's.

"Do you have a lot of them?" she asked.

"Only about a hundred head."

"Wow. That's a lot. Are they purebreds?"

He smiled. "Yes."

She put her refuse in the trash and sipped coffee. "I made coffee, if you want some," she said. She frowned. "I thought you were taking the day off."

"I was. Grace had to be back for a meeting, so I thought I'd go by the gun store and pick up the .28 gauge shotgun I ordered."

"That's a lightweight gun."

He looked exasperated. "And how would you know that?"

"Granddaddy was a triple A skeet shooter," she said. "I used to go to the gun club with him to watch him practice." She made a face. "He could shoot all four classes of shotguns, even an antique Colt .45 he owned, but he wouldn't let me use anything except that .28 gauge."

He scowled. "You can shoot a shotgun?" he asked.

"Well, it's not that hard," she began defensively.

"I've found very few women who would even pick one up," he returned, "and that includes my sister. They're afraid of the kick and the noise."

"Granddaddy had them put a padded stock on mine, to lessen the impact of the kick, and we always wore earplugs on the range. I really enjoyed it. Shooting, I mean."

She loved guns and cattle, and Grace thought both were unacceptable. He'd never been so depressed. It showed, too.

"Do you still have his guns?" he asked after a minute.

She shook her head. "Ben sold every one of them," she said tautly, "to help pay for Morris's lawyer." She frowned. "Well, all but the .45 double-action Colt," she amended. "That went missing just after Granddaddy disappeared. We never found it. Ben was really mad about that, because it was in a hand-tooled, very old gun belt that belonged to my great-great grandfather. The pistol was an antique, as well. It was worth a lot of money."

"You think Morris took it," he speculated.

She drew in a breath. "I'm not sure, but he probably did. Morris was an addict. He'd have sold me if it would have made him enough for more drugs. And if he did have it, he certainly wasn't going to tell his father."

He studied her for longer than he meant to. She was

pretty. He liked the way she dressed, the way she smiled. He liked a lot of things about her.

"Have you heard from Morris?" he asked abruptly.

She nodded.

His face hardened. "When?"

She drew in a steadying breath. The question was painful. "He called me last night on my cell phone," she said miserably.

"Why didn't you tell me that this morning?"

She gave him a long-suffering look. "You were in a hurry this morning," she replied.

He grimaced. "I guess I was. What did he say?"

"That he was going to pay me back for sending him to jail, and that he had no plans to go back, no matter what. He made threats about Tad, as well."

Banks moved closer to her desk. "He'll never get Tad," he said.

She nodded. "Cal has people watching him. A couple of them are ex-mercs."

"We have people in law enforcement who can do that," he returned, irritated.

Her eyebrows went up. "On our budget?" she exclaimed. "Well, we could probably afford a guy off the street who'd be willing to work for pizzas and beer…"

"And if he's after you, I'll guarantee he's after Darrell Tarley, as well," he continued. "Have you told Hollister?"

"Not yet…"

"You call him. Right now," he added curtly. He turned on his heel.

She started to ask where he was going and then realized that it was his day off and bit her tongue.

He stopped at the steps and turned back to her with a scowl. "You're alone down here," he said abruptly.

"No kidding," she said with mock surprise. "I'll tell the guy hiding in the closet to go home, then."

He gave her a dour look. "I'm serious. We can't lock you in. I don't like you being down here by yourself."

"I could go work in the lieutenant's office, but who'd man the phones here?" she wanted to know.

He was disturbed. Morris Duffy was vindictive, and he had contacts in the criminal community. What he could do to the sweet, kind girl sitting there was unthinkable. Banks felt his heart jump at the thought of Clancey lying dead on the floor of her own office.

"I've got the pistol," she said, because he looked so concerned. "It's loaded and I know how to use it. Cal took me on the firing range a lot. Before that, Granddaddy taught me how to handle all sorts of weapons. I'm not helpless."

He still looked worried. His black eyes narrowed on her face. "I've gotten used to you," he said gruffly.

She stared at him. "Imagine that, when you were trying to send me back to work for Cal just a few months ago."

The mention of her former boss made him angry, but he kept it from showing. "Nobody's taking you out on my watch," he said shortly. "Not you, or Tad."

She was genuinely touched by his concern. She smiled. "Thanks, Mr. Banks."

So formal. It set him off even more. "You're welcome. Nasturtium," he added with a hint of his old sarcasm.

"I am not a nasturtium!"

"A likely story," he huffed. He started up the steps. "I'll work this out, one way or the other," he murmured to himself as he left.

SHE SAT THINKING about him after he'd left. She didn't want to. He was involved with another woman, a saintly woman, at that. Clancey was just a minor irritation who did his busywork. Besides all that, her life was so complicated that there was no room in it for a man.

Morris worried her. Not for herself, but for Tad. She knew that despite all the precautions she'd taken, Morris had friends who could ferret out information for him. If he had Tad, Clancey would do anything to save him, even trade her own life for the child's.

She hoped it wouldn't come to that, but Morris had been very firm about not going back to prison. If only they could connect him to her grandfather's disappearance. If they could, they'd probably lock him up for twenty years or so—long enough for Tad to grow into a man, at least.

She studied her short, neat fingernails and thought with real longing of her guitar. She remembered Cal's invitation to Thanksgiving dinner. It was only a week or two away, and it would be a nice, big meal, the sort Clancey and Tad couldn't really afford these days. Of course they'd go. She just had to make sure that Cal picked them up at Tad's after-school program instead of the shelter. He'd be furious at the thought of the two of them living there.

But she didn't want to make Cal responsible for them. He needed to get married again, to a good woman, and have children while he was still relatively young. She wanted to tell him that. She didn't dare.

She went back to work, forcing her fears to the back of her mind. *One step at a time, one day at a time*, she told herself. Worrying was a one-way street to despair. She had to keep moving and stop brooding. Everything would be all right, she told herself.

EXCEPT THAT, JUST BEFORE it was time to pick up Tad at school, she had an unexpected call.

"Where's your little brother?" a familiar voice drawled.

Her heart skipped wildly. "He's at school," she said doggedly. "And they have standing orders not to let him leave with anyone except me!"

"Anyone except you and Hollister," he chuckled. He sounded high as a kite. She wondered if he was. "I told them Hollister sent me to get the boy because he was at a crime scene. It must have been a new woman, because she just smiled and said okay."

Her heart stopped beating. "I told Tad to scream if anyone tried to take him...!" she said frantically.

"I told him what I'd do to you if he did," he said with an unsteady laugh. "He thought I had you locked in a bedroom at home. So, now what are you going to do, tattletale?" he asked in a cold, angry tone.

Her mind was racing. Her heart was racing. She gripped the phone. "I'll come over there. You can trade Tad for me. I won't even make a fuss," she said, trying not to think about what Morris might do to her. "Please!"

"I'll think about it and let you know," he said.

"Don't hurt him!" she burst out.

"Well, that depends on you, doesn't it?" he asked, slurring his words, and hung up.

She was shivering with fear. It was quitting time. Morris had Tad. What should she do?

Her first instinct was to call Cal, and she did. But amazingly, what Morris had told her was the truth. Cal actually was at a crime scene and the switchboard said he wasn't answering his phone.

Banks might have helped if he'd been in the office. But he was gone, too, and she didn't know where to find him.

There was nobody else.

So she sat and sweated and felt sick all over as she contemplated what Morris might be doing to her little brother. She could call the police. But Morris could say the boy wasn't there and refuse a search unless the police had a warrant. By the time they got one, he'd have Tad somewhere else.

Tears of impotent fury ran down her pale cheeks. She had to do something! She couldn't just sit in her office and hope Morris would suddenly come to his senses and let the boy go. Kidnapping was a federal offense. He'd go up for life if they caught him at it. She could call the FBI. But Morris could just hide Tad. Or make him disappear, as her grandfather had disappeared. He'd already mentioned that.

She put her face in her hands and wiped away the tears. Her mind refused to think. She was devastated.

While she was cursing her own fate, her cell phone went off. She fumbled it to her ear. "Morris?" she asked at once.

"Sis?"

It was Tad! "Oh my God, are you all right? Has he still got you? Has he hurt you?" she burst out, frantic.

"He and his friends are stoned," he said, his voice a little shaky. "I opened the window in the room Morris locked me in. I had my cell phone in my pocket, so I called that cab driver who's always so nice. He's bringing me to your office. You still there?"

"Oh yes," she sobbed. "Yes, I am Oh, Tad!"

"We're almost there. Don't cry, sis. I'm okay. Really."

She swallowed down a dozen fears. "All right. I'll be waiting when you get here. It's quitting time anyway."

"The cab can take us on to the shelter, right?"

She didn't argue. She had just enough to pay him, with a tip, and a little of her check would be left over for food. "Yes, he can," she said softly. "Oh yes."

SHE LOCKED UP with shaking hands, thanking God over and over again for returning her brother to her.

The cab pulled up at the sidewalk. Tad opened the door and she almost dragged him out and hugged him and hugged him until she embarrassed him.

"Sorry," she said as she let him go. "Muscle spasm."

He smiled gently. "If you say so."

She looked him over critically. He had a couple of bruises, which made her angry, but he was otherwise unharmed apparently. "Okay. Let's go home."

She climbed in the cab with him and thanked the driver profusely for picking him up so quickly.

"It was nothing," he said easily. "He's a good kid. Where you going?"

She told him.

He grimaced. "Such a sad place. There are apartments all over town."

"Apartments cost money," she said with a smile and a sigh. "We're poor."

His face tautened. "As so many of us are," he agreed quietly.

"It's not so bad," she said, ruffling Tad's hair affectionately. "We have family. That's worth more than gold."

"You are very wise," the cab driver said with a smile. "Very wise, indeed."

HE DROPPED THEM off at the shelter. She paid him and rushed Tad inside the building and up to their room. She locked it. She leaned back against the door with a long, heavy sigh.

"I thought he might kill you," she said miserably.

"Me, too," he confessed. "But all he did was lock me in Ben's old bedroom. He just forgot to lock the windows," he added. He hugged her for comfort. It had been a scary experience. "I heard him stumbling around in the hall, talking to one of his friends."

"Could you hear what he said?"

"He was bragging about how smart he was. He said he'd killed a man with an old gun that wasn't even registered, and nobody would ever know where it was." He grimaced. "I think he meant Granddaddy, Clancey."

Her heart stopped and then started again. "Did he say anything else?"

"Just that he was going to make you pay for putting him in prison. He said you'd never see me again. But that didn't work out the way he planned." He drew in a breath. "I'm just glad he didn't lock that window. I was so scared..."

She gathered him close. "I tried to trade myself for you. I'd have done anything to save you!"

He hugged her back. "Me, too," he said. "He was so high he didn't know where he was half the time. He put on a good act for Mrs. Marvin, at my school, but she didn't know him. She was so sweet. She believed what he said about Cal sending him to pick me up, and he looked cold sober when he said it. Mrs. Marvin was new and she didn't know any better. I was afraid to say anything. Morris gave me that look he used to have...and when we got in the cab, he said he already had you. I didn't dare try to get away then." He paused. "Poor Mrs. Marvin. She's nice. I hope they don't fire her," he added worriedly.

She didn't echo his sentiments. Tad could have died because a new worker didn't check out the man who'd claimed he was a friend of Cal's. She swallowed, hard. "I've never been so scared. Not since that night," she confessed brokenly.

"I'm okay," he repeated. He drew back and looked up at her. "But if he could find me at school, he could find us here. What are we going to do? He's going to be real mad because I got away. You know how he is, even when he's not using drugs."

"I do, indeed." She let him go and paced, while she tried to think of ways and means to save them. She paused and looked at her little brother, at the light of her life. "I'll find a way. I promise."

BANKS WENT BACK into the office. The door was locked. Clancey had gone home. He'd been trying to find someone willing to tail her little brother night and day, and without luck. Then he remembered that Cal Hollister had mentioned that he'd already done that.

He pulled out his cell phone and punched in numbers.

Hollister picked up on the third ring. "Hollister," he said curtly.

"It's Banks. Have you still got somebody watching Clancey and her brother?"

"I did," he said angrily. "Two guys. They had a disagreement, got into a fight and ended up in jail for creating a public disturbance." He let out an angry sigh. "I've been trying to find somebody to take over for them…"

"Tomorrow's Friday. I'm going to take them down to

the ranch with me after quitting time. I'll speak to my sister and have her move in with us for the time being to keep Clancey from worrying about her reputation."

Cal let out a breath. "I offered for them to come here, but she won't," he said. "She's so damned proud. It's hard to do anything for her, because she thinks it's just charity, or worse, pity. She and Tad are sort of like family. I don't really have anybody else."

Banks ground his teeth together. He felt sorry for the man and he didn't want to. He felt jealous as well, and that set him off.

"I'll talk to my sister and then I'll drive over to the Brandiff Apartments and persuade Clancey."

Cal chuckled. "Good luck."

"I can be persuasive," he said. "I've got a big, friendly Maine Coon cat named Miss Kitty and my sister, Brenda, fosters stray cats. Right now she's got a big furry kitten that's homeless. I'll have her bring it down here, too. Clancey loves animals."

"Yes, she does. Let me know how it comes out, okay? I'll be at the office until late. We're working another homicide."

"Will do."

He locked up the office and went to see his sister at her apartment.

Brenda was overjoyed and trying very hard not to let it show. Grace was a friend, and she admired her, but she was no match for Brenda's impulsive, mercurial brother. Clancey was a far better match for him.

"I can go tonight, in fact," she said. "I don't work tomorrow. The boss gave me the day off, and a trainee's taking my place while they teach her the ropes."

"That will work out nicely," Banks said. He grinned. "Clancey loves cattle," he added.

"She's a country girl," Brenda replied. "Her mother was born down around Floresville and her father commuted to his job in San Antonio. Clancey doesn't really like living in town, but when her mother remarried, she had no choice. She was still in high school at the time."

"We'll take her riding this weekend. If I don't get called out," he sighed.

"Get married, have a lot of kids and suggest that they call one of the unmarried Rangers when they need assistance," she advised.

He made a face at her and went to the door. "I'll call you before I swing by to pick you up."

"I really would like to take my car, just in case," she said. "Can't I follow you down to the ranch?"

"Sure," he said easily. "I'll call you when I'm on the way. And bring that stray kitten you're trying to find a home for. Clancey loves cats."

She laughed. "Okay. See you in a bit."

"Fair enough."

HE WENT BY the office at the Brandiff Apartments and asked for Clancey and Tad's room number.

The manager looked at him curiously. "Who?" he asked.

"Clancey Lang. She has a little brother living with her. He's nine…"

He frowned. "We don't have any Langs here," he said. "There's a Carlie Lang, but she's in her fifties."

Banks felt his face go taut. "Are you sure?"

He nodded. "I've been manager here for sixteen years," he said. "I know everybody, and I mean everybody, who lives here. Sorry I can't help you."

"Thanks just the same," Banks said. He forced a smile and went back out to his vehicle.

He called Hollister. "She's not here," he said tautly. "She never was here."

"Where are you?" Cal asked.

"The Brandiff Apartments," he said curtly. "Something's going on. This doesn't feel right."

"No, it doesn't. Okay," Cal said after a minute. "Let's logic this out. She's within walking distance of your office and Tad's school. The Brandiff Apartments are the only low-rent housing within a three mile radius—I know, because I've been trying to help her find a place she could afford. If she couldn't afford Brandiff, there's only one place left that she's likely to be living."

Banks took a deep breath. "The homeless shelter," he said icily.

"Exactly," Cal replied. "And when you find her, you give her hell for me, too, because I offered twice to bring them both down here until I could find her a place in town!"

"I'll give her both barrels," Banks promised.

"And then call me so I can be sure she's all right," he added quietly.

"I'll do that, too."

HE DROVE TO the homeless shelter. He knew it because he'd had to interview a reluctant witness there just two weeks earlier. He asked for Clancey by name and was given permission to go to her room, after showing his credentials and mentioning that she worked for him.

He knocked on the door and waited patiently.

There were footsteps. The door was unlocked and opened. And Clancey stood there in sweatpants and a thick T-shirt with her mouth open, gaping at him.

TWELVE

BANKS WAS THE last person on earth Clancey had expected to find at her door. She couldn't even find words.

He didn't seem angry. His dark eyes weren't exactly friendly, though. "Well?" he asked. "Can I come in?"

"Oh." She opened the door reluctantly and let him inside. Her phone was ringing. Again. She knew it was Cal. She hadn't answered it out of fear that he'd found out what had happened earlier. Now that Banks had found her, she had another hint about why Cal was calling.

She wasn't wearing shoes. She seemed even shorter and more fragile to Banks, who was still wearing his boots with two-inch roping heels on them. He looked down at her coolly.

"You lied," he said curtly.

She bit her lower lip. She felt sick all over. She drew in a quick breath and started to speak.

Tad came out of his room and saw Banks and actually ran to him. Banks went on one knee to meet the charge and picked the child up.

"I was so scared," he sobbed into the big man's chest.

He'd been upset ever since they got to the shelter. He'd put on an act for Clancey with the cab driver, but when they got home, it all caught up with him. He'd been crying on and off ever since.

Banks hugged him. He felt odd. It was really the first time in his life that anybody except Brenda and, later, Grace, had needed him. He rubbed the boy's back. "Calm down, now. Tell me what happened."

"Morris took him from the after-school program," Clancey said miserably. "There was a new woman. She didn't know that only Cal or I had permission to pick him up. Morris drove him home, locked him in a room and called me to gloat. I tried to trade myself for him, but Morris wouldn't." Tears choked her. "I was afraid to call anybody. Morris sounded drugged up and he's unpredictable. I thought if I called the police and they rushed the house, Tad would be the first to…"

"Then how…?"

Tad pulled back, rubbing his eyes. "Morris was so high that he didn't take my cell phone away. He locked the room, but he forgot to lock the window. So I opened the window, called a cab driver who's been nice to me and sis, and he took me to your office. We picked up sis and the cab driver brought us here."

"You brave kid," Banks said, with visible admiration.

Tad actually flushed. "I didn't feel brave. I was scared to death Morris would catch me."

Banks smiled gently, pulling out a handkerchief to mop up Tad's face. "Everybody's afraid when they're under fire," he said softly. "The definition of courage is doing what you need to do, regardless of how afraid you are."

Tad drew in a shaky breath. "Thanks." He winced. "What are we going to do? He'll hurt us when he sobers up and finds me gone…!"

"No. He won't." Banks got to his feet and looked down at Clancey. "Pack up your things. You're both coming home with me."

Clancey flushed scarlet and searched for words.

"We're picking up my sister at her apartment on the way," he said in a long-suffering tone.

"Oh." She just stared at him. She would have argued, but he looked more formidable than usual and she was too unnerved to marshal an argument.

"She's waiting for us," he prodded.

"Oh! Sorry!" She took Tad with her to pack up the few personal items they'd brought with them, including Tad's schoolbooks.

They dressed and then went out to the living room with all their possessions.

Banks looked at them with an ache in his heart. It was painful to see how little they had. Both of them had dark circles under their eyes. He could only imagine how afraid they'd both been this afternoon. Well, Morris wasn't touching them again. Ever.

"Let's go," he said gently.

They went back down to the lobby. Banks had them wait for him while he talked to the woman in charge and explained what had happened. She was very supportive. They could always come back, anytime they needed to, she added, smiling at Clancey and Tad.

"Thanks for everything," Clancey said gently.

She nodded. "You're very welcome."

Banks herded them out to the SUV, put them inside and started toward his sister's apartment.

"Call Hollister," he said curtly as he drove. "He's been half out of his mind with worry."

She grimaced. "I didn't answer when he called earlier…"

"Just do it."

She glared at him. "You are very bossy," she said shortly.

"Comes from years of ordering people around," he murmured.

She sighed, opened her phone and called Cal.

"Where the hell have you been?" he exploded.

"At the homeless shelter," she said, wincing. "I'm so sorry…"

"I was worried sick. What happened?"

She hesitated. "I'll tell you later," she said in a minute. "Mr. Banks is taking us home with him…"

"I know. His sister's going with you."

"Yes, we're going to pick her up now," she added.

"I had two men watching you. They got into a fight and they're in jail, but I'll find someone else. You and Tad will be safe."

"Morris kidnapped him," she blurted out.

"What!"

"He locked him in a room. Tad climbed out the window and called a cab on his cell phone. The cab driver brought him to me and then drove us both to the homeless shelter. I didn't know what to do…"

"You should have called me! Or Banks! Or the FBI…!"

"Morris might have killed Tad when they rolled up to his front door," she said miserably.

He relented. "We need to have a long talk when you feel like it."

She managed a smile. "Okay."

"I'm glad you're both safe," he added gently.

"Thanks. So are we. I'll talk to you later."

"You bet."

She hung up.

Banks glanced at her. "Furious, was he?"

"A little worse than that," she said. "I should have called for help. I just panicked," she added.

"It's okay, sis," Tad said. "We're safe, now."

"Yes." She glanced at the tall man beside her in the front seat. "We're safe."

He glanced at her and felt his heart shift ten degrees. Tired, frightened, her hair ruffled, no makeup on, and she was the prettiest woman he'd ever seen. He made a sound deep in his throat and averted his eyes.

He sent Brenda a text. "She's on her way down," he told his passengers.

Brenda came out a minute later with a small carrier. "I'm bringing the kitten," she called.

"You got a kitten?" Tad exclaimed. "Can we play with it?"

She laughed. "Of course you can. I'll be right behind you on the way to Jacobsville. Don't run any more red lights," she cautioned her brother.

He made a rude sound.

She just laughed and climbed into her small foreign car with the cat carrier.

"I do not run red lights," he told Clancey.

"You don't?"

"Never."

"Okay."

He glanced at her with twinkling brown eyes. "Well, I did once. Brenda was with me when the city police caught up with us." He made a face. "I got a ticket and she's never let me forget it."

Clancey smothered a laugh.

"Don't you do that," he cautioned. "Or I'll bury you in old files when we get back to the office."

"Tomorrow," she began.

"Not tomorrow. Not you," he added. "You're staying at the ranch and so is Tad. I'll go by his school and speak to the principal. Meanwhile, I'm going to speak to the FBI and assistant DA Darrell Tarley and see how much trouble I can make for your stepbrother. He can't be allowed to get away with kidnapping a child!"

"It's Tad's word against Morris's," she said miserably.

"It is not. I'll find the woman who gave him into Morris's custody."

"Yes, but see, she gave him custody," she pointed out. "He didn't take Tad away without permission."

"Graduated law school just recently, did you?" he drawled sarcastically.

She glared at him. "You're just mad because you didn't think of it," she replied haughtily.

Tad chuckled.

"Okay, no petting the kitten for you," he said over his shoulder.

"I'm sorry!" Tad exclaimed. "Really!"

Banks chuckled, too. "Okay."

IT WASN'T A long drive to the ranch. It sat back off the highway on a long, graveled road between fences and cross fences. The full moon gave Banks's passengers a much better view of the land than a dark night would have.

The house was Victorian, two stories high with towering trees all around it. There were several outbuildings, one of which looked like a barn.

"I love Victorian houses," Clancey said excitely. "My grandparents used to live in one outside Floresville!"

He chuckled. "This one has a history. I'll tell you it one day." He pulled up at the steps. There was porch furniture, including a swing. Clancey could only imagine how much fun it would be to sit out there on lazy summer nights.

"And we're here."

He got Clancey and Tad out and carried their bags inside the house. Brenda pulled up right behind Banks's SUV and cut off her engine. She picked up the cat carrier and bounded up onto the porch with an overnight bag over her shoulder.

Banks opened the door. There was a blur of red fur. He knelt and picked up Miss Kitty. "Did you miss me, baby?" he teased as she purred and rubbed her head against his chest.

"She's so pretty!" Clancey exclaimed. The cat looked at him with soft amber eyes.

"Can I pet her?" Tad asked excitedly.

"She's a little nervous of people, just at first," he began as he put the cat down. But she went right up to Tad and rubbed against him.

"Well!" Banks said, stunned.

"And here's Bumblebee," Brenda added, opening the cat carrier. A little ball of yellow fur trundled out of the cage, so fat that her little sides bulged. She meowed softly.

"Oh my goodness!" Clancey exclaimed. She bent and

picked up the little cat, rubbing her head against it. "What a sweet baby!"

"She's just two months old," Brenda said. "Somebody found her walking across a parking lot at a shopping center and brought her in to the vet for adoption." She grimaced. "We haven't found anybody yet. I'd love to take her, but I'm not allowed pets in my apartment."

"We aren't allowed to have them in the shelter, either," Clancey said sadly.

"Shelter?" Brenda exclaimed, horrified.

Clancey went scarlet red.

"She wrote the book on pride," Banks huffed as he glanced at Clancey. His eyes went back to his sister. "Hollister offered her a temporary home, too, but she lied to both of us about having a nice apartment over near the office." He was glaring at Clancey now.

"Don't be mean, Colt," Brenda chided. She slid an arm around Clancey's shoulders. "He isn't really an old bear," she assured the other woman. "He just does a really dandy impression of one."

He was glaring at both women, now.

"Miss Kitty likes me!" Tad exclaimed, entranced with the big cat.

Banks chuckled. "So it seems. Come on. Let me show you to your rooms. This is a huge house. We have three extra bedrooms besides mine and the one Brenda uses when she comes down on weekends. You can choose whichever ones you want."

"Do you have one with a connecting door?" Clancey asked worriedly, with a speaking glance at Tad, who was still looking at the big cat on the floor.

Banks understood at once. "Yes. There's one."

He led them upstairs and down the hall to a room that overlooked a long fenced pasture that ended at what was obviously a barn. It had a twin bed with a simple chenille bedspread and a dresser. There was a closet and, in the bedroom that was beyond the open door, there was a larger bed with a quilt covering it, and a bathroom.

"It's nothing fancy," Banks began.

"Oh, it's a palace compared to our house," Clancey broke in gently. "These floors are oak, aren't they?"

His eyebrows lifted. "Yes, made the old-fashioned way, with long thin strips."

"Granddaddy's house had floors like this." She turned. "I can't thank you enough," she said. "I don't know what we'd have done. I wasn't sure that Morris wouldn't track us down…" She stopped dead. "But we'll be putting both of you in danger if we stay here," she added with obvious worry.

He pointed to the star on his white shirt.

Brenda pointed to the star on his shirt.

Clancey sighed. "Okay." She swallowed. "Thanks," she added huskily.

"This is awesome," Tad exclaimed, running between the rooms. "Gosh, it's so big! You could play baseball in here!"

"Don't you even think about it," Banks told him with twinkling black eyes.

"It's okay—I don't even have a bat," he assured the tall man. "Do you got horses?" he added with bright eyes.

"Lots of them," Banks said. "I'm off Saturday. I'll take you both riding." He glanced at his sister and laughed. "You can come, too. I've got a nice new rocking horse."

She glared at him. "If you can put a saddle on it, I can ride it," she said huffily.

"That's true," Banks had to admit. "She did barrel racing in her teens."

She laughed. "That was a while back. Can you ride?" she asked Clancey.

Clancey nodded. "It's been a long time, but Granddaddy always had a couple of saddle horses on the ranch." Her face was sad. "He was a grand rider."

Banks began to understand her. She'd loved her grandfather. It must have been hell on her, not knowing if he was alive or dead, even though he'd vanished five years earlier.

"We'll find out the truth," he assured her. "One way or another."

"Thanks," she said.

"Do you like cartoons, Mr. Banks?" Tad asked hopefully.

His eyebrows arched. "Why?" he asked.

Tad flushed.

"Saturday morning cartoons are his whole life," Clancey teased. "Well, except for his video games." She stopped and grimaced. They'd had to leave the equipment and the games at the house that now belonged to Morris.

Banks raised both dark eyebrows. "What sort of games do you like?"

"Destiny 2," the boy said at once.

Banks chuckled.

"Why are you laughing?" Clancey wanted to know.

"Put your stuff down and follow me."

He led them downstairs to the living room and pointed to a console on the entertainment center below the big screen television.

Tad caught his breath. "It's an Xbox One!" he burst out.

"And you'll find *Destiny 1* and *Destiny 2* installed on it," he told Tad. "I don't have a lot of time to play, but it's one of my favorites."

Tad's eyes grew wide with anticipation.

"You can play as much as you like," Banks told him. "As long as your homework's done first," he added firmly.

"I'll do my homework first thing every day, I swear!" the boy promised solemnly.

Clancey could have hugged the tall man for that. She knew how badly Tad had missed his games. But she was afraid to take anything out of the house in case Morris knew the equipment had been there and accused his siblings of stealing it. He still had friends in the neighborhood, and Clancey couldn't be sure that Morris hadn't had somebody pick the lock and take a look around to see what was in the house.

"I wish they hadn't let Morris out," Tad said sadly.

"The law is the law," Clancey reminded him gently. "You can't keep people locked up forever. Not even Morris."

"I guess not."

"You'll both be safe here," Banks assured them. "I have two full-time cowboys who live on the ranch. One of them," he added with a smile, "is a former Texas Ranger."

Brenda's face tautened. She didn't say a word, but Clancey recognized irritation when she saw it.

"He won't come near the house unless I ask him to," Banks assured her. "And I won't ask him when you're home."

Brenda didn't reply. She just stared at her brother.

"He did apologize," he added.

She made a huffy sound and started toward the kitchen. "I hope you've got something to cook in here," she said, turning on the light. "I didn't have time for supper."

"Freezer's full," Banks said, tossing his hat onto the hat rack. "Don't you touch it!" he added.

Clancey and Tad stared at him.

"She can burn water," he said, giving his sister a glare. "No way I'm turning her loose with the contents of my freezer!"

"I can cook a steak," Brenda protested. "Anybody can cook a steak!"

"It has to be defrosted first…"

"You just use the auto defrost on the microwave," Clancey said gently.

"You don't own a microwave, so how do you know?" Banks asked.

"When Ben…my stepfather, was alive, he had one. I had to cook after Mama died. If I hadn't, we'd all have starved to death. Ben and Morris couldn't cook."

"You can cook?" Brenda asked her, and her eyes lit up.

Banks glowered at her. "I can cook, too," he reminded her.

"You can cook steak and potatoes. I'm sick to death of steak and potatoes. It's steak for breakfast, steak sandwiches for lunch, steak and potatoes for supper…!"

"Steak is good for you, and besides that, I've got two sides of beef in the freezer that will go bad if we don't eat it!"

"Chicken is very nice," Brenda began.

"I'd rather eat feathers!" Banks shot back.

"Where's the freezer?" Clancey asked.

Brenda walked around her brother and led Clancey to it.

IN LESS THAN an hour, Clancey had made fresh biscuits and herbed chicken with mashed potatoes and seasoned green beans.

Banks was almost moaning with pleasure as he ate. Brenda watched him covertly, grinning at Clancey when he wasn't watching.

"Who taught you to cook?" Brenda asked.

"My grandmother," she said with a smile. "She was a wonderful cook. I have one of her cookbooks in the backpack I keep my things in." She grimaced. "We don't have a lot of our stuff left. Ben got really mad at me for testifying against Morris, so he threw out most of the things I had left of my grandparents."

Banks grimaced. "That's petty," he said harshly.

"That was Ben," she replied. "He wasn't really a bad man. He just loved Morris more than anybody else."

"I don't remember him much," Tad said as he finished a mouthful of buttered biscuit. "I remember Morris, though." He shivered.

"How old were you?" Banks asked him.

"Almost four, Sis said," he replied. "I don't remember much else about when I was little, but I remember Morris hitting me."

"He has nightmares," Clancey said, without adding that she had them, as well.

"I'm not surprised," Banks replied. He finished cleaning his plate and sat back to sip coffee. "Clancey, you're in a class of your own as a cook," he said flatly. "You could open a restaurant."

"Oh, not me," she said, flushing. "I love to cook, but there's lots of people who cook better than I can."

"Not that many," he countered. He smiled at her.

She averted her eyes. "Thanks," she said huskily.

Brenda watched them both with a secret glee that she was careful not to let them see.

LATER THEY WENT into the living room. But instead of turning on the television, he went out of the room and came back with a big, spruce-topped acoustic guitar.

"Oh!" Clancey exclaimed.

Banks handed it to her. "It's old," he said.

"I can tell."

"And you should hear him..." Brenda began, but her brother silenced her with a look and a quick shake of his head.

"This," he told Brenda, "you've got to hear to believe."

Clancey looked up at him.

"Come on," he said softly, and settled into a rocking chair that was obviously his, with a tender smile.

Clancey took a deep breath. "Okay."

Brenda was curious. Her brother must think that Clancey could play. A lot of people could, she reminded herself.

But then, Clancey positioned the guitar and began to play.

Brenda sat on the very edge of her seat, her lips parted with surprise, her eyes wide, as the exquisite melody flowed out from the guitar and all around the room. Tad grinned, watching her play.

She drew to a close and opened her eyes. Brenda was spellbound.

"How did you ever learn to play like that?" the other woman exclaimed. "That was beautiful!"

"My grandfather taught me," she said. "I still have his guitar."

She handed the guitar back to Banks with a smile. "It has a beautiful sound. Who plays it?"

He sat down on the edge of the big coffee table, tapped one toe and broke into a rendition of "San Antonio Rose" that had Clancey gasping.

Brenda chuckled. "Isn't he great?" she teased. "He knew a man in the service who'd trained under Chet Atkins."

"I thought that technique sounded familiar," Clancey laughed. "You're great!" she added.

He grinned at her and wound up the final riff.

"We need another guitar," Brenda said. "So you two can do duets."

"I can't play country," Clancey said sadly.

"And I can't play classical," Banks agreed.

"There's always a way to find common ground," Brenda pointed out.

"Not a bad idea. But it's getting late and I have to go to work in the morning. We don't keep late hours around here," he added to Clancey.

"Neither do we," she replied. "We're both in bed by nine at night."

Brenda didn't say anything. But she was smiling secretively.

CLANCEY HEARD A SOUND. A long moan. A cry. She opened her eyes. She was wearing her sweatpants and a thick T-shirt to bed, as she always did. The sound was coming from the bedroom through the connecting door.

She turned on the lamp, got up and walked through

to the smaller bedroom. She paused at Tad's bedside. He was crying.

She knew the nightmare. She'd comforted him through it for years. She turned on his lamp and touched his shoulder gently. "Tad, it's okay. Wake up, honey. It's okay. You're safe."

His eyes opened. They were wet. "Clancey?"

She sat down on the bed beside him. "It's okay," she said softly, and pulled him to her. She rocked him while he cried. "I hope Morris gets what he deserves one day," she said softly.

"Me, too." He sniffed. "I'm sorry I woke you up."

"Don't be silly." She smiled against his hair and rocked him some more.

The bedroom door opened softly, and Banks was standing there, in burgundy pajamas with a matching robe belted at the waist. His dark hair was tousled, as if he hadn't slept much, either.

"Is he okay?" he asked gently.

"Nightmares," she said.

He grimaced.

A door opened down the hall and Brenda came into the room a minute later, wearing a gown and a thick chenille robe. "Is everything okay?" she asked.

"Gosh, I'm sorry I woke everybody up," Tad said, with tears streaming down his cheeks.

"Come on," Banks said. He moved Clancey to one side, picked up Tad and carried him into the living room. "How about a glass of milk?"

"Thanks. That would be nice," Tad said, still choked from the tears.

"Chamomile tea?" Brenda asked Clancey. "It's the only

thing I can make really well. It helps me to sleep. It might help you, too."

Banks glanced at her with Tad in his lap. "Coffee. Black. Double strong. Put a horseshoe in it and if it floats, make it stronger."

Brenda rolled her eyes and laughed.

She and Clancey waited for the water to boil and the coffee to make. Brenda found a wooden tray to put everything on.

Tad was talking to Banks about his nightmare. Brenda came back into the kitchen and pushed the door shut, just a little.

"What happened to Tad?" she asked softly.

"When Tad was three years old, Morris was playing a video game and Tad interrupted him, crying. Morris picked up a steel shovel by the fireplace and hit him with it several times." She swallowed hard. "I ran and got in the way, and Morris hit me, too. I had two broken ribs. Tad had concussion. Morris was arrested, tried and convicted and sentenced to six years in prison, although he got out in five."

"Oh my goodness! How terrible!" Brenda said with genuine sympathy.

"I hoped maybe Morris might not want to come back here. But he wants to get even with me for putting him away," she added sadly. "I'm not worried about me, but Tad would have to go into foster care...!"

"He would not," Brenda said firmly. "But you stop thinking like that. Morris is not taking you out. If he tries to, he'll think he walked into a prickly pear cactus. My brother will have him roasted!"

Clancey managed a smile. "Your brother is a kind man," she said quietly.

"He has a soft heart. It just doesn't show." She drew in a long breath. "Grace has him tied in knots," she muttered. "She wants him to take an administrative position and give up raising cattle and living on a ranch." She made a face and shook her head. "He's been hung up on her for years, but she's changed. She's not the same woman he remembers from Houston."

"She seems very nice," Clancey said.

"She is very nice. But she's so involved in her work that nothing else matters to her. If you want to know what I think, I think she'll never get married. She has a job that makes her feel useful and gives her a purpose in life. She finds things wrong with the men around her to keep them from getting serious." She glanced through the door to make sure her brother was still talking to Tad. She turned back to Grace. "She'd already talked Mike Johns, her fiancé, into giving up police work and anything to do with guns. He wasn't happy about it. I'm not sure she would ever have married him. She was already very involved with church work. Colt said they'd had a nasty fight the day before Mike was killed, about his job."

"That's so sad."

"It would be even sadder if she ended up with my brother," Brenda said flatly. "You can see how unsettled he already is by her. She hates his job, she hates cattle ranching, she hates guns…but it's all just excuses. Her heart's where she left it, in the work she was doing in South America. No man in the world is ever going to be able to replace it. Colt hasn't figured that out yet. I hope he will, before he lets her ruin his life."

Clancey didn't know what to say. Which was just as well, because Tad came running into the room to see if his milk was ready. Miss Kitty and the kitten were right behind him.

"It's a parade," Clancey teased, smiling at her little brother.

"Aren't they cute?" he exclaimed. "Mr. Banks says that the kitten can stay here and I can come visit it and Miss Kitty whenever I want!"

"That's kind of you," Clancey said softly.

He grinned at her. "I'm very kind," he pointed out. "Not that you ever notice it. Nasturtium," he added deliberately.

THIRTEEN

"I AM NOT a Nasturtium," Clancey said belligerently.

"A likely story," he returned.

"What's a nas…nastu…?" Tad asked.

"Nasturtium," Banks told him as he reached for the coffeepot and poured himself a cup. "It's a flower."

"That's what Clancey's name means," Tad said. "Her whole name is Calanthé," he added. "It's Greek. It means pretty flower."

Banks looked surprised. Clancey flushed.

"It sounds like Clancey with a lisp," Tad chuckled.

"It suits her," Banks said after a minute, and his black eyes were quiet and intense as they met hers.

"I'm not pretty," Clancey said gruffly. She got up abruptly. "Is the tea ready?" she added, nervous. "I'll take mine back to bed with me, if that's okay."

"Of course it's okay," Brenda said, smiling. "Here. Do you want sugar in it?"

"No, thanks. I like it plain. Tad, ready to go back to bed?"

"You bet!" He looked up at Banks. "Is it okay if Miss Kitty and the kitten stay in my room?"

Banks chuckled. "Sure."

"I won't have nightmares if the kitties stay with me, I know I won't," he added.

"Just leave the door into the hall cracked. So they can get to their facilities if they need to," Banks added.

"Facil…facilit…?" Tad was struggling.

"The litter box," Banks whispered loudly.

"Oh!" Tad chuckled. "Okay. I will. Good night! Sorry I woke everybody up!"

He ran down the hall, with the cats pacing him.

"He's a good kid," Banks told Clancey. "You've done a great job with him."

"Thanks," she said. "I've done my best."

Brenda patted her on the shoulder. "He really is a good kid. I have to get back to sleep. I don't have to get up early, but I'll need to get him some breakfast before he leaves."

"I can cook," he said shortly. He studied Clancey. "But those biscuits were pretty good. I haven't had a biscuit like that since our mother was alive."

She felt a glow all over. "I could get up and cook you something. If you wanted me to," she added quickly, in case she sounded too forward.

"I'd like that. If you don't mind," he added in a husky, deep tone.

"I'd like that, too, because I can sleep late!" Brenda laughed. "Good night, then. Colt, you'll turn off the cof-feepot…?"

"Sure."

"Good night!"

They called good-night back, but neither of them moved.

Clancey felt as if she were rooted to the floor. Banks was feeling a similar inability to leave the room. He stared down at Clancey with black, glittery eyes in a face wiped clean of all expression. The only sound in Clancey's ears was the wild, heavy beat of her own heart and her quick, audible breathing.

She was violently aware of her state of dress, or undress. She was barefoot, just wearing sweatpants and a thick T-shirt that was, however, revealing. In fact those glittery black eyes were looking at it now, intently.

He took the teacup out of her hand and put it on the table beside them. One lean hand went into the hair at her ear. He bent, hesitantly, but she wasn't resisting. She seemed as spellbound as he felt.

Clancey's eyes closed helplessly as his hard, warm mouth settled gently on her lips. And then it was like the last time, outside her front door. Fire and fury. Storms. Lightning. An elemental response that brought them close together, with her soft body riveted to his hard one, her mouth drowning under the hungry expertise of his.

She moaned helplessly. His arms tightened. He lifted his head and looked down at her. He felt a shock of pleasure all the way to his toes as he felt her firm, taut young breasts pressed against his chest. Her mouth was slightly swollen, her pale gray eyes wide and intent on his.

"I shouldn't do this," he whispered, caressing her chin with his thumb.

She nodded.

He bent. "Or this," he added, lowering his mouth to hers in a long, sweet, tender kiss.

He lifted his head.

She nodded.

He smiled. "Are you listening to me?" he asked.

She nodded.

He chuckled and bent to pick her up, holding her tight in his arms as he kissed her hungrily one last time.

"Get your tea," he said, bending so that she could pick it up in its thick mug.

He started out of the room. "Get the light," he added softly, pausing to let her switch it off.

He carried her down the hall to her own room, the one just before Tad's. The door into her brother's room was oddly closed. But she wasn't paying a lot of attention. She felt warm and safe and shaken up, all at once.

He sat down on the side of the bed while she put her tea down. Then he turned her, and lowered her onto the tumbled sheets, sliding alongside her.

She stiffened, just at first.

"The door's open," he teased, indicating the hall door.

"Oh." She looked all at sea.

"Besides, my sister will have heard me come down the hall. About five minutes from now, she'll make a lot of noise coming out into the hall pretending to ask if you got your tea." He grinned at her expression. "She's got your best interests at heart."

"My best interests?" She was listening, but her eyes were on his hard, chiseled mouth. She was still hungry for it.

"Um-hmm." He bent, opening her lips under his while one lean hand snaked its way under her thick T-shirt.

Her hand caught his wrist instinctively. The eyes that met his were huge.

He just smiled. "It's part of the process," he whispered.

"The...process?"

He nodded. "You'll see."

His mouth was back on hers, hungry and slow and soft, and bit by bit she let go of his wrist and gasped when she felt his hand teasing around her soft breast. She thought about removing it. It was very intimate. But it was sweet heaven, kissing him, and his fingers were making her body sing a song it had never learned.

But his touch was ghostly. She wanted it where her body ached for it, and all he did was tease around that peaked rise that was desperate to feel it. Involuntarily, her young body twisted up, shivering, as she tried to get it where she wanted it.

And he knew, the beast. He was nice about it, not even snickering when he lifted his head and looked down at her. But he knew.

"You haven't done this," he said quietly.

She managed a slow shake of her head.

"Once we start, there's no going back," he said, his voice deep and slow. "It's a beginning."

Her slight brows slid together.

"You don't understand."

She sighed. "Not really," she confessed in a tone that sounded shaky and weak.

"You will, honey," he whispered. He bent again, so that his face filled her eyes. It went taut just as his hand slid tenderly over her naked breast and teased the hard peak. "Oh yes, you will."

It was the last coherent thought she had. Because in seconds, it was like flash fire, like lightning striking. She felt his hands moving the T-shirt up, felt the jolt of his body, so close to hers, as he looked down on her for the first time.

Her eyes opened. She had a quick glimpse of his taut, spellbound face as he studied her pretty, pink-tipped breasts. But then his head moved, and she felt his mouth open and take her soft little breast inside.

She couldn't have imagined the sound that weened its way out of her throat as he did that.

He laughed helplessly, even in thrall to the passion she kindled in him. He lifted his head. "Shhh," he whispered. "You'll raise the house."

She flushed. "Sorry."

"Oh, I'm not," he assured her with a wicked grin. "But it's not the sort of sound you really want to share with other people…" He grimaced. "Oh damn."

He sat up, jerked her T-shirt down and threw the sheet and cover over her just seconds before quick footsteps came down the hall.

A dark-haired woman peeked in the door. "Did you remember to get your tea?" Brenda asked a tousled, flushed Clancey. She only barely managed not to burst out laughing, because her brother seemed to be in a similar condition. She was delighted. Poor Grace!

"Yes, thank…you," Clancey stammered, and blushed even more.

"Yes, she did, and thank you very much, baby sister," Banks added with a hard glare.

"You're both very welcome. You going to bed now?" she added.

Banks looked at Clancey, grimaced and sighed. "I guess I am. Good night, Clancey."

"Good night. I'll make breakfast," she blurted out. "What time?"

"I get up at five."

She nodded. "Okay. Five."

He smiled tenderly and shooed Brenda out the door.

"Saint Brenda to the rescue," he grumbled as he walked toward his room.

"Now, now, she's like a saint herself, in some ways," Brenda chided.

He stopped and turned. "And am I the sort of man who starts anything with an innocent just for fun?"

She searched his black eyes. She smiled. She shook her head. "She's very special, our Clancey," she replied. "We can't let Morris get her."

"No way. I'm calling in everybody who owes me favors. She'll be safe. Here, at work, anywhere."

"This man, Hollister, who looks out for her," she began a little worriedly.

"Her big brother," he said, and he smiled. "He's looked after both of them for years. She worked for him before she worked for me."

"I see."

"You'd like him," he replied. "I hated his guts at first, of course, until I realized that he didn't have designs on Clancey..." He stopped dead, realizing that he'd given himself away.

But Brenda didn't tease him. "She's a lot like you," she said. "And she doesn't judge people the way Grace seems to these days."

He grimaced. "Grace isn't the woman I remember." He sighed. "The thought of her coming home was turning my life upside down. I thought it was all I wanted from life. And then I drove Clancey and Tad home from a movie just before Halloween." He averted his eyes. "She got pneumonia from walking with Tad to school and on to work in freezing cold without a proper coat. I took her to the hospital." He smiled wistfully. "It's been a long time since I had to take care of anybody besides you."

"She's frail, for all her fierceness," Brenda replied. "Morris must have been a horror to live with. She and Tad have had a challenging life."

"It's going to get better from here on out. Do you have plans for Thanksgiving?"

She shook her head.

"You can come down here." He drew in a rough breath. "I'll have to invite Hollister. If I don't, they'll feel obliged to go over to his place for it, because they promised."

"You just said he was nice."

"Well, he's nice as long as he thinks of Nasturtium in there as just a little sister," he added, and he wasn't smiling.

Brenda didn't laugh until she was in her room, with the door closed.

It wasn't daylight when Clancey, fully dressed, went into the kitchen to make breakfast for Colter.

She made biscuits and shot them into the oven before she started on bacon and eggs. He came into the kitchen yawning, just pulling on the long-sleeved white shirt he wore with dark pants.

She stopped in the middle of reaching for an egg and just stared at him. He was the most gorgeous thing she'd ever seen. Broad, muscular chest covered with thick, curling black hair, narrow waist, lean hips, long, powerful legs…

"What an expression," he mused with a chuckle. He

moved to her side, pulled her hands to his chest and pressed them there, enjoying her expression. Obviously, this was something new, as well. He loved first times with her. She brought out a tenderness in him that he'd rarely felt with any woman, even Grace.

"You're hairy," she whispered breathlessly.

"I noticed." He bent and brushed his mouth over hers. "I like kissing you, Clancey," he added softly.

She caught her breath. Her pale silver eyes looked up into his black ones. "I like kissing you, too," she confessed.

He drew in a breath and half lifted her against him. "I'm starving…"

The kitchen was quiet. There wasn't a sound except her quick breaths and the beat of his heart, unnaturally loud as his mouth settled on hers and opened just enough to make her gasp.

She felt a strange new throbbing in the lower part of her belly, something swollen and a little frightening. She stiffened, just enough that he noticed.

He lifted his head and met her eyes. "It's as natural as breathing," he whispered, anticipating what she was afraid to admit. "I have no plans to give it up. Just making you aware of my intentions," he added on a soft chuckle as he bent his head again and kissed her hungrily.

"You know, I haven't ever… I mean, I don't…" she faltered against his firm lips.

He lifted his head. His eyes were stormy, but full of affection. "You know me by now," he said quietly. "Am I the kind of man who'd take advantage of an innocent woman?"

"Oh, of course not," she replied immediately, and watched his eyes glimmer with some dark, deep affection.

"So stop worrying," he whispered against her mouth. "Come on and kiss me. I have to eat and finish dressing."

"I love you, undressed," she murmured and then flushed and laughed self-consciously at what she'd blurted out.

He grinned, pressing her hands closer to his broad, hair-roughened chest. "I'd love you the same way," he whispered. He removed her hands and kissed them before he let them fall. "But one of us has to be sensible. Breakfast. Please."

She laughed and went back to her cooking. But she felt newborn, elated beyond measure. Until they sat down to breakfast and she sipped coffee and suddenly worried about the future.

"Now what is it?" he teased, watching her expressions change.

"Morris," she sighed. "Colt, we can't…"

"What did you just call me?" he asked softly.

She went red. "Oh, sorry, I…"

"I love it," he replied solemnly. "That's the first time you've ever called me anything but 'mister.'"

"You don't mind?" she asked breathlessly, drowning in his black eyes.

"I don't mind," he reassured her.

She smiled. "Okay."

"So. What were you saying about Morris?" he asked, finishing his eggs and part of a biscuit.

"I have to go back to work Monday," she said miserably. "And Tad has to go back to school. We can't stay away forever."

"I'm getting that covered," he said with a smile. "Things will be in place Monday. Trust me."

"I do," she said. "With all my heart."

His own heart lifted. He loved the way she looked at him. Her eyes were as expressive as her pretty face. He grinned.

"Tomorrow, we're all going riding," he added.

She grinned. "I'll try not to fall off."

He chuckled. "If you do, honey, I'll catch you. I promise."

She beamed at that word. It made her feel warm all over; it filled all the empty places inside her.

He was feeling something similar. In the middle of a fervent exchange of eyes, his cell phone went off.

He grimaced as he saw the number displayed. He answered it. "Hello, Grace," he said, but not in any affectionate way.

Clancey started moving empty plates off the table and to the sink. Her heart sank as she overheard what he was saying to the woman who had first place in his heart. Had she totally mistaken his feelings? Was he just missing Grace and Clancey was handy?

"No, I'm sorry," he was saying, his eyes on Clancey's stiff spine. "Yes, I know it's important to you. But we have guests and we're taking them riding tomorrow. Another time, perhaps? Yes, I know you leave soon. I'll try to make time for lunch one day—how about that?" There was a pause. He grimaced. "Grace, there's nothing wrong with the way Brenda dresses. And I'll remind you that she goes to church every Sunday. Well, you're entitled to your own opinion. Just don't expect me to share it. Yes. Fine. I'll see you." He hung up. His expression was thunderous.

Clancey understood at once. "Brenda has pretty legs," she said shortly. "And if she wants to show them off, it doesn't make her a prostitute," she added curtly.

He laughed softly, his bad mood dissipating. "You're a tonic, honey. I was just getting irritable. You make everything so easy."

She smiled. "I love Brenda," she said. "She's been very kind to me."

"She loves you, too," came a mischievous voice from behind them. Brenda came in, hair tousled, robe fastened over long blue pajamas, yawning. "Oh boy, food, and I didn't have to cook it! Clancey, you're a wonder!"

Clancey laughed. "I love to cook."

"Was that Grace on the phone?" Brenda asked her brother as she sat down at the table and filled a plate.

He made a face. "It was." He fastened his shirt. "She has some of the most rigid beliefs," he added on a sigh.

"She loves her work," Clancey said simply. "It's more important to her than anything else. She feels needed." She sighed. "I think she sabotages relationships so that she can keep doing what she wants to do with her life."

Colter and Brenda exchanged amused looks.

"She's very nice," Clancey added nervously.

"So are you, pet," Brenda replied gently. "You look right at home in the kitchen."

"Thanks." She smiled gently. "I love it here."

"Yes, poor oppressed milk cows and all," Brenda teased. They all laughed.

COLTER FINISHED DRESSING and strapped on his gun belt before he stuck the big 1911 Colt .45 in the holster and pinned on his Ranger star.

"You look very nice," Clancey said softly when he cocked his white Stetson over one eye.

He smiled. "You're not bad yourself, kid," he teased, eyeing her spotless white T-shirt and jeans that outlined a beautiful figure.

His phone rang. Again. He pulled it out and scowled. "Banks," he said abruptly. He listened, made a face, glanced worriedly at Clancey. "Yes, I'll be right there. Are they badly injured? Thank God. On my way."

He hung up. "It's the Martins," he said, anticipating Clancey's anxious expression. She'd gone to church with them for years. They were elderly, and Mr. Martin was crippled. "Someone roughed them up, trying to find you and Tad."

"Morris," Clancey said miserably. "It had to be Morris! Oh, the poor things! They've been so kind to us." She choked on tears. "Will they be all right? And what if Morris comes back?"

He put his big hands on her shoulders. "I'll handle it," he said softly.

It was all he had to say. She looked up at him through a faint mist, but with perfect trust. "Okay," she replied.

Brenda, watching them, had to hide a smile. They were already like two halves of a whole. Not that she didn't share Clancey's concern for the Martins, who went to church with them. They were kind people.

"Are you going in today?" Colter asked Brenda.

"No. I've got the day off."

"Miles is in the bunkhouse. Billings is in position some damned where, he won't say where, with a sniper rifle. We're pretty much covered here, but you can call Sheriff

Hayes Carson if anything happens while I'm gone," he added grimly.

"We'll be all right," Brenda said quietly. "I promise we will."

"Okay." He looked down at Clancey, bent with a smile and kissed her tenderly. "I'll see you later."

Clancey flushed. It was the first time he'd kissed her right in front of his sister. It was, in fact, a statement of intent that she totally missed. She just smiled. "Okay."

He chuckled, called a quick goodbye to his sister and went out the door.

"Gosh," was all Clancey could manage.

"Gosh, indeed," Brenda laughed. "And here I've been worried to death that Grace was going to get her sweet hooks into him and remake him into Mike Johns."

She turned from the sink where she was soaking dirty dishes. "Mike Johns?" she asked.

"Grace's fiancé. She turned his life upside down. He was killed off duty in a bank robbery. He was a Houston police officer. Grace was trying to get him away from a job he loved because she didn't approve of guns. She'd already started on Colt the minute she got back into town." She smiled gently. "I'm sorry you got sick, Clancey, but I'm very glad at the same time. Grace was the last thing he needed. He was stuck in the past with her. You brought him into the present when he had to take you to the hospital and then look after you and Tad."

"He's...very masculine," Clancey said. "And very nice."

"I think so," Brenda laughed. "Although I have to admit to some prejudice."

She poured herself another cup of coffee, warmed

Brenda's and sat down at the table. "I hope the Martins aren't badly hurt," she said worriedly. "I'm really fond of them. So is Tad."

Brenda put a gentle hand over hers. "They've been good to you. I love them, too. They'll be all right. And Morris will trip himself up sooner or later. He can't get to you. So he may try to get to the assistant DA. That will be the biggest mistake of his life."

"Yes, it will, because that will involve Cal Hollister. He has some really shady friends," she added on a laugh.

"You're fond of him," Brenda noted.

"Very fond. When I worked for him, he sort of adopted me and Tad. He's like the big brother I never had."

"Colt's jealous of him—did you know?"

She grinned helplessly. "I noticed." She sighed. "I was jealous of Grace. I mean, she's really a good person. Lots better than me. I was afraid he was going to marry her."

"So was I," Brenda confessed. "But I don't think that's going to be a concern ever again," she added with a wicked smile at Clancey.

Clancey, glowing with feeling, just laughed.

THE MARTINS HAD been taken to the emergency room. Mrs. Martin was only shaken, but Mr. Martin had been roughed up to the point of a sprained arm.

Colter was outraged on their behalf. Mr. Martin knew Morris and at least two of his cohorts, and he could pick them out in a lineup, he assured Colter. They were after Clancey and Tad. Even if he'd known where they were— and he didn't—he'd never have given them up, he added.

Colter took a steadying breath, one big, lean hand resting idly on the butt of his Colt .45 in its hand-tooled leather holster. "We need to put both of you in a safe house for the time being," he told the elderly couple. "Morris will know that you'll likely be willing to testify against him. He's vindictive."

"My sister lives in Baton Rouge," Mr. Martin said. "We could go there for a few days, or a couple of weeks, until you need us to testify." He hesitated. "But even if he's arrested for assault, you know, he could get out on bail."

"That's unfortunately true," Colter said solemnly. "Besides that, flying or taking a train or car to Baton Rouge is a bad idea in your physical condition," he added to Mr. Martin.

The elderly man smiled whimsically. "In my youth, I taught Tae Kwon Do. I was a twelfth-degree black belt, in fact." He shook his head. "Old age gets more dangerous all the time. But what about Clancey and Tad?" he added worriedly.

"They're safe. Morris would need a small army just to get to them," he added with a smile.

"Thank goodness," Mrs. Martin said. She put a hand on her husband's shoulder. "Mr. Banks, I hope you can do something about this wild young man. He almost killed Tad, you know. Poor Clancey didn't fare much better. It's such a shame about her grandfather. The not knowing, you see."

"I do see," Colter replied. "People with missing children go through the same agony."

"Funny about that antique gun Clancey's grandfather owned," Mr. Martin said. "He showed it to me once. It had a long history in his family, passed down from lawman to lawman." He frowned. "Clancey said it went missing about the same time her grandfather did. Morris wouldn't have dared sell it, the thing was so rare and valuable. But then, if you can't find the body, the gun would do you no good, would it?"

Colter sighed. "Not much, no."

"Pity we don't have one of those psychics here," Mrs. Martin said whimsically. She touched her husband's hair. "When I was sixteen, a fortune-teller told me who I'd marry and when. I just laughed. But everything she told me came true, right down to his initials and the scar on his left knee."

Colter frowned. He was remembering something he'd heard from one of the local lawmen, about a man named Dalton Kirk, up in Wyoming, whose wife had something of a reputation for knowing things she shouldn't.

"You know," he said after a minute, "that isn't a half-bad idea."

"Do you know somebody who has that ability?" Mrs. Martin asked.

"In fact," he replied with a smile, "I think I do. Thanks for the suggestion." He added that he was going to put them under immediate protection as material witnesses in a possible murder case. That would involve federal marshals, and even Morris wouldn't be crazy enough to go up against those guys. He made the call before he left the hospital and was assured that an agent would be on his way over before the Martins ever left the area.

HE FOUND LIEUTENANT RICK MARQUEZ in the middle of a staff meeting, so he lingered around the hall until the meeting was over.

Marquez grinned at him. "Loitering is prohibited."

"I'm not loitering. I'm investigating your floors to see if anybody dropped pocket change in the cracks."

Marquez burst out laughing. "No chance. It would be snapped up before you could reach for it. We're all un-derfunded and underpaid in law enforcement, but we do the job because we love it."

"All true."

"So, what can I do for you?" he asked, leading Colter into his office.

"We had an assault on a material witness today. Mor-ris Duffy and a couple of his cohorts burst into a home owned by the Martins and roughed the old man up pretty good. I persuaded the Martins to take out a warrant for Duffy's arrest, for assault."

"Why did Duffy and his friends attack the Martins?" Marquez asked.

"Because Duffy's trying to locate his stepbrother, as well as the stepsister whose testimony put him in jail for five years," he said simply. "He's also a suspect in the dis-appearance of the stepsister's grandfather, Dalton Reed, five years ago."

"They're Clancey's relatives," Marquez said, making the connection. "Are she and her little brother safe?"

He nodded. "They're staying at the ranch with me. Morris won't get within binocular distance, even if he finds out where they are. I've got Chet Billings some-where on the property with a sniper kit."

Marquez let out a whistle. "Billings was up here with Rourke during a similar case, helping protect a vet's as-sistant, Cappie Drake, from Jacobsville whose brother was assaulted by her former boyfriend. The perp threatened Cappie, too. You might know her. She's married to Dr. Bentley Rydel."

"Miss Kitty, my cat, is Bentley's patient," he said with a grin. "I know Cappie. Her brother recovered nicely from the assault, even managed to walk again after surgery. He's a tactics expert in a group of international mercs headed by a man named Bojo. They're good people."

"So I've heard. I remember Billings, however. Smokes like a furnace. I would have asked him not to, but a lot of high buildings overlook my living room window," he added with a chuckle.

"He does have a bit of an attitude problem. Expert marksman, however."

"Indeed. What about the Martins?"

"I asked the local US Marshal's office for help. The Martins are potential witnesses in a murder case. Morris Duffy was, apparently, the last person to see Dalton Reed alive. The man had an antique Colt .45 in an equally antique holster, worth a lot of money for its history alone. The gun went missing along with its owner. I think the Martins may be able to help us pinpoint some connections. They've known Clancey and Tad for years. I don't want them to go missing."

"Neither do I. Are they going to be staying at their own house?"

"They'll have to. Mr. Martin's in no condition to travel. Marshals are sending an agent to stay with them."

"Give me the address," Marquez said, reaching for the notes app on his cell phone. "I'll put on extra patrols, as well."

"Thanks for the help."

"Oh, it will help me, too. Darrell Tarley wants Morris

really badly, after the death threats he made. Since Darrell is running for DA in the next election, he's going to use the case as a platform." He pursed his lips and smiled. "Not a bad idea. It might help us."

"Indeed it might." He checked his watch. "I've got to report to my boss and tell him what's going on. I had Clancey and Tad stay at the ranch today, so I'll have to handle the office by myself."

"Just put a big sign on your door that reads Out to Lunch, and don't go back."

"Wasn't it you who came up with that idea about traffic improvement?" Colter asked suspiciously.

"It was," Marquez agreed. "I suggested that we make all the roads and streets one way only, leading out of town." He smiled.

Colter just shook his head and laughed.

FOURTEEN

"THERE WAS ONE other thing, before I go," Colter told Marquez.

"Shoot."

"A man named 'Tank' Kirk who lives up in Wyoming is married to a woman who has, well you might call them visions," he began. "My cousin is sheriff up near Catelow, where the Kirks live, but he's out of the state on a case and I can't call him about her."

"That would be Merissa," Marquez replied at once. "We all know about her. She helped us solve the case of another assistant DA who was murdered. We solved it with a designer watch and a couture shirt, both stolen from the victim. She put it all together and told us how to find him."

"Amazing ability," Colter said. "Do you think she'd talk to me?"

"I'm sure she would." He pulled out his cell phone, wrote down a telephone number and handed it to Colter. "She won't mind." He chuckled. "In fact, she'll probably be expecting the call even before you make it."

Colter sighed. "If I could find that gun and gun belt, I'll bet you a nickel I could find the body of Clancey's grandfather. If Morris was afraid to try to sell the gun, it's probably with the body."

"Nice deduction," Marquez replied. "But that would be a long shot. The body's been missing for, what—five years?" He grimaced. "You'll need a forensic archaeologist if you find anything."

"I know where to find one of those, too," Colter chuckled. "So it's not a lost cause. Not yet." He got up and indicated the phone number on the slip of paper. "Thanks."

"No problem. Good luck."

HE STOPPED BY his superior's office to tell him what was going on with Clancey and made sure she was excused from work for the day without any penalty. He also outlined the case concerning Morris and his assault on the Martins, who could identify the missing gun and gun belt and who might have other information about Clancey's grandfather's sudden disappearance.

Then he went to his own office and phoned Merissa Kirk.

"Hello, Mr. Banks," she said in a soft, gentle voice. "How can I help you?"

He drew in a breath. He hadn't told her his name; he'd just asked for her and another woman had called her to the phone.

"I have a missing man…" he began.

"Yes," she interrupted, her voice changing just slightly. "Dalton Reed. He was a sheriff's deputy until he retired. He disappeared five years ago. There's a young man. The deputy was his stepsister's grandfather. Oh…the young man did terrible things to his stepsister and stepbrother. He went to prison?"

"Yes," he returned, spellbound.

"There's a deserted church. He hates churches, that's why he chose this one. It sits off the road between San Antonio and that little town Tank went to, when he was being stalked by a killer. What was it called? Jacobsville, yes, that's it. It's in a grove of pecan trees. There's a crooked log fence and an old well that sits in front of a burned-down house that's on the way to the church. The gun and gun belt are there, but he wants to sell them. He thinks it's safe now, so long from the crime. The poor old man's body is there, under the boards, near the altar." She stopped and sighed heavily. "I'm sorry. That's all I have. It comes and goes…"

"That's more than I had, much more. I can't thank you enough."

"You're more than welcome. And congratulations."

"Excuse me?"

There was a smile in her voice. "She's very sweet, your assistant. She loves you very much."

"She does?" There was a catch in his voice.

"Oh yes. But watch out for her," she added. "There's something—I can't see what. Keep close to her."

"I'll do that," he said huskily. "Thanks!"

"Oh, and that man you have watching her, the one with the rifle… I'm so sorry. He's going to have to use it. Desperate men do desperate things. He's already said he's not going back to jail. When you find the body, he'll know that it's all over for him. But your sharpshooter will not miss."

"Mrs. Kirk, you are…"

"A witch?' she teased and laughed wholeheartedly. "Yes, but I'm a good witch and I don't curdle milk."

"I would never have accused you of it, even if I was drinking buttermilk right now."

She laughed again, delighted. "If I think of anything else that might help, I'll phone you, if I may?"

"You certainly may. One last thing," he added quickly. "There are two elderly people, the Martins…"

"He won't bother them again. There's a federal agent with them. He's very…imposing," she said. "Honestly, if I were a career criminal, I'd think twice about going into the same room with him, even armed. They'll be fine."

He laughed. "I'm reassured now. Thanks again."

"It's no problem at all."

HE FINISHED HIS work for the day and stopped by to check on the Martins on his way out of town.

The man who answered the door was tall and husky, with broad shoulders and a face that seemed chiseled out of stone. He had wavy black hair and pale gray eyes, and he was carrying a .357 magnum in a holster at his waist.

"You'd be the deputy US Marshal?" Colter asked. "I'm Colter Banks, Texas Rangers."

They shook hands. "McLeod," the agent introduced himself. He stood aside to let Colter inside.

He found the Martins in their living room, with all the blinds and curtains drawn. Mr. Martin was lying on the sofa, in obvious pain. Mrs. Martin was trying to coax him into eating something.

"Didn't they give him anything for pain?" Colter asked.

Mrs. Martin grimaced. "All these drug dealers helping addicts to an early death, so the government has to try to stop an opioid epidemic. But people who are suffering chronic, terrible pain are paying their price. Even some people with terminal cancer can't get painkillers because the doctors are afraid of losing their jobs if they prescribe any pain medicine at all. It's such a shame," she said, wincing as she saw her poor husband trying to get comfortable. "What a world we live in!"

"Well, it's the only one we've got," Colter said with a gentle smile. "So we just have to soldier on."

She laughed. She turned back to her husband. "I made you some chamomile tea, sweetheart. It's not as good as a pain capsule, but it will help a little. Come on, now."

"Torment," her husband teased. "All right, I'll drink it." He glanced at Colter. "Any leads?"

"In fact, I've got a good one. I can't mention where I got it, but it's something I'm going to check out." He moved closer. "Did Clancey's grandfather ever mention an old church, by any chance…?"

"Well, yes," Mr. Martin said after a minute, frowning. "He was baptized there when he was a boy. He said he liked to stop there once in a while and walk around. It was a peaceful place. His wife was buried in the cemetery. I think he went there to visit her."

Colter's heart leaped. "Do you know where it was?"

"Somewhere down around Jacobsville, is what he said," Mr. Martin replied, wincing as he moved. "On a farm road. I think he called it the Victoria Road. It ran by a roadhouse where he liked to stop for a beer after work."

"Shea's," Colter said, nodding.

"That sounds like what he said," the older man agreed.

"If you're going out there, better take backup," the fed said quietly.

Colter turned, curious.

"They told me about the boy and his family." He indicated the Martins. "If he's got the *cajones* to threaten an assistant DA and kidnap a small child, he won't stop at murdering a lawman."

"I suppose you're right."

"I lost a partner who thought it was going to be perfectly safe to check out a potential crime scene. It was broad daylight. He walked into an ambush. There were three of them. He was shot twenty times."

Colter grimaced. "I lost a partner in a similar fashion some years back. It never hurts to be cautious, I agree."

The big man nodded. "Meanwhile, I'm going to teach Mr. Martin here the finer points of draw poker."

"I don't need teaching, young man. I'll bet I can beat you," he added with a grin.

"Not likely."

"I could draw a royal diamond flush," the older man chuckled.

"Yeah? Well, I could match that with two deuces and a .357 magnum," he replied, stone-faced.

They all laughed. Even the fed.

COLTER HADN'T PLANNED to take anyone with him to look for the old church, and Mrs. Kirk hadn't even suggested it. But he thought the fed might have a point. He made a call before he left the city.

On the way out of town, he went slowly by Morris's house. There were lights on inside it, although it wasn't dark yet. He heard loud music and drunken voices. Poor Clancey and Tad. Had it been like that when they had to live with Morris? He recalled what the Martins had said, and he felt sick at his stomach. There was no telling just what Clancey'd had to put up with. Well, Morris wasn't going to hurt her ever again, or Tad, either. He'd make sure of it.

He wasn't aware of a curtain moving as he sped up, or a conversation that led three men outside to a car.

THE CHURCH WAS on the Victoria Road back in a grove of pecan trees, just as Merissa Kirk had described it. Colter got out of the SUV and closed his eyes. He used his hearing often when he tracked animals and men. In a quiet place, even the snap of a twig was loud.

He listened but he didn't hear a thing. Until he was tapped on the shoulder and almost jumped out of his skin.

"How do you do that?" he demanded as Reverend Jake Blair came up beside him.

"Long years of practice. I wasn't always a minister," he added with a mysterious smile.

"Have you seen anyone around here?"

"Not yet. But there's an old blue Chevy back on the highway that keeps going up and down the road. It hasn't seen me. I've certainly seen it, however. I imagine your being here is provoking some interest." He didn't add that the car might have been following Banks down here.

"I had a tip. It may lead to the solving of a five-year-old murder," Colter replied.

"Hence the curious Chevy," the reverend replied.

Banks's eyes narrowed. "I went by Morris Duffy's house on the way out of town. If he knew my SUV from my visit with the Martins, he might have recognized it and followed me."

"I thought about that myself," Jake said.

"This could be dangerous," Colter began.

The reverend pulled his jacket back over a deadly looking combat knife. "I don't kill people. But I can wound them, in a good cause," he added with a grin. "Come on."

"I did phone Cash Grier," Colter said.

"He's in Houston at a workshop," the minister replied. "My daughter works for him, so she heard your message on the answering machine."

"Now I get it."

"Let's get to this."

THEY WALKED INTO the deserted church. The front doors would close, barely, but with gaps. Colter had his tire tool with him. The curved end would be good to use if he had to pry up boards.

"What a shame, to see a piece of history like this just allowed to decay," Colter murmured.

"It truly is. This was the first church ever organized in Jacobs County, too," Jake Blair said. "I need to get a fund going to restore it."

"Not a bad idea."

Colter walked up toward the altar. His foot met no resistance on one of the boards. He exchanged a long look with Jake. He knelt and started pulling up boards.

CLANCEY WAS SITTING with Tad in the dining room, playing checkers on a board Brenda had found for them. Brenda was on her cell phone, texting a friend.

Clancey had something on her mind. It was her grandfather, and the gun belt and the old Colt .45 that he wore in the holster. Her grandfather had a favorite spot where he liked to visit when he had time off. He'd taken Clancey and Tad with him a time or two. It was an old, deserted church, near the Banks ranch.

Her hand stilled on the checker she was about to move. "Tad, do you remember the church Granddaddy took us to? The one where Grandma was buried. He used to go see her there."

"I remember. We went with him sometimes," Tad replied.

She frowned, her mind not really on the checker pieces. "It was an old church, falling apart. It's not far from here, either." Her heart skipped. "It would be like Morris to pick a spot like that if he was going to kill somebody..."

Tad's face tautened. "You mean, he might have killed Granddaddy there."

"He might have." She stopped and picked up her phone to call Colter.

But he'd cut his phone off when he and Jake reached the church, in case Morris or any of his friends were nearby and heard it ringing at an inopportune time. She phoned Cal, but he wasn't in his office. In desperation, she called the Martins.

Mr. Martin himself answered. "Clancey," he said when she spoke. "Are you and Tad all right?"

"We're fine, Mr. Martin. How are you and Mrs. Martin?" she asked.

"We're a little shaken, but we're okay. Mr. Banks found an agent to stay with us, in case Morris turns up."

"Oh thank goodness," she exclaimed. "I've been so worried about you. I'm sorry you got dragged into this mess."

"It will be worth it if Mr. Banks can find evidence of your grandfather's murder. I told him about the church where your grandfather said he used to go see your grandmother, in the cemetery. He was going out there on his way home. He's just been gone a few minutes. We all told him to take backup, so don't worry," he added.

"Thanks so much. Was it that old church on the Victoria Road, here in Jacobs County?" she asked.

"Yes, in fact it was…"

"I'll talk to you both soon. Thanks!"

She hung up. Her whole body felt tight and shaky. Morris was a past master at setting people up. Colter was very good at his job, and he might have backup, but Morris had several friends. What if they'd seen Colter leave the Martin house and followed him to that old church? Morris would have absolutely nothing to lose if Colter found evidence of a murder there. It was the sort of place Morris would have picked if he'd planned to kill her grandfather.

She stood up. Her first impulse was to go rushing over there, to make sure Colter was okay. But she had no car, and she wasn't reckless enough to put Brenda in the line of fire.

"How can we get in touch with that sniper Colter has on the place?" she asked worriedly.

Brenda's eyes widened. "The sniper?"

"Yes. His name is Billings, isn't it?"

"I think so. I don't know how to contact him."

"Who does he work for?"

"Eb Scott, I think," Brenda said. "Why? What's going on?"

"Colter was going by the old church where Granddaddy used to visit Grandma's grave, at a deserted church on the Victoria Road. Mr. Martin said he was on the way there now. If Morris and his gang follow him…!"

"Listen, it's okay," Brenda said softly. "Colt can take care of himself. He's a good lawman, and a terrific shot."

"Morris won't come at him head-on," she said stubbornly. "He'll do it from hiding, like the coward he is. Who can get in touch with Mr. Billings?"

Brenda got up, concerned now. "I'll call Eb Scott," she said. She pulled up the numbers on her keypad and dialed—fortunately for both of them, Eb was one of the people Colter kept on both their lists in case of an emergency.

The phone rang and rang. Clancey chewed on a fingernail while Tad sat by worried and unsettled.

Finally, a deep voice answered. "Scott."

"Mr. Scott, it's Brenda Banks," she said. "One of your men, Mr. Billings, is over here at the ranch with a sniper rifle, protecting us from our houseguest's stepbrother. Colt's on his way to a deserted church where we think he may be ambushed..."

"Where is it?" Eb asked at once.

She told him. "We understand he's probably there now."

"I'll take care of it. Try not to worry." He hung up.

"He's going to take care of it," Brenda said on a relieved sigh. "Thank goodness!"

Clancey was still chewing on a fingernail. She wanted more than anything to go to the church. But that was insane. She could walk into an ambush herself, be taken captive by Morris and used to put Colter in danger. She couldn't bear the thought of anything happening to him.

Brenda put an arm around her. "It's going to be all right. Trust me."

She looked up at the other woman. "The light would go out of the world..." she began, and swallowed, hard. Tears threatened.

"Sometimes all we have is faith," Brenda reminded her.

Clancey took a deep breath. "Yes," she said, and felt herself calming.

"He won't get hurt, will he?" Tad asked, joining them.

Clancey wrapped him up tight. "He won't get hurt," she said, with more conviction than she felt.

MEANWHILE, COLTER AND JAKE had pried up enough boards to disclose what was very obviously a collection of human bones. Some had been scattered, probably by foraging animals. The victim was clothed in casual clothes—khaki pants and a white shirt and belt and boots. The dry area had left him more mummy than corpse.

Beside him, nearby, was a suitcase. After documenting the crime scene with photos from his cell phone, he opened the suitcase, sad at the thought that any fingerprints would have long since deteriorated. Inside it was a pristine gun belt with a holster and an antique Colt .45.

"Pay dirt," Colter told Jake. "We need to get the crime lab out here with all their…"

"No need for that," a sarcastic voice interjected from the back door of the church. Three armed men stood just inside the doorway. One of them was Morris Duffy, obviously high as a kite, with two other men backing him.

Jake and Colter exchanged glances. This was a situation they could handle, but it was going to take some finesse. It could also go either way. Colter thought of Clancey and how tragic it was going to be if he were killed here.

"You thought you'd hide my stepbrother and stepsister, and all your worries would be over, didn't you, lawman?" Morris drawled, advancing with the small pistol in his hand pointed straight at Colter's stomach. "Well, two can play at that game. We had the Martins' house bugged while they were at the hospital. We heard everything you said."

"How enterprising," Colter drawled.

Morris glared at him. "You had no business interfering," he snapped. "But it doesn't matter anymore. We'll just cover up what you found, dispose of you and your friend, and then I'll even up with Clancey and that stupid assistant district attorney."

"You don't kill a Texas Ranger and get away with it," Colter said quietly. "They'll hunt you down like a dog."

"I'll be out of the country long before they can find me. I got it all planned. That gun and gun belt are going to buy me safe passage out of Texas." He indicated them, lying on the floor.

"I wouldn't bet on that."

"Who's your friend?" Morris asked, glancing at Jake. "Isn't he that Methodist minister?" he added.

"Yes, I am," Jake said. He even smiled. "You might benefit from a few hours a week in church."

"Church," Morris spat. "What good is that in the world? Nobody believes in fairy tales any longer!"

"God is no fairy tale," Jake said with quiet conviction. "And anybody can be forgiven and saved, even at the end of the line."

Morris burst out laughing. "Hear that, guys? I can be saved at the very end!"

They laughed, too.

Colter was thinking of ways and means of dealing with the three, who were less than sober. "Lieutenant Marquez in San Antonio knows I'm here," Colter said calmly.

"Well, it won't do him any good, because you're about to disappear, just like that meddling old man did. I spent five years in prison on account of his stupid granddaughter and my even stupider baby brother. Somebody's going to pay for that!"

"Pay for it yourself," Colter said icily. "It was your crime, not theirs."

"Stupid little kid, pitching a tantrum when I was just about through the worst scenario I ever played. I was winning, and he had to start screaming. I told him to shut up—I even shook him, but he wouldn't stop. He wouldn't stop! Anybody would have hit him!"

"With a steel shovel," Colter recalled.

Morris looked briefly disconcerted from the way Colter was looking at him. "Well, it doesn't matter now. Jon, Harry, find a good place to plant these two somewhere nearby. Get out those shovels we bought, too."

"Sure thing," one of the men returned. They both left.

Morris still had the gun on Colter and Jake. "Any famous last words? Something tender for my idiot sister, maybe? I hear you're sweet on her."

"I am."

"Pity it will come to nothing." Morris glowered at him. "Five years in hell, all because little miss purity couldn't keep her mouth shut! Everything would have been fine if she hadn't spilled her guts to that police officer!"

"Clancey didn't beat up herself or Tad," Colter said icily.

"Five years of hell," Morris repeated. "Five long years! You don't know what it's like inside!"

"I know," Colter said, and he smiled.

Morris's hand clenched on the handgun. His eyes glittered with pure hatred.

"Boss, we dug a grave out here." One of Morris's men stuck his head in the door. "We need more than one?"

"Nah," Morris said. "We'll just chuck them both in together. No need to waste space. You got it in a concealed place?"

"You bet, in between a couple of trees where there's bushes. Real sandy place."

"Fine." Morris moved back, to make sure he wasn't jumped, because his two prisoners looked dangerous. "Okay, you two, out back." He gestured with his head.

It looked as though time might have run out for them, Colter thought, and it made him sad that Jake Blair had become involved. The man did so much good in the community. His son-in-law was a physician, his daughter worked for the chief of police. They were a tight family, and now there was a little boy, a grandson. If Jake died, Colter would never get over the guilt. On the other hand, he wasn't ready to die. And if there was even a slim chance, he was going to take it.

He glanced at Jake and saw the same cold resolve in the other man's eyes.

"Once we take care of you two, I'm going after Clancey," Morris said. "I have plans for her. Real plans. And even worse ones for that stupid kid who climbed out the window and ran away. I'll get them all, every one!"

Colter felt really angry now. If he failed, he doomed the three people most dear to him in the world, because Brenda was there with Clancey and Tad. No way would Morris spare Brenda. She'd be a witness to what he planned for his stepsister and little stepbrother.

They walked out into the sunlight, with Morris still pointing the pistol at them. He glanced to one side just long enough to see that the grave had been dug, and the shovels and mound of dirt were waiting.

He stepped back another couple of feet, just to make sure the men wouldn't have a chance to rush him. He smiled sarcastically. "Turn around," he said curtly. "Let's see you beg for your lives."

"In your dreams, Duffy," Colter said simply.

"Same song, second chorus," Jake replied, nodding.

Morris glowered. "Well, it doesn't matter. I can always tell Clancey that you begged for your life, with tears in your eyes. Boo hoo."

"You know, you really should make sure of your surroundings before you attempt a murder," Colter said, having seen just a bare flash of sunlight off a rifle barrel, missed by his companions.

"Oh? Why's that?" Morris asked carelessly as he raised the pistol to the level of Colter's chest.

A shot rang out.

Morris looked stunned. He just stood there, with blood suddenly gushing from his throat. He grabbed at it, but he was bleeding out at a phenomenal rate.

"Oh my God," one of his cohorts exclaimed, running to him. "Morris, Morris, can you hear me?" He looked up at the other men. "We have to get an ambulance!"

"Who shot him?" the other cohort yelled, looking all around for another gun.

Jake took him down in a heartbeat, with no warning whatsoever.

Colter had the other man on his feet and cuffed in the same time frame.

"Morris will die if we don't get help!" the last man exclaimed.

After taking their guns and cuffing them, Colter turned back to Morris and went on one knee to examine him. "The bullet hit the carotid artery," he said, rising. "No power on earth can save him now."

Morris managed a laugh. "At least… I won't…go back…" He turned his head and died.

Colter got on his cell phone and called for assistance. Minutes later he had an ambulance, the coroner, the crime scene unit, and half the lawmen in Jacobs and surrounding counties.

Into this mixture, strolled Chet Billings, with his sniper rifle slung over one broad shoulder. He was pale, but otherwise unmoved.

"I owe you my life," Colter said simply, shaking hands.

"Me, too." Jake returned the gesture. "I loathe the taking of a life, but that man would have scored two if you hadn't acted. However, I do feel for you. I know how it is, to throw down on another human being," he added softly.

"Thanks," Chet sighed. "It's never easy, having to do that."

Colter frowned. "What are you doing over here?" he asked.

"Brenda called Eb Scott and told me where you were," he said simply. "Clancey was very upset when she couldn't reach you. She phoned the Martins and they told her where you were going. Smart lady," he added. "She figured it all out."

"Smart, indeed," Colter had to agree. He felt warm inside that Clancey had been upset enough to send the troops in.

"Uh, I might just mention that I'm available for weddings," Jake said in a low whisper.

Colter laughed. "I'll keep you in mind. I think that's going to be the next thing on my agenda. Meanwhile, thanks for the backup."

"Anytime."

FIFTEEN

CLANCEY WAS ALMOST climbing the walls. There had been no calls or texts on either her cell phone or Brenda's. Brenda had tried to phone Eb Scott again, but he wasn't answering. Neither was Colter. What if he'd been killed, or badly wounded? Wouldn't somebody call to tell them? Brenda, like Clancey, was chewing her nails. The waiting was horrible.

An hour went by and then another hour. Just when she was ready to throw caution to the winds and ask Brenda to drive her to the old church, she heard an SUV drive up outside.

She went running out, blind and deaf and dumb to anything except Colter's dark, handsome face. She changed direction and ran straight into his arms, to be swept close and kissed to within an inch of her life.

"Did you arrest him? Morris, I mean?" she asked worriedly. Because she knew, as he did, that many men were released on their own recognizance. If that happened, Morris would throw caution to the winds and come after her and Tad with a vengeance. She'd have to worry about Tad even more…

But before her mind could torture her anymore, Banks wrapped her up in strong, warm arms and just stood rocking her.

"Morris?" she whispered into his chest.

"Dead," he said quietly.

She lifted her head and her pale silver eyes were tormented. "Dead?"

"He had Jake Blair and me at gunpoint. His men had dug a single grave and he was at the point of killing us. Chet Billings blew him away, not a minute too soon, I might add."

"God bless Chet Billings," she said fervently.

He hugged her close again. It had been a tragic day, almost a fatal one. He'd thought about dying many times in his life, but this was truly the closest he'd ever come. The thought of never seeing Clancey again had flashed through his mind while Morris taunted him and Jake Blair. He knew that Jake was thinking about his daughter, Carlie, and his new grandchild that he might never see again. Nothing ever looked as big as the barrel of a gun when it was pointed at you. He could still feel the fear. He hated it, hated his own helplessness against it. At the same time, he mourned for Morris. The boy, with the right parents, might have turned out totally different. It was a damned shame.

"We'd better go tell Tad," Clancey said, drawing back. "I'm sorry that Morris was the way he was," she added quietly. "Except for what happened today, Tad and I might be the ones dead."

"Yes," Colter replied. His chest rose and fell deeply. He was still in a sort of fog from the standoff. "We found your grandfather," he added gently. "Morris had buried him under the planks at the altar of the old church."

Tears stung her eyes. She'd been expecting it for five years, but during that time she'd had hope that maybe her grandfather had just lost his memory, that he'd been carried off somewhere and hadn't found his way home. They were illogical hopes, but they'd kept her going.

Now she had proof that he was really dead. It was so unfair. He'd been a kind, gentle man. *Why?* she asked. "Why?" she moaned aloud.

Colter dried her tears with a handkerchief. "Nobody understands why criminals do such horrible things. Hundreds, thousands of books have been written about motivation, DNA, upbringing. But in the end, it's still mostly a mystery, even to people in the criminal justice system who've dealt with them for years."

"My grandfather was such a good man," she choked.

He hugged her close in his strong, warm arms and rocked her in the silence of the front porch, broken only by the distant lowing of cows and the snuffling sounds the horses made in the nearby corral.

A minute later, the front door flew open and Brenda and Tad came out. "Mr. Banks!" he exclaimed. "You're okay!" He ran to the big man, to be picked up and hugged. Tad held on for dear life.

Brenda hugged him, too, and stood back with Clancey, sighing with relief.

Tad's eyes were red. "They said you went after Morris. You sure you're okay?" he added, fighting tears as he pulled back enough to see the tall man's face.

"I'm okay." He smiled. The boy's affection was obvious. It made him feel good. The way Clancey was looking at him felt good, too. He drew in a steadying breath. It was going to be all right. Everything was going to be all right. THERE WAS NO way to identify Deputy Sheriff Dalton Reed's body except by a forensic archaeologist. There was one in San Antonio, who showed up at the crime lab in time for the autopsy. Colter was there as well, along with Alice Mayfield Fowler, the head criminalist for the forensic unit.

"Did you know him?" Alice asked as they proceeded.

"Yes," Colter said. "Not well. I heard him play the guitar at a retirement dinner some years ago. His granddaughter, Clancey, has the same skill. She plays classical guitar."

"Your sister, Brenda, noted that on her Facebook page," Alice mused. "She said Clancey could give you a run for your money."

"She really could," Colter said. "But I play country."

"Guitar is guitar," she said.

"Not at all. The guitar I play has steel strings. Clancey's has nylon. The playing styles are different, as well."

"Hmm," Alice said. Her eyes were on the delicate work the forensic archaeologist was doing.

"How long had the body been missing?" the archaeologist, Den Mitchell by name, asked as he worked.

"Five years, more or less," Colter told him.

"Explains the desiccation," he murmured. He moved aside a piece of parchment-like tissue to reveal a large hole, right where the victim's heart was—that poor, shriveled, dried-out thing that seemed to have been shattered by the round. A few minutes later, he pulled out a bullet that was lodged in the spine of the corpse. He put it into a bowl.

Colter studied it. "We'll need ballistics on that, but I know a .45 slug when I see one," he said. "Unless I miss my guess, he was shot by his own antique Colt .45. We found it with the body."

"That would be a good guess," the other man replied. "At least, death was most likely instantaneous. That might be some comfort to his surviving family."

"I'll make sure they know," Colter replied solemnly.

"Clancey and Tad have been staying with you and Brenda," Alice remarked.

"Yes." He felt a pang in his heart. "They'll have to go back to work and school. Now that the danger is past."

"They'll miss you, I'm sure," she said, eyeing him covertly.

He drew in a sad breath. "I'll miss them, too," he said.

HE LOADED THEM up and took them back to the house that would be Clancey's now, since Morris, the legal owner, was dead. He hated leaving them there. The danger was past. They had Morris's two cohorts in jail as accessories to attempted murder, and they wouldn't be getting out soon. In fact, they were singing like birds to Darrell Tarley, whose own life had been under threat by Morris. Tarley would prosecute the case, also giving him a load of free publicity as he ran for DA.

"I don't like leaving you here," Colter told Clancey as they walked through the house. "Good God, what a mess!"

It was. There were stains on the floor, even on the walls. The beds had been slept in and the sheets not changed for God knew how long. There were cigarette butts and whiskey bottles and the remains of what looked like bongs all over the place.

"It's just a little cleaning. Honest," she told Colter. Her heart was breaking at having to be away from him. She'd gotten used to being around him. This really hurt. He'd been going to take them horseback riding today. Instead, Morris had died and Colter and Reverend Blair had almost died. It was a sad, solemn day.

"We'll have to bury Morris. And my grandfather," she added, almost choking on the thought of the old man's last minutes.

"I'll help with that. We don't need to do it today, right?"

She nodded. "No. Not today. And I'll have the weekend to get everything put to rights here."

"Check the fridge and the cupboards and see what you need. I'll run to the store for you before I leave," he said.

She drew in a steadying breath. "That's very kind of you."

Tad had gone exploring. He came back, subdued but with shining eyes. "Morris got a new Xbox One and new games for it. I guess those are ours now, huh?" he asked.

"Indeed they are," Colter said, smiling at the boy.

"My room's a mess. It stinks of something sweet and nasty."

Colter went with him and took a whiff. He made a face. "Marijuana," he concluded. "Open the windows and air it out. I'll get some air freshener while I'm at the store."

"We should call the Martins also," Clancey said. "I want to know how they are, and let them know we're home again."

"Good idea. Make me a list for the store," he added.

"Okay." She went to find a pencil and paper, trying not to think of how empty her life was going to be without Colter in it. Just a little while ago, she'd thought they were surely heading for something permanent. But now he was withdrawn and polite, barely even affectionate, except with Tad. She felt alone. Terribly alone.

She came back with a short list. "That's all we need right now," she said, and pulled out a twenty-dollar bill and handed it to him. "I pay my own way," she said, and forced a smile. "Okay?"

He managed a smile. He already missed her. "Okay."

He started for the door when his phone rang. He checked the caller ID and grimaced. "Hello, Grace," he said.

"Why don't you come and have supper with me?" she asked softly. "We can talk over old times. There's a nice little Italian restaurant about a block from here…"

"I know the one. I'll meet you there about six. Or do you want me to come pick you up?"

"I could use a ride," she confessed.

"Okay. I'll come and get you about five forty-five. I've got a couple of chores to finish first."

"All right." There was a pause. "Is that woman still living with you?"

"Clancey and Tad were staying with Brenda and me at the ranch while her life was in danger," he bit off.

"Still, you know, it looks bad. And with Brenda dressing the way she does…"

"I'll see you after a while, Grace." He hung up without waiting for her to speak. He didn't even look at Clancey as he went out the door. It was a good thing. Her heart was breaking, and it was very noticeable.

HE DROPPED OFF the groceries. Clancey thanked him politely and said nothing else when he left.

He got into his SUV and took a deep breath. He'd been

distant with Clancey and Tad. They wouldn't understand. He'd probably given Clancey the idea that he didn't care. That wasn't it at all. He was going through some trauma. He and Jake had been standing beside Morris when Chet Billings shot him. It had been disturbing, in a lot of ways. Morris had looked so young, so fragile, lying there on the ground in a pool of blood. Even though he'd been in combat and seen many such wounds, it had worked on Colter like acid. If Chet Billings hadn't made the shot, Colter and Jake Blair would be dead. If Colter and Jake hadn't poked their noses into the church, Morris would still be alive.

Sure. Still alive to threaten Tad and Clancey and the assistant district attorney who'd sent him to jail.

Colter drew in a long breath. There were no easy answers in life. And now he had to go and have supper with Grace and listen to her rattle off her prejudices against his sister and Clancey. That wasn't going to end well.

"WELL, AT LEAST it smells better, doesn't it?" Clancey asked Tad, forcing a smile. She'd cleaned the rooms, sacked up the trash and taken it to the trash can outside, sprayed with Lysol, and aired out the bedrooms and the living room, despite the cold temperatures.

"It smells lots better. Is it our house now?" Tad asked.

She smiled sadly. "It's our house." She hugged her brother. "We have to have some sort of funerals for Granddaddy and Morris," she added quietly. It was hard to realize that her grandfather really was dead, after years of hoping that he might be alive somewhere, with amnesia or something. Irrational hope, but hope nevertheless. "I'm not sure if I can handle planning a funeral."

"We could ask Mr. Banks to help us," Tad suggested.

"Mr. Banks has done so much already. I hate to ask him to do anything else," she said, thinking about Colter's date with Grace tonight and his coolness to herself. She picked up her phone and called Cal Hollister.

"Why the hell didn't you call me sooner?" he asked, exasperated.

"I was busy…"

"Lame excuse," he muttered.

She grimaced. "I know. Listen, I have to do something about funerals for Granddaddy and Morris." She paused. "Granddaddy's body was in really bad shape, too."

"What do you want to do about him?"

She was thinking about expenses. She had hardly any money coming in and funerals cost thousands of dollars. "Cal, I can't afford big funerals," she confessed, strangling on pride.

"I know that," he said gently. "Why not a simple memorial service for both of them? You can have the remains cremated and urned. It's not that expensive, and if you go to Lunsfords, they'll let you clear the debt over as much time as you need."

She let out a breath. "That's such a relief," she said. "I didn't know how to manage."

"Call Lunsfords," he suggested. "They'll handle it."

"You're such a nice man," she said.

There was a hesitation. "Clancey, why didn't you call Colter?"

She bit her lower lip. "He's been, well, cool since the shooting," she began.

"He's traumatized," he said simply. "He watched a man being killed in front of his eyes. Even for a lawman, that's hard." He sighed. "I watched two of my men blown away by an incendiary bomb in Africa some years ago, men I'd worked with for a long time. I got drunk and couldn't lift my head for three days. Even if you don't pull the trigger, it's still traumatic."

"Oh." Could it be that simple? On the other hand... "He's going out with Grace tonight," she added heavily.

Hollister knew about that old romance. He had his own issues with a woman he'd loved and pushed out of his life, a woman he still loved after all the years in between, despite what she'd done. If Banks loved Grace, there was nothing Clancey could do but accept it.

"Life happens," he said finally.

She grimaced. "Yes. Life happens. Thanks for the advice."

"You're welcome. Still coming over for Thanksgiving next week?"

"You bet," she said. "Thanks for the invite."

"I thought you'd probably be having it with Brenda and Colter."

"Not much chance of that," she replied. "He'll probably celebrate with Grace." She sighed. "She thinks Brenda is promiscuous because she wears short skirts and she was livid that I was 'living' with Colter at his ranch, even though his sister was there."

"Some people take religion more literally than others."

"I guess. I go to church, but I think we should live and let live."

"A good philosophy," he chuckled. "If you need me, just call. Otherwise, I'll expect you and Tad on Thursday."

"You cooking the turkey?" she asked suspiciously.

"What? You don't think I can cook?" he asked with mock indignation.

"Snake and rats, maybe…"

"Stop that," he huffed. "I can cook. I'd have starved years ago if I hadn't learned how. My wife was too busy drinking to do anything in the kitchen."

"I'm sorry about that," she said.

"Life happens," he repeated. "Thursday. Call me if you hit a roadblock. And you'll need an attorney, too. You'll have to be appointed executrix of your grandfather and Morris's estates."

She groaned. "More expenses," she said heavily.

"Go see Darrell Tarley," he suggested. "He's still a practicing attorney and he was Morris's potential victim, as well. He'll probably do it pro bono." He didn't add that he was going to call Darrell himself and suggest that.

"Gosh, thanks!" she said with relief. "It's just so complicated!"

"Not really. It's a matter of organization. For now, get some sleep. I'll talk to you later."

"Okay, Cal. Thanks."

"No problem."

COLTER, MEANWHILE, WAS SITTING at a table with Grace in downtown San Antonio, listening to her rave about going back to South America, to the village where she was working.

His mind was on what had happened that afternoon. He was seeing Morris's throat explode, over and over again, in a horrible slow motion bloody movie in his head.

"You could come with me," Grace said, dragging him back to the present.

He blinked. "Excuse me?"

"You could come to South America with me," she said

softly, sliding her fingers over the back of one big lean hand resting on the table beside his plate. "It's nice there. They always need people. You wouldn't even need to carry a gun. You could give up all this violence and have a job that was nurturing instead."

He looked at her as if she'd taken off her ears and flung them at him. "Grace, I've been in law enforcement since I was seventeen," he pointed out.

She made a face. "I know that. But people can change. It's not too late."

"I love my job," he said. "I don't want to change."

"But you have to carry a gun and shoot people," she said. "I finally persuaded Mike that he needed to get a job in administration and stop wearing a gun all the time," she added. She sighed sadly. "He'd already put in an application when he was...killed."

"Mike loved police work, Grace," he said after a minute. "He would have made the change, because he loved you. But you're missing the point. You can't change people to suit you. You have to take them as they are."

"No," she returned. "It's our duty to turn people's lives around and bring them back to faith."

He gave her a long, sad look. "I'm proud of you, for the work you do," he said. "You're suited to it. You don't really want a relationship with a man, Grace," he added quietly, watching her face react to the shock of the words. "You do everything in your power to push men away. You want me to give up law enforcement, even though I felt called to do it from the start. You wanted Mike to give it up. The plain fact is that you like your life the way it is, and you don't want to give that up. You're devoted to your job. It takes the place of marriage and a family for you. It…" He searched for the right words, "It completes you. Makes you whole."

She sat back in her chair and just stared at him for a minute. She didn't say anything.

"You know I'm right," he told her.

She drew in a long, slow breath. "Yes, I think you are." She studied his hard face. "You're in love with that woman, Clancey, aren't you, Colt?"

He laughed softly. "I'm afraid so."

"Well, as they say, you don't choose who to love. At least she goes to church…" she began.

"Let's agree to disagree on some issues," he interrupted. "How about dessert?"

HE DROPPED GRACE off at her hotel and kissed her gently on the cheek. "You and I felt guilty about what happened the day before Mike got killed," he said. "I kissed you and you kissed me back. It was a spur-of-the-moment, impulsive thing, but both of us overreacted to it. It's tied us up for years. But I think we've finally worked it out."

She smiled. "I think we have. You're a wonderful man, Colt," she added softly. "I'm sorry things didn't work out for us. But you're right. I feel that I'm doing what I'm meant to do with my life. Some of us are made to do service for others, like what I'm doing in South America. It's good, useful work, and it does complete me. I'm glad you understand."

"You take care of yourself."

"You, too. I hope you'll be happy."

"I hope the same for you."

HE DROVE BY Clancey's house on the way back to the ranch, but all the lights were off. *Poor kid*, he thought. She'd had to face the loss of her grandfather along with the loss of her stepbrother. Regardless of her feelings, Morris had lived with her, been part of her family. She was certainly grieving for her grandfather. He wished he'd stayed and talked to her instead of going off with Grace on a date that meant nothing. He'd have to call her tomorrow and try to smooth things over.

But she didn't answer her phone the next day. He knew the calls were going through. She was ignoring him. Brenda had moved back to her apartment in San Antonio. The house was quiet and morose. And he had too much time to think about what had happened. A knock on the door surprised him.

He opened it. Jake Blair was standing there.

"Got a spare cup of coffee?" the minister asked. "I've just finished my sermon and I'm really thirsty."

Colter chuckled. "Come on in. I just made a fresh pot."

They sat at the kitchen table. Jake studied him carefully. "You're all alone here and you're brooding about what you saw yesterday," he said. "I thought you might need somebody to sit and listen while you talked."

Colter let out a long breath and smiled. "I think that's just what I need."

CLANCEY AND TAD and the Martins went to church. It felt good to Clancey, who hadn't been able to go while Morris was on the loose. The minister was a surprise. It was Jake Blair from Jacobsville, who was filling in for the resident minister, who'd gone down with a bad case of the flu. Jake's assistant pastor was taking over for him in Jacobsville in the meantime.

She and Tad sat with Brenda and the Martins, and

Clancey said a silent prayer for her beloved grandfather and for her troubled stepbrother. She'd talked to the funeral home the day before and made the arrangements, which were much less of an expense than she'd dreamed possible. Tomorrow she'd talk to Darrell Tarley about the disposition of Morris and her grandfather's property. Details were getting taken care of, but she hadn't spoken to Colter. She felt bad about not answering the phone. She'd been hurt that he'd been so cool with her and so eager to get to Grace. It was always going to be Grace, she'd realized. He loved the woman. Well, if he did, and if she loved him, which she did, she should want him to be happy. If Grace could make him happy, fine. It was just that Clancey was grieving as much for Colter's loss as for her grandfather. Her heart was breaking.

"Colt misses you two," Brenda said as they walked out of the church, Clancey pushing Mr. Martin's chair.

"We miss both of you," Clancey said.

Jake Blair shook hands with all of them. He glanced at Clancey. "I went to see Colter yesterday," he said. "He was taking it hard."

Clancey stared at him.

"He watched a man die, Clancey," Jake said softly. "Even though the man was a criminal, and meant to kill him, he saw it happen. It's traumatic, even for a lawman," he continued. "I sent him to counseling. He'll need to work through it."

Clancey caught her breath. She hadn't realized any of that. "I looked, but I didn't see," she said vaguely.

Jake smiled. "You're grieving for your grandfather."

"Yes. There was always hope, before, even if it was irrational," she tried to explain.

"We can have a memorial service for him, and for your stepbrother, in Jacobsville anytime you're ready, if you'd like to do it there," he told her.

"I would. Granddaddy was a deputy sheriff in Jacobs County once," she replied. She sighed. "I miss him so much. And I'm sorry Morris turned out the way he did."

"They're both at peace now."

She smiled. "That's comforting."

"It's meant to be," he replied. "And if you ever need to talk, I'm as close as your phone."

"Thanks, Reverend," she said.

"You're most welcome."

Brenda walked them all to the Martins' car. "You and Tad can come over for dinner any night you want to," she told Clancey. "I can't cook, but we have a great Chinese takeout place right next door to my apartment."

Clancey smiled. "You can come have dinner with us sometime, too," she said. "I can cook."

"Can you ever!" Brenda said. She sighed. "Until the reverend explained it, I hadn't thought about how hard it was for Colt to watch Morris get shot," she said.

"Me, neither," Clancey said. "Maybe it's why he was so distant. Well, he had another date with Grace, too," she added miserably.

Brenda's eyes widened. "With Grace?"

Clancey nodded. She smiled sadly. "We can't help who we love," she said. "I want him to be happy. Whoever it's with."

Brenda hugged her. "Me, too, but I don't want it to be Grace," she whispered in Clancey's ear. "She wants him to give up law enforcement and be a mission worker. It will never work out."

"You think so?" Clancey asked, her eyes hopeful.

"Wait and see," she replied. "Just between you and me, I think Grace's attitudes are wearing just a bit thin. Besides, you go back to work tomorrow, right?" she added.

Clancey's heart jumped. "I do."

"Best way to find out what a man's thinking is just to ask him."

"I'll remember that," Clancey laughed.

COLTER WAS SITTING at his desk when Clancey came down the stairs the next morning. She felt uneasy. It was the first time she'd seen him since his date with Grace and she wasn't certain what to say.

"You doing okay?" he asked.

She nodded, standing by his desk. "You okay?" she replied.

He sighed. "A little better. I'm going to see a counselor today, just to get a few things straight in my mind."

"I'm sorry I…well, I didn't think about what it would be like, to have to watch Morris…well, you know," she rambled, and flushed a little.

"It would have been worse if I'd had to pull the trigger." He grimaced. "Billings is holed up in his apartment with two fifths of bourbon and a bad attitude. He says he's going to stay drunk for a week and see if he can get the sight out of his mind. Odd man to be a sniper. He doesn't really have the temperament for it."

"Poor guy," she said. "Does it help to remember that Morris and his friends would have killed you and Jake Blair without a second thought?" she added. "After which, he'd have come after Tad and me. We'd all be dead."

His black eyes searched her pale gray ones. "It helps,"

he said quietly. "If I lost you…" He bit the words back. It was hard.

She moved a step closer. Her heart raced. "If you lost me…?" she prodded, holding her breath.

He got to his feet, towering over her. He framed her face in his big, lean hands. "All the color would go out of the world, Clancey," he said in a husky, deep tone. "And I'd mourn you for the rest of my life. Which, frankly, wouldn't be that long. I don't want to live in a world that doesn't contain you, too."

Hot tears stung her eyes. "You never…"

His mouth was warm and slow and hungry on her lips, stopping the words before they could get out. She didn't want to talk anyway. She reached up to him, to be lifted and kissed to within an inch of her life. She held on, moaning softly as the kiss went into depths of feeling she'd never imagined.

He groaned, too. But he finally drew back.

"We have to work," he ground out.

She nodded and reached up to kiss him again.

His heart was hammering in his chest. "This isn't appropriate behavior for people in an office," he tried again.

She nodded a second time and kissed him harder.

"Oh, the hell with it," he bit off, and kissed her back.

SHE SAW DARRELL TARLEY, who was as relieved as she was to be rid of the threat of Morris. He did take the case pro bono, and she was appointed executrix of not only her grandfather's estate, but of Morris's, as well. Nothing was left of her grandfather's few possessions, but Morris had quite a few expensive things. Clancey took down the serial numbers and called them in to Cal Hollister to see if they were stolen. At least two were, and she turned them over to the police.

Meanwhile, Colter invited her and Tad down to the ranch for Thanksgiving, adding that he'd also invited Cal Hollister. Brenda was there, too, and also the Martins, who'd been given a lift with Brenda.

It was a delightful, uproarious meal. Clancey and Cal had prepared it all themselves, to applause and delight as turkey and all the accompaniments were served up. Cal had done the turkey and dressing and gravy at home, so he just packed it up and carried it over to the ranch. Clancey did homemade rolls and potato salad and green beans. Colter had brought two pies home from the bakery in San Antonio. It was a big meal.

After lunch, Colter took Clancey riding and they dismounted near a stream on the ranch and he tied up the horses. He took Clancey to a grassy spot and sat her down.

He took a box out of his pocket and put it in her hands. It was a jeweler's box. Small and pretty, made of polished wood.

"It isn't expensive," he said quietly. "Even with the ranch, I'm not a wealthy man. But it's the best I could get."

She looked at him with her heart in her eyes. "I don't care about expensive things," she said softly, which made his black eyes light up.

She opened the box. There was a small but perfect diamond engagement ring and a matching wedding ring in yellow gold. She had a little, inexpensive pair of pierced gold studs that she wore all the time. She loved yellow gold. Apparently, Colter had noticed.

Her throat felt full of thorns. She could barely breathe. It was a proposal of marriage.

Tears rolled down her cheeks.

Colter ground his teeth together. Was she going to refuse? Had he completely misjudged her feelings?

Even as he thought it, she took out the engagement ring and put it in the palm of his big hand.

"Will you put it on for me?" she whispered, looking up at him with her whole heart in her eyes.

He let out the breath he'd been holding. "Damned straight, I will," he said huskily.

He slid it onto her ring finger and kissed it hungrily. "Is that a yes?" he asked softly.

She laughed and caught him around the neck and kissed him with more fervor than skill. "It's a yes," she whispered. And she said nothing else for a very long time.

SIXTEEN

THERE WAS A solemn memorial service for Morris and Clancey's grandfather at the Methodist church in Jacobsville. It was well attended, because a lot of older residents of the county remembered Deputy Sheriff Dalton Reed. The urns containing both sets of remains were buried in the cemetery, next to Clancey's mother and father. She shook hands with Reverend Blair and reminisced with people who'd known her grandfather.

Later, she and Colter stood back from the small graves in the cold wind.

"He was a terrific grandfather," Clancey said quietly. "I loved him even more than my mother and father."

He put an arm around her and drew her close. "I'm sorry you lost him in the way you did."

She nodded. "I'm sorry Morris turned out to be such a bad man. If Ben had been a better father, if he hadn't spoiled Morris to death, he might have turned out differently."

"That's a hard call," Colter said. "We can't go back. We have to go forward."

She looked up at him and smiled. "Forward sounds very good. When are you going to marry me?"

He pursed his lips. "How about Saturday at the Methodist Church? And if you don't mind, I'm going to invite the lieutenant. I'm hoping he'll give us Monday and Tuesday off so we can have a nice, long honeymoon."

"Where are we going on our honeymoon?" she asked.

He chuckled. "Galveston. To the beach. It's too cold to swim, but the scenery's terrific."

"That suits me just fine," she said, and hugged him. Secretly, she was still a little worried. She'd gone to her doctor two days before and been examined. The visit had required a little minor surgery, which was still just a little sensitive. But by the weekend, she'd be all healed up and ready for an adventure with her new husband. Hopefully, she could stop being afraid of what would happen. She was all nerves already. Well, she told herself, women had been doing it for thousands of years. It was natural. She just had to think of it that way.

THE WEDDING WAS well attended. Clancey wore a white dress and a hat with a veil, and she carried a bouquet of white roses. Friends had set up refreshments in the church's fellowship hall, as well.

Clancey said her vows, watched her brand-new husband lift her veil and look at her with black eyes so full of affection they made her knees weak. He kissed her very softly and then they ran down the aisle to be showered with white rose petals all the way out the door.

They fed each other cake, had photographs taken, visited with the guests and then climbed into Colter's big

SUV to go back to his house and change clothes for the drive to Galveston.

Tad was staying with Brenda at her apartment in San Antonio, so there was nobody in the house. Colter had taken Clancey's suitcase full of clothes to the ranch the night before, so that she'd have everything packed for the trip. He'd packed, as well.

She started to change out of her dress when she felt big, lean hands on her waist, pulling her back against a hard, warm body.

"Mrs. Banks," he said softly, and chuckled.

She turned, smiling. "Mr. Banks," she replied, her eyes searching his. She bit her lip. "Listen, I need to tell you something."

His eyebrows arched. "You're on your period?"

"Colter!"

He chuckled. "Sorry. Bad choice of words. Go ahead."

She was flushed. "I had to see my doctor, you remember?"

He nodded.

"Well…he had to do a little minor surgery. I was, well, sort of intact," she stammered.

"Are you healed?"

"Yes." She looked up at him, worried. "It will be all right, won't it? I mean, I've never, and I'm scared," she blurted out.

"Honey," he said gently, "everybody's scared the first time. Even boys."

Her eyes widened. "Really?"

He nodded. "Really. If it helps, I know what to do. I won't hurt you. I promise."

She relaxed a little. She nodded. "Okay."

He started to unbutton the coatdress.

"But it's daylight," she burst out.

He chuckled deeply. "In five minutes, you won't care."

She was about to question that when he bent his head and slid his mouth under the coatdress, under her slip and bra and right onto her soft, firm little breast.

She gasped. Her head fell back. She moaned harshly as the motion of his mouth and tongue caused the most exquisite sensations she'd ever felt in her whole life. Then he began to suckle her, and she went under like a swimmer drowning in passion.

She was so aroused that she never noticed or cared that the curtains were open. She lay on the bed nude, twisting and writhing with a need she'd never known she had while Colter undressed. He turned toward her, and even the sight of him without clothing didn't embarrass her. She was too hungry. She held out her arms, arching her back as he came down to her, hard and powerful and demanding.

Minute after blistering minute, she clung to him, arching and moaning and sobbing as he aroused her to fever pitch. When he went into her, the last thing in the world she was thinking about was whether or not it would hurt. She wrapped her legs around his and moaned with every hard thrust until the rhythm increased to madness and, at the last, she cried out so loudly in her pleasure that he covered her mouth with his kiss to muffle the sound so that it wouldn't carry.

She wept when it was over, still clinging to the tanned, muscular, perfect body still joined to hers in the sweaty, lazy aftermath.

"Were you scared?" he teased.

She laughed secretly. "I forgot to notice. Where did

you learn that? Never mind," she added quickly. "I don't want to know!"

His mouth brushed her throat softly. "It was long before I met you, when I was young and curious." He lifted his head. "There will never be anybody else except you, as long as I live. I promise you that on my honor."

She traced his jaw. "It's the same for me." She looked up into his black eyes. "I love you, Colter."

He flushed. He bent and kissed her softly, hungrily. "And I love you. Nasturtium," he added wickedly.

"Don't you…!" she began in mock anger.

His hips moved very slowly. She felt him inside her, felt him swell, watched his eyes as it happened and caught her breath.

"It's all new and fascinating," he whispered. "Even for me."

She shivered. "It's…beyond words, trying to describe how it feels," she replied.

"Oh yes," he murmured as his mouth found hers and the rhythm began all over again.

THEY GOT UP, showered and dressed in their traveling clothes. She hugged him close before they went out the door.

"We forgot to talk about something," she said.

His eyebrows rose.

She colored, just a little. "You mentioned my period, remember?"

"Yes," he said.

"Well, I'm halfway between periods," she said.

He was a cattleman. He knew a lot about female functions. He pursed his lips. His black eyes twinkled. He smiled.

She laughed. "I guess you read minds, too, huh?" she asked.

He caught her by the waist and pulled her close. "We can get something to use, if you want to."

"Do you want to?" she asked.

"I love Tad. I think it would be nice if he had company growing up."

She beamed. "Me, too!"

He laughed. He bent and kissed her softly. "Then let's leave it to fate. I haven't been around kids much, but I'm crazy about Tad. I think I'll love having babies in the house."

"I know I will," she said with a sigh. "I took care of Tad from the time he was born."

"And you were worried that nobody would want you with your so-called baggage," he chided.

"That's what I thought," she agreed. "Then I got sick."

He smiled. "You'll never know how much I enjoyed taking care of you." He grimaced. "Or how jealous I was of Cal Hollister," he added.

"Cal's like my brother," she said lazily. "You know that now."

"Of course I know it now. But I didn't know it then," he emphasized. "He's a good cop. I like him a lot."

"He likes you, too."

"Nice of the lieutenant to give us those two days off," he said, changing the subject. "I wish it was warm weather. You could wear a bathing suit and I could just lie on the beach and look at you and fend off other men."

"Flatterer," she teased.

He bent and kissed her. "Don't you even know that

you're beautiful, Clancey?" he whispered. "Because you are. Inside and out."

"I'm not. But I'm glad you think so. I think you're the most gorgeous man I ever saw in my whole life. And I still can't believe I'm married to you."

He chuckled. "I can." He pursed his lips. "I've got scratches on my butt to remind me..."

She hit him. "Oh, you!" she exclaimed.

He just grinned. "Let's go. It's a long drive to Galveston."

"Not so long, if you have good company on the ride," she replied.

"Just what I was thinking," he said, and he went to get the suitcases.

THEY HAD A great honeymoon. They walked on the beach, hand in hand, and visited all the touristy places. Mostly, they stayed in their hotel room and explored each other.

By the time they got home, they were closer than they'd ever been, like two halves of a whole.

Clancey moved down to the ranch with Tad and invited the Martins to move into the house Morris had owned. Their own little house was falling apart. The roof leaked and the plumbing was failing, along with the wiring. They accepted gratefully and insisted on paying rent. Clancey agreed, to save their pride, but she set the amount at a figure they could easily afford.

"That was nice of you, to let the Martins live in the house," Brenda commented when she came down on the weekend to visit with Colter and Clancey and Tad.

"A house needs to be lived in," Clancey said simply. "And they're such sweet people."

"Yes, they are." Brenda cocked her head and looked at them. She smiled. "You look good together."

"Thanks," Colter chuckled.

"Grace went back to South America two days ago," she continued. She made a face. "After reminding me again that nice women don't wear short skirts."

"Nice men don't carry guns, either," Colter mused. "Or so she said."

"You are so nice," Clancey replied, and hugged him close.

He wrapped his long arms around her. "I'm glad you think so, honey."

"I think you're nice, too, Colter," Tad said with a grin. He'd come into the living room with both Miss Kitty and Bumblebee, the kitten. They followed him everywhere now. "When I grow up, I'm going to be a Texas Ranger, just like you."

"I'm very flattered," Colter said, and smiled at the boy. "How's the homework coming along?" he added.

"Awww, Colter, it's just Saturday," he groaned.

"And if you get your homework done, you can game all weekend," Colter returned.

"I didn't think of that." Tad laughed. "Okay." He ran back down the hall to his room. The cats galloped after him.

"Oh, you have a way with kids," Brenda remarked gaily. She studied them. "You two going to have kids?"

They nodded. They smiled.

"I'm always available to babysit," she replied with a big smile.

"We'll remember," Colter promised.

"We have another cat who needs housing," Brenda began.

"We have two cats," Colter pointed out.

She sighed. "The more the merrier?" she asked hopefully.

"Suppose we think about it?" Clancey asked, and sighed as she snuggled close to her husband.

"We can think about it," he agreed.

Brenda grinned.

THEY HAD A new kitten, an uproarious birthday celebration for Clancey the first week of December, when she turned twenty-four, and a wonderful Christmas celebration with a nine-foot artificial tree and company and lots of presents. Then, three months later, Clancey came home on Saturday morning after an appointment with Dr. Louise Coltrain.

"You look… I don't know, worried," Colter said, taking her gently by the shoulders. "Is something wrong?" he added, and now he looked worried, too.

"The rabbit died."

His eyebrows arched. "You killed a rabbit?"

"It's a figure of speech," she began. "You know, a metaphor."

"Is there a reason you're giving me this metaphor?"

"Sort of."

"What do you mean, sort of?"

She smiled secretively. "Well, Dr. Coltrain is sending me to see a specialist."

He lost color. "What sort of specialist?"

"A woman who does obstetrics."

All at once, he got it. "Dead rabbit, metaphor, obstetrician… You're pregnant!" he exclaimed.

She grinned. "Yes!"

He picked her up and kissed her and kissed her, walking around the room, in an absolute fever of joy.

Tad came in the door from outside, where he'd been helping the foreman feed the bottle calves. He stopped and just stared at them.

They stopped and stared back.

"What are you doing?" he asked curiously.

"Celebrating," Colter said.

"Celebrating," Clancey added.

"Celebrating what?"

"The coming occupation of our spare bedroom," Clancey told him mischievously.

"We're taking in renters?" Tad, obviously, didn't get it.

"We're putting in a bassinet and diapers…"

"We're going to have a baby?" Tad burst out, radiant. "A real baby? Oh my gosh! That's just great! I won't be an only child anymore!"

He hugged Colter, who still had Clancey up in his arms, and they all laughed.

THE FOLLOWING CHRISTMAS, besides the colorfully wrapped presents under the big tree, there was another present that capped the spirit of celebration and joy. Clancey and Colter brought home the newest member of their household. Their son, Jacob Dalton Colter Banks. He was, Clancey told her delighted husband, the nicest Christmas present she'd ever had in her life. Smiling, he bent and kissed her so sweetly that she felt tears brighten her eyes. She looked up at him with her heart in her eyes. And she smiled back.

* * * * *

*Can J.C. Calhoun open up his heart—
and his home—to Colie Jackson, the woman
who wrecked his life once before?*

Read on for a sneak preview of Wyoming Winter,
part of the Wyoming Men series from
New York Times *bestselling author Diana Palmer*

COLIE THOMPSON WAS in a mild panic. Her brother Rodney was bringing over his friend J.C. Calhoun. J.C. was thirty-two, pretty much at the end of his Army Reserve service—the cutoff age was thirty-two. He and Rodney met in Iraq, almost four years ago. Both men were with the same Army unit. Rodney was serving his first tour of duty. J.C.'s Army Reserve unit had been called up for limited duty, and he was assigned to the same area as Rodney. In one of those wild coincidences, they started talking and discovered that they lived in the same Wyoming town, J.C. having taken a job with another Catelow resident, Ren Colter, whom he'd met during his first tour of duty. Rodney looked up to J.C., who was a little older. The older man had been a police officer before he went into the Army the first time, almost twelve years earlier.

Rodney left the Army before his tour of duty was officially up, never saying why. He'd been home for several months. After J.C. finished his overseas duty, he came home with him sometimes, although they'd grown apart since Rodney started a new job. They still went around together, but not often. One memorable visit to the Thompson home was on Colie's birthday, when J.C. had unexpectedly given her a cat. It was the high point of her recent life. She named the huge gray Siamese cat Big Tom and it slept on her bed every night.

Even though he didn't come home with Rodney much, Colie often saw J.C. around Catelow, which was a small and very clannish town. There were only a couple of restaurants, and Colie, whose real name was Colleen, worked as a receptionist and typist for a law firm downtown. Inevitably, she saw J.C. from time to time, occasionally with her brother. And since he was single, and handsome, and mostly avoided women, he was the subject of much gossip.

He always made time to talk to Colie if he saw her. He was polite, teasing, friendly. He made her glow inside. Once, when he brought Rod home after his car had quit, J.C. had helped her into her jacket when she was going outside to get the mail. Just the touch of his hands was like an explosion of pleasure. The more she saw of him, the more she wanted him.

Rodney had invited J.C. to come to supper before this, but he'd always had an excuse. This time, he accepted. It had been just after Colie had started walking back to the office, in the snow, and J.C. had stopped and given her a ride the rest of the way. Sitting with him, in the cozy warmth of the big black SUV he drove, she'd been hesitant to get out again. They'd talked about the upcoming presidential election, the state of the country, the beauty of Catelow in the snow. He'd teased her about wearing high heels to work instead of sensible boots, with snow already piling up and she'd retorted that boots would hardly complement the pretty pantsuit she was wearing. He'd pursed his lips and looked at her, long and hard, and said Colie would look good in anything. She'd gone inside the law office, reluctantly, flushed and beaming after the unexpected pleasure of his company.

J.C. worked full-time locally, but he went back overseas periodically to train troops in Iraq in police procedure. He was supposed to go back in a few months to do it all over again with a new group. J.C. worked as security chief for Ren Colter, who had a huge cattle ranch, Skyhorn, outside Catelow, Wyoming. Ren was ex-military as well, and he had somebody fill in for J.C. while he accommodated a former commander by drilling new recruits.

Giving orders was something J.C. was very good at. He was also gorgeous. He had jet-black hair, cut short, and eyes so pale a gray that they glittered like silver. He was tall and muscular, but not like a bodybuilder. He had the physique of a rodeo cowboy, lithe and powerful. Colie liked to just sit and look at him when she had the opportunity. She'd never known anybody quite like him. He had a unique background, about which he rarely spoke. Rodney had told her that J.C.'s father was a member of the Blackfoot nation up in Canada. His mother had been a little redheaded Irish woman. Quite an uncommon pairing, but it had produced a handsome child. J.C. never spoke of his father, Rodney added.

Colie wanted a family of her own, badly. She and Rodney had lost their mother two years previously to bone cancer. It had taken her a long time to die, but even then, she'd been cheerful and upbeat around her children and her husband. Colie's father was a Methodist minister, a pillar of the community. Everybody loved him, not just his own congregation. They'd loved Colie's mother, too. The little woman, named Beth Louise, but called Ludie, had always been the first to arrive if there was a sick person who needed caring for or a child who needed a temporary home. She even fostered dogs that were picked up by the local no-kill animal shelter, while they waited for an adoptive family.

All that had passed, along with her. The house was suddenly empty. Jared Thompson, Colie's father, had been almost suicidally depressed after his wife's death, but his faith had pulled him through. It was, he told Colie, not right to mourn someone who had lived such a full life and had gone on to a happier, more wonderful place. Death was not the end, for people of faith. They simply had to accept that people died for reasons that were, perhaps, not quite clear to those left behind.

Colie and Rodney had grieved, too. Rodney had been overseas for almost four years, with only brief visits. He couldn't come home for his mother's funeral, although he Skyped with his father and sister after the services. He was a sweet, biddable boy until he went into the service. When he came home, he was...different. Colie couldn't figure out why. He became fixated on fancy cars and designer clothes, neither of which fit in his small budget. He'd obtained a job at the local hardware store when he came home, because it was owned by a friend of the Reverend Thompson. Rodney seemed to be a natural salesman. But he complained all the time about getting minimum wage. He wanted more. He was never satisfied with anything for long.

The one thing that bothered Colie most was that her brother wasn't quite lucid much of the time. He had redrimmed eyes and sometimes he staggered. She worried that he might have been hurt overseas and wasn't telling them. She knew it wasn't from alcohol, because Rodney almost never took a drink. It was puzzling.

During Rodney's tour of duty in the Middle East, J.C. and Rodney hung out together when Rodney was off duty. Rod didn't write often, but when he did, he mentioned things he and J.C. had done overseas during the time J.C. was there. They went out on the town when Rodney was on liberty. Odd thing about J.C., Rodney had commented. He never drank hard liquor. He'd have the occasional beer, but he didn't touch the heavy stuff. Like Rodney. But the brother who used to tease her and bring her wildflowers and watch television with her seemed to have gone away. The man who came back from overseas was someone else. Someone with a darkness inside him, a lust for things, for material things.

He'd been vocal about the old things in the house where he lived with his sister and father. It was primitive, he scoffed.

Colie didn't find it so. It looked lived-in. The small house was immaculate, Colie thought as she looked at her surroundings. The sofa had a new cover, a pretty burgundy floral pattern, and her father's puffy armchair had a solid burgundy cover. The spotless wood floors had area rugs, which were beaten clean by Colie on a regular basis. There were no cobwebs anywhere. The marble-topped coffee table that her father had found at an antiques shop graced the living room, where an open fireplace crackled with orange flames and the smell of burning oak.

Colie didn't look too bad herself, she reflected, glancing in the hall mirror at her wavy collar-length dark brown hair. It never needed curling. It was naturally wavy. She had an oval face, sweet and pleasant, but not beautiful. Her eyes were large and dark green under thick lashes. Her mouth was a perfect bow. She had an hourglass figure, with long legs always clad in denim jeans. She had only a few dresses and a couple of nice pantsuits, which she wore to church and to work at the local attorney's office where she was a receptionist and typist. Around the house, she wore jeans and boots and pullover sweaters. This one was a nice medium green, long-sleeved and V-necked. It showed off Colie's small, firm breasts in a nice but flattering way. She never wore low-cut things or suggestive dresses. After all, her father was a minister. She didn't want to do anything that would embarrass him in front of his congregation. She didn't even curse.

Rodney did. She was constantly chastising him about it.

Just as she thought it, he walked in the door, stomping snow off his big boots on the front porch as he stood in the open doorway, letting in a flurry. He closed it quickly behind him.

"Damn, it's cold out!" he swore. "Snowing like a son of a…"

She interrupted him. "Will you stop, that? Daddy's a minister," she groaned. "Rodney, you're such a pain!"

He had her dark green eyes, but his hair was straight and thick and a shade lighter than hers. He was tall, with perfect teeth and a rakish smile. No choirboy, Rodney, he was always in trouble throughout high school. Presumably, he'd been better behaved in the military, since he was discharged early.

"Daddy can curse," he retorted. "Haven't you heard him?"

"Yes, Rodney, he says 'chicken feathers!'. That's how he curses." She glowered at him. "That's not what you're saying when you lose your temper." He lost it a lot lately, too.

He shrugged her off. "I have issues," he said easily. "I'm working on it. You have to remember that I've been around soldiers for several years, and in combat."

"I try to take that into account," she said. "But couldn't you tone it down, just a little bit? For Daddy's sake?"

He made a face at her. "God, you're hard to live up to, do you know that?" He sighed, exasperated. "You've never put a foot out of line. Never had a parking ticket, never had a speeding ticket, never even jaywalked! What a paragon to try to live up to!"

She grimaced. "I just behave the way Mama taught me." The thought made her sad. "Don't you miss her?"

He nodded. "She was the kindest woman I've ever known. Well, besides you." He chuckled and hugged her, and just for a minute, he was the big brother she'd adored. "You're just the best, sis."

She hugged him back. "I love you, too." She sniffed and her nose wrinkled as she drew back. "Rodney, what's that smell?" she asked, frowning as she sniffed him again. "It's like tobacco, but not."

He let her go and averted his eyes. "Just cigarette smoke. Some of that imported stuff. I have a friend who gets them."

"Not J.C. He doesn't smoke," she said, curious.

"Not J.C.," he agreed. "This is a guy I know from Jackson Hole. He and I pal around sometimes."

"Oh." She smiled. "Sorry. I thought it was marijuana."

He raised both eyebrows. "If I smoked marijuana in this house, Daddy would call Sheriff Cody Banks and have him lock me up in the county detention center in a heartbeat! You know that!"

"Well, yes, I do." She didn't add that plenty of men did smoke that awful stuff, and managed to keep their parents from suspecting. She'd had a girlfriend in high school who even bragged about it.

Colie had never used drugs of any sort, especially not any kind that had to be smoked. She had weak lungs. She didn't smoke, period.

"Didn't you say J.C. was coming to supper?" she asked after a minute, trying not to sound as excited as she felt.

"He is," Rodney said, pursing his lips as he saw the excitement she was trying so hard to hide. She was an open book, especially about his best friend. "He'll be here in a few minutes. He had to run an errand for Ren."

"Oh. Okay. I've still got leftover turkey from Thanksgiving that we have to eat, and mashed potatoes and a green salad, with apple pie for dessert. He does like turkey, doesn't he?" she added worriedly.

"He's not fussy about food," he said, smiling down at her. "Actually, he said snake wasn't bad if you had enough pepper…"

"Yuck!" she burst out.

"He was spec ops, back when he was in the Army," he laughed. "Those guys can eat anything, and have, when they're out on a mission. Bugs, snakes, whatever they can catch. There was this guy attached to his and Ren's unit overseas, years ago, who cooked an old cat for them when they couldn't find anything else."

"Oh, that's heartless," she said, wincing.

"It was a very old cat," he replied. "They were starving." He hesitated. "He said it tasted awful, and they got sick."

"Good!" she returned enthusiastically.

He laughed and hugged her again. "You softy," he mused. "You're just like Mama. She loved her cats." He frowned, looking around. "Where's Big Tom?"

"Out back, chasing rabbits," she said. The big seal point Siamese cat loved the outdoors. He slept inside at night, because there were predators all around, including bears and foxes and wolves. The Thompsons' home was outside Catelow, nestled in a forest of lodgepole pines, with no really close neighbors except Ren Colter. Ren's ranch ran right up to the Thompson property line, but he didn't run cattle close enough to worry any of the residents.

"Funny," Rodney mused, thinking about Big Tom.

"What is?"

"J.C. giving you a cat," he remarked.

It had touched Colie, that unusual gift from J.C. It had been a birthday present, the cat he'd found wandering around near his cabin. He'd had the vet clean him up and give him his shots, and he'd brought him over to Colie, who was a sucker for stray animals. Big Tom turned out to be housebroken and he never used his claws on the furniture. He was a lot of company for Colie while her father was visiting his congregation, which he did often. Rodney had been away in the military, so there was just Colie in the small house. Well, Colie and Big Tom.

"He's a very nice cat," she remarked.

Rodney laughed. "J.C.'s not big on animals, although he likes them. He's good with cattle. Even Willis's wolf will let him pet him. That's an accomplishment, believe me," he added with a huff. "Damned thing nearly took my hand off when I tried it…"

"Rodney!"

He ground his teeth. "Oh, hell."

"Rodney!!"

He let out a breath. "Set up a jar," he said with resignation, "and I'll put a nickel in it every time I forget."

"If I do that, we can have a Tahiti vacation in a month," she accused.

He laughed. "Not nice."

"I'll find a big jar," she returned. "And you'll put a quarter in. Every time."

He drew in a long breath and just smiled. "Okay, Joan of Arc."

She chuckled and walked back to the kitchen to check on her apple pie in the oven.

J.C. LOOKED INCREDIBLY handsome in a shepherd's coat, jeans and boots, with snow dusting his thick, black, uncovered hair.

"You never wear a hat," Colie mused, trying not to let her hands tremble as she took the coat to hang up for him. He was so tall that she had to stand on her tiptoes to pull it back off his shoulders.

"I hate hats," he remarked. He glanced at her as she put the coat on the rack in the hall, his pale gray eyes narrow and appraising on her slender, sexy body. She dressed like a lady, but he knew all about women who put on their best behavior around company. She was just out of school; college, he was certain, because she had to be at least twenty-two or twenty-three. Catelow had several thousand people, and J.C. didn't mix with them. He only knew what Rodney told him about his sister. And that wasn't much.

"I noticed," Colie said as she turned, smiling.

His eyes flickered down to her pert breasts and he fought down a raging hunger that he hadn't felt in a long time. He had women, but this one stirred him in a different way. He couldn't explain how, exactly. It irritated him and he scowled.

"It wasn't a complaint," Colie added quickly, not understanding the scowl.

He shrugged. "No problem. What are we eating?"

"Leftover turkey with cranberry sauce, mashed potatoes, salad and apple pie." She hesitated, insecure. "Is that okay?"

He smiled, his perfect white teeth visible under chiseled, sensuous lips. "It's great. I love turkey." He chuckled. "I like chicken, too, although I usually get mine in a bucket."

Her eyes widened. "You put it in a pail, like you milk cows with?" she asked, shocked.

He glowered at her. "There's this chicken place. They sell you chicken and biscuits and sides…"

She went red as fire. "Oh, gosh, sorry, wasn't thinking," she stammered. "Let's go in! Daddy's already at the table."

Rodney went ahead, but J.C. slid a long finger inside the back of Colie's sweater and gently stopped her. He moved forward, so that she could feel the heat and power of him at her back in a way that made her heart run wild, her knees shiver. "I was teasing," he whispered right next to her ear. His lips brushed it.

Her intake of breath was visible. Her whole body felt shaky.

His big hands caught her shoulders and held her there while his lips traveled down the side of her throat in a lazy, whispery caress that caused her to melt inside.

"Do you like movies?" he whispered.

"Well, yes…"

"There's a new comedy at the theater Saturday. Go with me. We'll have supper at the fish place on the way."

She turned, shocked. "You…you want to go out with me?" she asked, her green eyes wide and full of delight.

He smiled slowly. "Yes. I want to go out with you."

"Saturday."

He nodded.

"What time?"

"We'll leave about five."

"That would be lovely," she said, drowning in his eyes, on fire with the joy he'd just kindled in her with the unexpected invitation.

"Lovely," he murmured, but he was looking at her mouth.

"Colie? Supper?" her father's amused voice floated out from the dining room.

"Supper." She was dazed. "Oh. Supper! Yes! Coming!"

J.C. followed close behind her, his smile as smug and arrogant as the look on his face. Colie wanted him. He knew it without a word being spoken.

He seated Colie, to her amazement, and then pulled out a chair for himself.

"Good to have you with us, J.C.," the reverend said gently. "Say grace, Colie, if you please," he added.

J.C. felt stunned as the others bowed their heads and Colie mumbled a prayer. He wasn't much on religion, but he did bow his head. When in Rome...

IT WAS A pleasant meal. Reverend Thompson seemed shocked at J.C.'s knowledge of biblical history as he mentioned a recent dig in Israel that had turned up some new relics of antiquity, and J.C. remarked on it with some authority.

"My mother was from southern Ireland. Catholic," he added quietly. "She was forever asking the local priest to loan her books on archaeology. It was a passion of his."

"She couldn't get them off the internet?" Rodney queried.

J.C. laughed. "We lived in the Yukon, Rod," he told

him with some amusement. "We didn't have television or the internet."

"No TV?" Rodney exclaimed. "What did you do for fun?"

"Hunted, fished, helped chop firewood, learned foreign languages from my neighbors. Read," he added. "I still don't watch television. I don't own one."

"Do you hear that?" Reverend Thompson interjected, pointing to J.C. "That's how people become intelligent, not from watching people take off their clothing and use foul language on television!"

"It's his soapbox," Rodney said complacently. "He only lets me have satellite because I help pay for it."

"The world is wicked," the reverend said heavily. "So much immorality. It's like fighting a tsunami."

"There, there, Daddy, you do your part to stop it," Colie said gently, and smiled.

He smiled back. "You're my legacy, sweetheart," he said. "You're so like your mother. She was a gentle woman. She never went with the crowd."

"I hate crowds," Colie said.

"Me, too," Rodney added.

J.C. just stared into space. "I hate people. The best of them will turn on you, given the opportunity."

"Son, that's a very harsh attitude," the reverend said gently.

J.C. finished his turkey and sipped black coffee. "Sorry. We're the products of our environment, as much as our genetics." He glanced at the older man with dead eyes. "I've been sold out by the people I loved most. It doesn't encourage trust."

"You have to consider that we all have a purpose," the

reverend said solemnly. "I've heard it said that people come into our lives when they do, for a reason. Some bring out good qualities in us, some bring out bad. Life is a test."

"If it is, I've sure failed it already." Rodney sighed. He nodded toward Colie. "She's got a big jar. Every time I swear, I have to put in a quarter. I'll be bankrupt in days!" he moaned.

Reverend Thompson laughed wholeheartedly. "Now, that's creative thinking, my girl!"

"I'd take a bow, but the pie would get cold," she teased, as she served it up.

She noticed that J.C. seemed to love his. He glanced at her, saw her watching him and grinned. She flushed and fumbled with her fork.

The reverend watched the byplay with amusement and concern. Colie was an innocent. He knew things about J.C., who was vocal about his distaste for family life and children. Colie would want marriage and kids. J.C. wouldn't. It was a mismatch that could lead to tragedy for his daughter. He saw the danger ahead and wished he could stop it.

They had relatives in Comanche Wells, Texas, a small town in Jacobs County. He could send Colie there. She'd be away from J.C...

Even as he thought it, he realized how impractical it was. Colie had a good job. She loved Catelow. And if her continual sighing over J.C. Calhoun was any indication, she was already halfway in love. She'd never dated much, except for an occasional double date with an older girl-friend who'd later married and moved to Billings. She didn't go out these days. She worked and cooked and cleaned and read books. Even the reverend realized it wasn't much of a life for a young woman, who should be out learning about life.

It was just that she was going to learn things that he disapproved of. He looked at J.C., saw the way the man was watching Colie, and something inside him tightened like a rope around his throat. He averted his eyes. He didn't know what to do. He only knew that Colie was headed for disaster.

COLIE WALKED J.C. out onto the porch, where a small light burned overhead. Snow was falling softly.

"They say we're looking at six inches of snow," she remarked with a long sigh.

He smiled. "I can drive in six feet of snow," he mused. "If the theater is open, we'll get there. If it isn't, you can come home with me and I'll teach you how to play chess."

Her lips parted on a rush of excitement. He really wanted to be with her. He wasn't teasing. She looked up into narrow, pale silver eyes and wanted nothing more in the world than to be in his arms.

He saw the look. It amused him. She had her act down pat. Playing innocent, showing all the right sort of excitement for a woman headed for her first love affair. He didn't believe what he was seeing. He'd had too many experienced women tease him with displays of innocence, only to become wildcats once he had them in bed. It was a trust issue, he supposed. He didn't trust women. He had good reason not to.

But he was willing to play along. In fact, he knew tricks that Colie might not know. He moved closer, taking her gently by the waist and holding her away from him just a little.

"You'll get cold," he whispered, bending his head so that his mouth was just above hers, not touching, but taunting.

"It's not that cold," she whispered back, her voice unsteady as she looked up at his mouth, focused on it with all the pent-up hunger she'd been saving for the right man, the right time, the right place.

"Isn't it?" His voice was deep, dark velvet. He brushed his nose against hers, while his big hands smoothed up and down her rib cage, almost brushing her taut breasts—but not touching.

Her lips parted. They felt swollen. She felt swollen all over. She didn't know enough about men to understand what he was doing to her. It was a game. A very old game. Tease and retreat, to make a woman hungry for more.

"I have to go," he whispered, his breath mingling with hers, he was so close.

"Do you?" She was standing on her tiptoes now, almost begging for the hard, chiseled mouth so close to hers. She could almost taste the coffee on it.

"I do." He brushed his nose against hers again, teased her mouth without touching it, and suddenly put her away from him. "Don't stay out here. You'll catch cold."

"O...okay," she said. She was disappointed, frustrated.

He saw that. It delighted him. He smiled at her. "I'll see you Saturday. Five sharp."

She nodded. "Five sharp."

"Good night, Colie."

He went down the steps before she could reply and back to his black SUV. He got in, started the engine, backed out and drove away. He didn't look back. Not once.

COLIE WENT BACK INSIDE, frustrated and cold. Why hadn't he kissed her? She knew he wanted to. His eyes had been hungry as they stared at her parted lips. But he'd pushed her away. Why?

She wished she had a really close girlfriend, somebody she could trust, to talk to about men and their reactions. Well, there was Lucy, at work, the closest thing she had to a friend. But she'd be too embarrassed to ask Lucy, who was married, questions about men and sensual techniques. Lucy would know why she wanted to know, and she'd tease Colie, who was too shy to invite the attention. Still, she wondered why J.C. had been so hesitant to kiss her, when she knew he wanted to. Muffled gossip, movies and explicit television shows hadn't really educated her about how men felt and why they behaved in odd ways.

She started clearing the dining room table.

"J.C. get off all right?" her father asked.

She nodded and smiled. "It's snowing again."

"I noticed." He was still sitting at the table, with his second cup of black coffee. He took a breath. "Colie, I know how you feel about J.C.," he said unexpectedly. "But you have to remember that he's not a marrying man."

She stopped what she was doing and looked at him. Her expression made him wince.

"You've never really been exposed to anybody like him," her father continued quietly. "Most of the boys you dated were like you, innocent and out of touch with the modern world. J.C. has seen the elephant, as the old-time cowboys used to say. He's well-traveled and he's lived among violent men…"

"I know all that, Daddy," she said softly. "It's just that…" She bit her lower lip. "I've never felt like this."

"You're nineteen," he replied. "Such feelings are natural. But you should also remember that despite what you see in social media, people of faith live by certain rules. Ours teaches that we get married, then we have children. We don't encourage intimacy outside marriage."

"I remember."

"It's natural to feel such things. We're human, after all. But just because a lot of people do something immoral, that doesn't make it right. Any man who truly loves you will want to marry you, Colie, have kids with you, go to church with you. If you interact with a man who has no faith, you risk falling into the same trap that many young women do. I've seen the result of broken relationships where illegitimate children were involved. It is not something I want my daughter to experience."

She wanted to mention that there was such a thing as birth control, but she bit her lip. Her father, like many of his congregation, saw things in a different light than the rest of the world. He was out of touch with what was natural for young women today.

She wanted J.C. Why was it so wrong to sleep with someone you loved? It was as natural as breathing. At least, she imagined it was. She'd never been intimate with anyone. One date had fumbled under her blouse, but his efforts to undress her had been interrupted and Colie hadn't been sorry. She was curious, but the boy hadn't stirred her with his kisses.

J.C., on the other hand, made her wild for something she'd never had. She wanted him. Her body burned, for the first time. He felt the same thing for her, she was sure of it. Except she didn't understand why he'd drawn back so suddenly, why he hadn't kissed her. It was disturbing.

"Think of your mother," the reverend added, when he saw that his arguments were having no effect.

She lifted her eyes. "Mama?"

"She was the most moral human being I ever knew," he said. "She waited for marriage. So did I, Colie," he added surprisingly. "I loved her almost beyond bearing." He lowered his eyes. "Life without her would be empty, except for my faith and my work. I carry on, because that's what she'd want me to do." He looked up. "She'd expect you to live a moral life."

Yes, she would, Colie agreed silently. But perhaps her mother hadn't been as hungry as Colie was, as much in love. Her parents had been together in a different time, when things were less permissive in small towns. Goodness, half the young people in town were in relationships. Few of them actually married.

"If you live with someone, you get to know them and you find out if you're suited enough to get married," she ventured without looking at him.

He drew in a slow breath and sipped his coffee. "It's your life, Colie," he said gently. "You're a grown woman. I can't tell you how to live. I can only tell you that many people who live in an open relationship don't eventually marry. There's no real commitment. Not like there is in marriage, where you bring children into the world and raise them. J.C. doesn't want children."

"He could change his mind," she said.

"He could. But I doubt he will. He's how old, thirty-two? If he still feels that way, at his age, he's unlikely to change. There's something else," he added quietly. "You can't involve yourself with someone with the idea that you can change things about them that you don't like. People don't change. Bad habits only grow worse."

"Not liking children," she began, moving silverware

around on an empty plate. "That might change, if he had a child."

He closed his eyes and winced.

Colie saw that. It wounded her. "Daddy, I can't help how I feel," she ground out. "I'm crazy about him!"

He drew in a long breath. "I know." He looked up at her and saw her stubborn resolve. He finished his coffee and got to his feet. He brushed a kiss against her cheek. "I'll always be here for you. Always. No matter what you do. I'm your father. I will always love you."

Tears sprang to her eyes. She put down the plates and hugged him, tears bleeding from her eyes.

He patted her on the back and kissed her hair, as he had when she was very small, and hurt, and she ran to him for comfort. It had always been like that. She loved her mother very much, but she was Daddy's girl.

"It will all work out," he said, trying to reassure both of them.

"Of course it will," she replied, fighting more tears.

Don't miss Wyoming Winter *by Diana Palmer,*
available wherever Harlequin® books
and ebooks are sold.

www.Harlequin.com

Copyright © 2019 by Diana Palmer

New York Times Bestselling Author

DIANA PALMER

Can love find the space to take root on the stunning Wyoming plains?

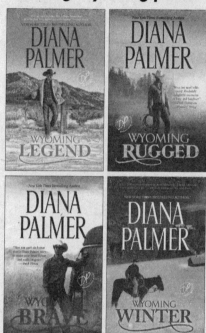

Bring these Wyoming men home today!

"Palmer returns with a splendid Western contemporary novel filled with passion, heartache and small-town life."
—*RT Book Reviews* on *Wyoming Brave* (Top Pick)

HQN

HQNBooks.com

PHDPWM1019MAX